# THE LAST NIGHTINGALE

ANTHONY FLACCO

SEVERN RIVER

PUBLISHING

Severn River Publishing
www.SevernRiverBooks.com

ISBN: 978-1-64875-549-1 (Paperback)

# ALSO BY ANTHONY FLACCO

**The Nightingale Detective Series**

The Last Nightingale

The Hidden Man

Vengeance For All Things

Gold in Peace, Iron in War

To find out more about Anthony Flacco and his books, visit

severnriverbooks.com/authors/anthony-flacco

*TO SHARLY*

*for the magic of believing*

*Even if The Last Nightingale could be revived,*
*How would it tolerate the cure?*
*Knowing Life merely awaits*
*To devour it again.*

—PRESUMED SUICIDE NOTE IN THE POCKET
OF TOMMIE KIMBROUGH'S LAST VICTIM,
WASHED ASHORE NEAR THE GOLDEN GATE.

# 1
---

THE FIRST SHOCK WAVE
April 18, 1906—5:12 a.m.

RANDALL BLACKBURN'S MUSCLED FRAME did not strain at the long uphill hike, even though the route led from his policeman's beat in the waterfront district all the way back to the City Hall Station. At thirty-two years of age, he was able to power his long legs up the steep terrain with such speed that he could leave his beat at five in the morning, traverse more than a dozen blocks uphill plus a few short connecting streets, and still be at his desk with enough time to jot down a brief nightly report and quit the shift by six.

The strenuous hiking routine usually helped to calm him down after a long night. This morning, it barely had any effect. He was coming off of an unusually rough beat patrolling the "Barbary Coast" district, whose grand name was a façade for a strip of bottom-feeder saloons and dead-end flop-houses down near the waterfront. The whole night had been filled with more violent rampage and general disturbance than he had ever seen on a single shift. He had spent most of his patrol hours dodging punches from drunken gamblers and avoiding knife blades flashed by syphilitic whores.

The mania in their faces was consistent among them on this unhappy shift, more so with every passing hour.

He had never gotten used to the place, even after all these years there. The dangerous foot patrol assignment was routinely meted out to him by his station chief. Blackburn knew the continual Barbary Coast beat was intended as some sort of an ongoing affront to him, and that it was being done for the benefit of the rank-and-file officers. He just didn't have any good ideas as to what to do about it. His reputation as a widower who was far too obsessive in his police work was naturally pleasing to the upper brass, but it also placed a lot of pressure on fellow officers: men with families, lives away from the job.

Then some bright soul up in the command office figured out that with Blackburn's overactive code of ethics, he would work just as hard in that dangerous seaport district called the Barbary Coast as he would anywhere else. And so week after week, Blackburn's dreaded assignments sent a morale-soothing message to the rank and file: *Don't worry about Sergeant Blackburn, no matter how much of a fanatic he might be. Look at where he is. Nothing matters unless the right people like you.*

While he strode along the sidewalk, Blackburn tried to tell himself that the real reason he constantly drew the graveyard shift and the Barbary Coast assignments was because of his superior physical capability. But a voice in his head accused him of being the author of his own predicament. The back of his neck tightened at the unwelcome truth of it.

On any night, it was a relief to leave the district behind at the end of a shift. That was especially true this morning. There had been a real "ladies' night" blasting along the Barbary Coast, and between the women and the men, the street corner hags were by far the most dangerous. Those bottom-rung females lived in a drunken haze, battered by lives of nonstop torment. He approached every one of them knowing they would eagerly offer sex to a policeman to buy his tolerance, or just as eagerly snatch away his sidearm and shoot him in the face. Most were prepared to live or die in the attempt and it appeared to be all the same to them.

Lately, while he kept a sharp eye out for their flurries of random rage, he also knew the department strongly suspected that at least one of these doomed women had somehow become highly skilled at throwing heavy-bladed knives. Blackburn himself had seen the grim products of the mysterious killer's work. Each of her victims had almost certainly fallen to the same knife, which left identically deep and wide cuts. The crime was always committed as a fast kill, performed under cover of darkness. The consistent knifepoint entry at the back of the neck indicated either surprise or ambush. The victim's spinal cord was usually split by the thick blade.

Over a dozen such victims turned up in less than nine months, with never a clue beyond a couple of reported glimpses of a "small-framed woman" seen hurrying away. No one even knew if this woman had any actual involvement in the crimes. That's how thin the evidence remained, even after all this time and all those victims.

Blackburn had personally found three of the bodies, on three separate occasions. Every one of the men was castrated postmortem, using surgical cuts executed with precision and skill. Not a single victim was robbed. It seemed as though the taking of the victim's life and the removing of his useless manhood were enough to complete the desired experience—one longshoreman's body was even found with a sizeable wad of cash right inside the vest pocket.

When the press got wind of the story, with macabre humor they dubbed the killer "The Surgeon." The SFPD publicly speculated that The Surgeon was almost certainly a physically fit young woman, probably one who had fallen into ruinous ways. Perhaps she grew up on a farm, where she had learned her skill with the knife. Possibly butchering hogs.

Since then, on most nights along the Barbary Coast, Blackburn had nothing more for company than the inevitable castration jokes that seemed to come from all directions. The night-beat clientele generally agreed that as long as they weren't the ones being killed, the best thing to do was to laugh it all off. And since Blackburn was under Chief Dinan's orders to keep an ear to the street, he had no choice but to spend his nights asking the same questions about the killings, over and over, and listening to the same handful of jokes in response.

No one actually voiced open approval, but he couldn't help noticing the sidewalk ladies were uniformly ignorant of any useful facts and free of any helpful theories. None was inclined to so much as guess who the ghoulish killer might be. And while they never went so far as to openly cheer The

Surgeon's grisly work, that extra bit about slicing off the cocks of the dead men usually made them giggle whenever the topic came up.

As for the killer—Blackburn still hoped there was only one. But he wondered if any other violence-prone whores might have started to find personal appeal in The Surgeon's behavior.

So tonight he was doubly glad when his shift ended without major trouble. He took extra-long strides back to the station, making good time even though the predawn light was absorbed by the fog. With the gas streetlamps still burning at every corner, he could see just well enough to keep up his pace between the isolated pools of weak yellow light while he moved through the chilled mist. The sound of his heavy boot heels ricocheted off the cobblestones and echoed around the silent brick storefronts.

The smell of early morning ham and egg breakfasts floated from a number of homes, tempting him to get back home to a meal of his own. He paused to check his silver pocket watch when he passed through a circle of pale gaslight near the corner post office at Mission and Seventh. He was still a few blocks away from the City Hall Station, but it was only twelve minutes past five: record time. He liked that. It felt as if more of the night's prickly energy had risen from the ground, soaking through the soles of his boots and filling him up as quickly as he burned it away.

He pocketed the watch and started to take a step outside of the lamplight, but just as he lifted his foot, the entire street jerked sideways and pulled itself out from under him. His footing vanished with such power that, for an instant, he thought he had stepped on some drunk's sleeping blanket and gotten it snatched out from under his feet.

Half a second later, the street's cobblestone surface jumped up and hit him with the rude force of a blind-side fist in a bar fight. His body slammed to earth and he took the pavement as a full frontal blow, barely reaching out in time to protect his face from the cold bricks. Spots filled his vision. His head rang with waves of pain that throbbed in time to his heartbeat. He heard his own voice cry out, "It's an earthquake!" even as he fought to avoid blacking out.

Instinct brought him to his hands and knees, moving his limbs with natural magic while the ground shuddered under him, but he remained in place. After a boyhood in Northern California, Blackburn had enough experience with earthquakes to know it wasn't time to get up yet. He reassured himself that at least he was awake and knew what was happening—he hadn't been ejected out of a warm bed and onto a cold floor, as most of the city's residents no doubt had been. He knew most of them were probably lost to confusion and panic at that moment.

He also knew there wasn't any safer place to go until the rattling died down. If he moved out of the range of falling bricks or stones from one building, he would only move into range of another. He thought about taking shelter in a doorway but rejected that. In the heavy stone buildings lining both sides of this street, a doorway could prove to be a good place to get buried alive when the keystones gave way. He knew if any structural damage took place during the bigger shock, any given building might only need another little rattle before coming apart.

He told himself that with any luck, this first shock wave would be the worst of it. But just as he began to rise from his hands and knees, the street began a hard swirl that threw him onto his side. This movement was much stronger, coming not thirty seconds on the heels of the first shock wave. It rolled with such power that the best he could do was scramble back down onto all fours and remain there on the ground.

Beyond that, the shuddering earth was already telling him everything he needed to know. That first wave, he now realized with a cold rush, had not been the real earthquake.

*It was only a foreshock.* Blackburn didn't know if he yelled the words or not.

And then it was more than just the idea of a major earthquake that leaped into his mind. It was all the dire implications that went along with it for a brittle city of bricks and mortar.

They quickly became real. The violent rolling motion of the earth was joined by a vertical rise and fall. The ground dropped out from under him, then slammed back up again. Blackburn found himself clutching the back of a lurching beast. It was all so unreal that the first icy shot of mortal fear had not yet struck. All he knew at the moment was that he had never been through an earthquake like this one.

Then abruptly, the ground's vertical movements slowed. All movement stopped.

Quiet descended...

Everything became shrouded in a deathly silence. The air felt like a thick wet blanket that did not transmit sound. There was nothing reassuring in the absence of noise.

The silence managed to hold out for a handful of slow heartbeats: pulse...pulse...pulse...

And then a deep rumbling began. It throbbed from far beneath the earth's surface, so low on the tonal scale, he felt it in his bones and deep in his chest before his ears heard anything at all. For an instant, his memory flashed a boyhood image of putting his ear to a railroad track, listening for the vibrations of a faraway locomotive. Except now there was no track and no train. This rumbling sound was wrong, completely out of place.

It was then that the first burst of real *fear* stabbed through him, stronger and colder than anything he had ever felt. It cut through his training and his mature life experience, and at that moment, if the rolling earth had allowed him to climb to his feet, the fear would have owned him and sent him screaming into the fog. His instincts already sensed what the rest of him was about to learn.

When he glanced down Mission Street, he stared into an impossible sight—a massive surge of energy was running toward him, travelling beneath the surface of the earth. It hurtled through the ground like a wave of curling surf.

Solid earth was rolling like the sea itself.

His brain seemed to freeze while the invisible monster shot toward him and trailed upheaval in its wake. Brick storefronts buckled and exploded. Granite paving stones blew upward like kernels of popping corn. By the time the energy wave hit him, Blackburn was a paralyzed statue of astonishment. The wave tossed him into the air. When he landed and the street curb crashed into his ribs, the blow knocked the wind out of him. He could do nothing more than lie helpless: ten seconds, twenty seconds, fighting the sensation of drowning on dry land.

He rolled onto his hands and knees and managed to take a clear breath, but by then the invisible wave was gone. The din of destruction overpowered his hearing. Behind him, the roof of the post office was gradually collapsing, and those sounds were only part of a much larger chorus. In all directions, buildings of every size were still shedding their stone exteriors like giant reptiles casting off skin. The ones that collapsed upon themselves expelled thick clouds of dust out the windows and doorways, coughing their guts into the streets before they died.

He turned his head in a circle and caught shadowy glimpses of Armageddon. Never since losing his wife and child had Blackburn felt the overpowering need to cry. Now the choking sobs took him as if they had only been gone for a day. He cried out in wordless despair. It was several seconds before he regained control and strangled the feelings back down. In a self-conscious flash, he felt thankful to know that even if anybody was awake and looking out of their window right at him, they were certainly far too distracted to have noticed his unacceptable slip of emotion.

Meanwhile, another eerie silence was returning to the ruined landscape. Silence itself felt especially unnatural, because people should have been calling out, screaming in pain or crying for help. But instead there was a complete absence of voices.

He knew survivors had to be out there: random miracles mixed in with the rubble. They were scattered underneath the ruined buildings all around, just as surely as the silent dead were buried alongside them.

But still nobody screamed. No voices at all. Random sounds of falling debris punctuated a deep silence as cold as the black waters of the bay. Blackburn had no idea how long it took him to stagger a block or so, but it was only then, after that much time, when sounds from the victims finally began to drift up from the giant piles of rubble. The first cry he heard was a long, ghastly wail. It started low, then quickly rose in pitch, like the sound of a distant hunting dog.

That initial outcry triggered a ghoulish chain reaction—now other victims sounded out from hidden and entombed places. Their voices carried a tone Blackburn had never heard in his twelve years of hard-scrabble police work. He knew those desperate sounds might as well be the wail of graveyard ghosts.

When a terrible scream sprang up through a pile directly in front of him, he couldn't help himself. He abandoned the trip back to the station and began clawing his way toward the trapped victim.

Just as he closed in on the anguished sounds, he glanced up from his work and saw the first living person since the earth exploded its skin—a healthy-looking young man was scrambling across the rubble. He looked like he was running from a rabid dog.

"Hey! Over here!" Blackburn bellowed to the man. "Police! Help me dig!"

When the man ignored him, Blackburn bellowed in his strongest voice, "I said *police*, damn it! Stop right there!"

The fellow scuffed to a halt. For an instant, the young man swung around and stared straight at Blackburn, eyes like saucers. He paused just long enough to adopt an attitude and make a decision. Then he spun on the balls of his feet and disappeared.

Blackburn swore in frustration. He resumed digging and didn't bother to call for help again. Within a few moments, he managed to pull a large man free. The victim was bleeding from several wounds and seemed too injured to get very far. The man immediately began to wail in a thick Greek accent, "My wife! Where she is? My wife!"

Blackburn could only holler for him to stay put until someone could carry him out of the area. Then he stumbled away in search of the next buried victim. In the space of a few moments, screams were beginning to rise from everywhere, and there was still no able-bodied help to be seen.

It only took another couple of steps for him to reach the next source of cries—children, clearly, two of them—their shrill voices penetrated his bones. He abandoned himself to such a fury of digging that he did not feel the skin shredding from his fingers and his palms. Any object that his hands could latch onto was hurled to the side, in movements he repeated over and over while the thick, dust-filled air seared his lungs.

But soon, in spite of all the distraction, he noticed a new smell in the fouled air.

Smoke. Oily and thick, the source was somewhere nearby. He resumed digging, but within moments, the screams of the other trapped victims began rising higher. By now these people smelled the smoke too, and they grasped what it meant for them if they failed to get out of the path of the fire. Every breath he took held less usable air. He began to go light-headed. His body began to fail him despite his determination. His hands turned into clumsy paws. His thoughts ran thick. He tried to force his memory to tell him what he was supposed to be doing. He got no answer.

It was the feel of a tiny hand that brought him back. He had opened up a pocket of space that held two small girls, perhaps six and seven years old. They pounced on him, crying out in a language he couldn't identify while they grabbed at his uniform sleeves to pull themselves free.

He saw that both girls were bleeding, but before he could think of how to help them, they scrambled over him and scurried away, hand in hand, shrieking in panic. There was nothing else he could do for them. More trapped victims were calling out everywhere around him, and his strength was quickly draining away. His only choice was to get to clearer air, and to gather reinforcements at the station: men, tools, water. Water most of all.

When he finally made it far enough up Market Street to a spot where random air currents carved a trough of better air, his thoughts began to clear. He felt some of his strength return. But when he stared through the faint light at the place where he knew City Hall was supposed to be, the sight stopped him in his tracks. Devastation.

Only a few days before, a fellow officer named Leonard Ingham told of a nightmare that kept him up for hours; the entire city was wiped out in one massive conflagration. Blackburn remembered laughing at Ingham and chiding him for spending too much time around the fortune-tellers down on the waterfront.

But here he was, staring at the spot where the high-domed City Hall was supposed to be, and most of it was reduced to rubble. The great dome's steel frame remained standing, but it had shucked most of its limestone covering, just as Ingham described. Worse, with all of the early morning cooking fires burning at the time that the quake struck, the massive blaze predicted by Officer Ingham's dream was certain to be close behind, fed by gas from all the broken underground lines.

Blackburn hurried over to the ruined building. A dozen or so able-bodied officers were clearing out space for a makeshift command center on the broad front steps. In their midst was Police Chief Dinan, pacing back and forth, bellowing orders at anybody within earshot. Dinan had already spotted him.

"Sergeant Blackburn! Thank God you're alive!"

"Yes, sir, I was almost back here when it—"

"We need a man with your strength!"

"I'll do whatever I—"

"Most of the city jail inmates are still under the building! We've opened a passage down to their cells. Check 'em out one by one. If they're dead, leave 'em. Any that are injured too bad to work, leave them too!" He dropped his voice down low and added, "I mean this, it's an order: Round up everybody else at gunpoint and march 'em all down to Portsmouth Square! Do it with a smile..."

"Portsmouth Square? Sir, that's a long way from—"

"Shoot any man who breaks ranks!"

"Sir, there are already fires. Maybe we could draft the prisoners to work the hoses?"

"What are they going to *do* with the hoses, Sergeant? Use 'em to beat the flames out?"

"What?"

"A runner from the waterfront just came up—most of the city's water mains are busted. There's not gonna *be* any water for these fires. But you can bet there'll be bodies to deal with. The graveyards on this peninsula are full. So you march those men down to Portsmouth Square and start digging trench graves!"

The chief grabbed Blackburn by the lapels and drew him close enough to blast him with a hoarse whisper. "We got *plague* down in Chinatown, you understand me? And now the rats will be coming up out of every busted sewer line! Think about that, will you? You want to know how important this is—even though we've only got one motorized patrol car, it's not gonna do anything but ferry bodies down to you. That means our rescue work is all gonna be on horseback or most likely on foot, hear me? Just so you can get the bodies we send you into the ground, fast as you can."

The chief dropped his voice again. "And make sure to cover them too deep for the rats. We can rebury everybody later. Somewhere off the peninsula. Oakland, maybe."

Blackburn felt a flicker of worry that Dinan had gone off the deep end. "Chief, if you mean the Black Death, I've never heard about any plague in San Fran—"

"You weren't *supposed* to hear!" the chief bellowed. He forced his voice back down to a croaking whisper. "Nobody was, except a few of us! We've been hoping that those few cases that came up were brought directly in, but that the plague itself isn't really here. Nobody knows for sure. Knew for sure. And now you can keep quiet about it too, or I swear I'll bury you right along with the—"

"Yes, sir! I'll go right now!"

"You sure as hell will if you want to stay upright, Sergeant! And mark me, now—these inmates, tell 'em you've got orders: If any man even *looks* like he might try to run, you're gonna *shoot him down*."

Blackburn hurried to comply. But there was hardly time to get down into the cell area and holler for the attention of the captive men before the next big aftershock struck. It was now thirteen minutes after the initial wave.

Just when he was opening his announcement to the inmates about a proposition to get them out of their cells, the aftershock rolled through with deep force. The basement area was claustrophobic on a good day, making this second quake feel much more powerful than the first. Blackburn was certain if it didn't subside within twenty or thirty seconds, the rest of City Hall would collapse into the basement and make a grave for all of them.

Luck gave them a nod; this shock wave faded quicker than the first, and when he was able to pick himself back up and peer through the dust, he realized his sales pitch to the men could have had no better opening. He saw the same feral panic in their eyes that he felt inside of himself. There was no need to use force. He simply asked for volunteers and got a universal show of hands.

They all smelled the thickening smoke.

He and his two officers were so heavily outnumbered, they had to move with great care in hooking up their chain gang. It used up valuable time to get the men organized by height, for equal stride length, and then shackled into teams on long leg bindings improvised with sections of a wagon harness. The sun was well over the horizon by the time the big sergeant and his young patrol officers marched away with their twenty-five conscripts.

By now massive smoke columns were rising up in every direction, joining together high over the city in a ruinous pall that blocked out most of the daylight. The three officers marched their charges into what was becoming artificial twilight, armed only with a rifle and a double set of sidearms for each man. Blackburn had instructed them to make it a point to look like they were itching to use their guns, and for a while at least, the simple theatrics worked. The trembling "volunteers" felt less fear of marching deeper into the burning city than of the bullet in the back they were convinced any man would receive if he attempted to escape.

At 8:14 a.m., another powerful aftershock set everything to rattling, and this time it was too much for dozens of the city's brick and stone buildings; they finally shattered and crumbled into the streets. Block after city block began to take on the appearance of a rubble-strewn artillery field.

A score of major fires now burned unchecked in every direction. Full daylight barely penetrated the shroud of smoke swelling over the ruined city. Blackburn lost large chunks of time in guiding his men around the worst of the damage and the emerging fires. The streets were so choked with obstacles that a hike which should have taken less than half an hour consumed nearly three. They only sustained that modest speed because they were marching under a firm order not to stop for any rescue work, no matter how vital it might appear to be. His confidential order from Chief Dinan was simple:

*Nothing gets priority over saving the city from a rampaging outbreak of the Black Death.*

The desperate focus of that order became plain when the same sea breezes that were feeding the fires began to lift the smoke clouds. Blackburn hated what his eyes told him. As far as he could see in all directions, the city's large buildings were in various states of collapse. The few still standing amid the billowing smoke swayed with every new aftershock.

Some of the city's able-bodied survivors had recovered enough of their humanity to begin working to rescue trapped survivors, but there were others who made no attempt to disguise their looting. From time to time, Blackburn fired over their heads to scatter them, but it was clear that they would only move on and strike again.

On three unique occasions he actively interfered with events by ordering one of his armed men to chase and shoot at gangs of looters. But each time, he remained within his orders by keeping the group of inmates moving while his assigned officer made sure the perpetrators either took a bullet or were frightened away.

It never slowed the group down. When he marched his men past one half-buried victim who stood trapped below his waist among twisted iron beams, the young man begged to be shot before the advancing flames could reach him. The approaching fire proved his fears were true. Blackburn didn't even have to issue the order—his corporal quickly stepped forward and shot the man through the back of the head. The convicts watched, astounded, and felt themselves reminded that the penalties today were swift and harsh. They fell into step with added determination.

Blackburn's group lost direction several times due to the lack of recognizable landmarks. They were picking their way across the crumbled remains of the Emporium Building before he realized that they were at the corner of Market and Powell Streets. He ordered the men to take the slight left turn onto Powell and corrected their course whenever he spotted something familiar. Still, by the time they reached the intersection at Jackson Street, a stone's throw from Portsmouth Square, it was already a quarter past ten—and they were off course again.

He glanced around at the beautiful neighborhood's simple houses. The modest family homes had survived, built with flexible wood beams instead of rigid bricks and mortar. He found himself hoping that the prevailing winds would change, just so these simple wood homes might be spared the swarming fires.

But just after his men rounded the corner and began to head down Jackson Street, he heard a woman's screams. The sounds stopped him cold. Piercing, deathly shrieks were coming from inside one of these peaceful-looking houses. The screams were as primal and intense as anything he had heard yet that day, an equal mix of terror and pain. The unreal aspect of it was that they were coming from somewhere inside an untouched house. No motion could be seen in the home, and the neighbors either failed to hear or were choosing not to react. The entire neighborhood was otherwise silent.

But Blackburn had already marched his men past so many other miseries, there was no time to investigate this one. Portsmouth Square was getting close, and the sour-faced inmates were starting to look as if they realized how heavily they outnumbered their captors.

He took a last glance back at the peaceful-looking house. Exhaustion pulled at him, and the main work detail hadn't even started yet. There was nothing else to do but make a mental note to come back later on and try to check into the source of those terrible, out-of-place screams.

If he ever got the chance.

# 2

FIVE HOURS AFTER THE GREAT EARTHQUAKE

AT THE SAME MOMENT Blackburn turned his men away from the house on Jackson Street, twelve-year-old Shane Nightingale lay trapped inside it. He curled his thin frame tighter inside the small kitchen pantry and tried not to listen to what was going on just a few feet outside of those pantry doors, but the words stabbed into him like nails.

"It's the end!" the stranger's voice hissed. "A day of atonement for you. You're starting to appreciate that now, aren't you? My job is to empty you out! But don't worry. We'll take all the time we need..."

The sounds coming out of Shane's adoptive mother mostly dissolved into babbling, while the madman responded to Mrs. Nightingale with icy precision, mimicking the noises of her mortal terror. He did it with such energy and skill that he seemed to be playing to an audience.

To Shane, it was as if the killer somehow realized a terrified and helpless twelve-year-old boy lay hiding only a few feet away, and the man was taking additional pleasure in his torments by drilling the event deep into Shane's mind, toying with him until the moment came to throw open the pantry doors and drag him out to suffer with the others.

Then abruptly, Mrs. Nightingale went quiet.

The room took on a silence as sour as old buttermilk. It was several long moments before the stranger began to speak again. This time he kept his voice to a reverential whisper.

"Ah! Now you're perfect! Safe from any more sin! The sins of that arrogant man you people call husband and father."

Apparently, the horrors laid upon Mrs. Nightingale were still not enough to satisfy the maniac, even though he had surely killed her by that point. Shane felt a vague sense of relief that she was finally at the end of her suffering, and the lovely lady who adopted him out of St. Adrian's would endure no more of it.

Shane knew she was the one who had influenced the family's decision to rescue him from that place. He overheard the adults once, in spite of their whispers. Her husband and daughters would have passed him by and left him there. And because he knew the secret, even though she never allowed any real closeness, he had always loved her for saving him.

His relief sank under an overwhelming flood of guilt. He knew perfectly well that even a scrawny kid of twelve was expected to find the strength to fight off such a monster. Instead, from the moment the brutal attack began, his terror owned him. His legs went numb and useless. His throat seized shut. He couldn't even control his bladder.

How long had it been? He could barely see inside of that darkened place, but the pocket watch he won by pitching pennies now hung from a little hook on the back panel. He had placed it there when he moved in because he could read it by a thin beam of light that penetrated the slight warping of the door frame. Now when he craned his neck to see it, the watch hands showed almost ten thirty.

Earlier that morning, once Father Nightingale saw that nobody in the family was injured, he ordered everyone to get out of the house and into the safety of the front yard, just in case another aftershock rolled through. He left the house carrying his shotgun and a sack full of ten-gauge shells, shouting that his dry goods store was at the mercy of looters. He rushed off in the family's four-seater buggy, calling over his shoulder for Shane to make sure everybody stayed outside until he returned.

The family obeyed him for a while, but eventually both girls convinced their mother to go back in and set about putting away the toppled things in the parlor and kitchen. Shane had no power to enforce his order. He stood in the ruined doorway, quietly reminding them of their father's command. They passed by him without so much as a glance.

It was as if they all somehow agreed the earthquake was the worst thing that could happen that day, and the rest was simply a matter of cleaning up. He let them work until they got tired, knowing they had no endurance for this.

Fatigue kicked in on them all before long, and while they refused to go back out into the yard and sit there as potential objects of pity, Shane was able to gently persuade them, one by one, to return to their rooms and rest. It was a far easier task. After that he went straight into the kitchen and crawled back into his usual sleeping spot inside the pantry. There he fell into an exhausted sleep.

He awoke to the sounds of the girls screaming...loud banging noises on the floors and walls...Mrs. Nightingale hollering in protest...people brutally dragged downstairs. The only words came from the intruder, who sounded like he was searching through the house, bellowing, "Where's your husband? Where is he?" Mrs. Nightingale cried out over and over that her husband was downtown guarding his store, but the intruder was determined to search the whole house himself. Shane could only lie paralyzed. He knew his grim hiding place was sparing his life.

Early on, Mrs. Nightingale had screamed Shane's name twice. After that, she kept herself mercifully quiet about him. The killer made no reaction to the name. Either he didn't hear her or he was already convinced nobody else was around.

Shane wondered if perhaps she hoped he would somehow escape and run for help. Maybe she thought that by keeping quiet, she was giving herself and her girls a chance at rescue. A chance for him to run.

The girls had no such chance at all. From the moment they were dragged into the kitchen, each one had only managed a couple of wordless screams before they were silenced.

Shane recognized those brief sounds, however. Not the words—the sounds. He knew them from his days at St. Adrian's. There, unsuspecting children who got themselves targeted for punishment frequently had the experience of a Helper coming up from behind and grabbing them—snatching them up off of the ground by an arm or leg, pulling them like a sack of grain. Sometimes the Helpers would yank so hard, the child made that same kind of involuntary yelp of shock and fear.

Back then, there was never anybody around to help either.

His adoptive sisters, Amy and Carolyn Nightingale, grew up in a loving household. They had no powers for battling vicious cruelty. Shane wondered if they were dead, unconscious, or if mere shock had sealed their lips; his own terror, after all, was keeping him silent and holding him frozen.

The intensity jumped higher when the perpetrator began a nonstop diatribe about his motives, as if to explain and justify his actions to the victims. Since there was no way for Shane to ignore the dreadful harangue, he was a captive audience at a demon's lecture.

Inside the pantry, the hanging watch showed it to be nearly three hours since the invader took Mrs. Nightingale and her girls captive. Obviously, the killer felt no concern about making a quick escape. In the general chaos going on all over the city, he was gambling that help was unlikely.

It went on and on, long after the woman of the house stopped making any sound.

When Shane finally realized what the madman was actually talking about, he had to bite his teeth into his tongue to silence himself. The girls were both still alive, because the man was actually asking his surviving victims to agree with him, to tell him that what he was doing was all right. The killer wanted to hear them concur that his reasons were sound.

Amy and Carolyn began kicking out at the floor, against the cabinets, against their restraints. At that point everything became more than Shane could take in. His need to escape the lunacy overtook him and his brain began to shut itself down. His eyelids turned to lead. He plunged into a sickened and delirious blackness. The ability to rouse himself was nowhere inside of him.

Later, when Shane felt himself coming back, his eyes were already open. He blinked hard and blinked again, stunned that the world had not somehow gone away.

Now it was quiet. An amber split of lantern light bled through the crack above the pantry door, and the thin beam showed his pocket watch: nearly straight-up midnight. A full day, gone. He wanted to think that Father Nightingale had somehow returned and vanquished the demon, and that it would now be safe to crawl out from hiding. Before the thought could fully form, he realized that of course the man of the house never came back. The sounds of the men fighting would have roused him. Shane wondered whether he could have made himself burst out of the pantry in that case and somehow join in the fight against the demon.

But it did not happen, and now the awful sounds were beginning all over again. The demon was killing Amy. Shane's blood pounded so hard beneath his skin that it felt as if it could burst through his own flesh. The demon rendered her unconscious again and again. Each time, he revived her at the last instant, godlike, and granted her another few minutes of life before starting the process all over. It was happening to sixteen years' worth of beauty and charm bundled into a feminine form so lovely, Shane spent his entire first year in that house trying to avoid falling in love with her. He squelched his feelings, never doubting that if he gave himself away the entire family would find his affections repugnant. Amy might have been repulsed. They could have sent him back.

He knew any worthy young man would leap out of that pantry, determined to fight like a warrior, all in the nick of time to save beautiful Amy. But Shane's legs wouldn't take him anywhere. He could barely feel them.

Briefly, he wondered if he could at least do something as simple as to cry out. Could he buy Amy a few more moments of life that way, while the startled killer left her to search for the source of Shane's voice? He began with a quick swallow, in hopes of opening up his parched and swollen throat a little bit wider. He braced himself to scream with all of his power.

"Stooooooooooppp!"

Nothing came out but a hiss of dry air. Hardly enough to penetrate the simple wooden doors. The sounds outside the pantry never even slowed down. They became more brutal than anything anyone should hear. Shane lay on his back and positioned his numb forearms to cover his burning ears. Amy's degradation was private. He would not listen to any more of it. Even without his sense of hearing, the powerful swirl of torment spun inside of him until it carried the rest of him away once again, pulling him deep into a trance.

More time passed.

When Shane finally came to, he snapped back to consciousness at the sound of the terrible voice.

"Time to wake up!"

*He found me!* Shane's heart slammed hard in his chest as he fought to focus his eyes inside the dim pantry—and then he realized that it was still dark in there. The doors were still closed.

And so the monster was not talking to him. Not talking to him. Not him. *Keep quiet and don't move. Try not to breathe.*

The only one left was Carolyn, the youngest. An instant later, Shane heard her muffled cries. *Where in God's name is Father Nightingale? What could keep him away for so long?* Shane noticed a strong smell of smoke drifting into the house. There was fire out there, a big fire, not far away.

Crashing sounds began in the kitchen. These were harder than anything he'd heard throughout the long ordeal, so despite his terror, Shane dared to peer through the crack just above the door. Through that razor line of sight, he saw Carolyn being whirled about the room in a profane dance with the devil.

Now she was crashing into furniture. Slamming into walls.

Shane caught glimpses of the killer but never saw enough to gather anything more than that the man was dressed in nondescript workman's clothing. He seemed to have a small and wiry build, but there was no hint of weakness about him. He moved like an attacking dog.

Shane pulled away from the dangerous crack and shrank back against the wall. A wave of delirium washed through him and held him in its power while the attack went on and on.

Daylight crawled by. Twilight fell. Only then, after all that time, did silence return to the Nightingale house. Most of the night passed before Shane's awareness drifted back into the moment. He found himself in the growing light of sunrise.

A day and a half had passed, and during all of that time Shane witnessed the Nightingale house continually used to stage a play more furious and foul than anything an earthquake could do.

---

*"Hello? Hello, inside! Anybody here?"*

*A man's voice. At the front of the house.*

*Scraping noises now, just outside the pantry. The demon is visible through the crack over the pantry door, staggering across the room in fear. The demon scrambles to the window and peers outside.*

*"Shit!" the demon hisses. Even from inside of the pantry, the demon can be heard while he stumbles to the rear of the house...throws open the back door... makes his escape out through the yard...*

And as quickly as that, it was over. The killer was gone.

There was more loud banging at the front door. Then sounds of the door being forced open.

"Hello, inside? Police! We're evacuating the area!"

Heavy boots entered the kitchen. A booming male voice called out, "Sergeant Blackburn! Three bodies here. No sign of life."

More boots thumped into the kitchen. Now Shane could see the sergeant through the door crack—he was big, strong-faced, with dark hair like Shane's. He and his men were all filthy, covered with streaks of dirt and blackened by smoke. They looked half dead with fatigue. But something else was wrong. The sergeant failed to show any surprise at the sight of the dead women. Shane could see all three police officers there in the kitchen, and none of them looked puzzled by what was on the floor in front of them.

Still Shane lay paralyzed. He could not make himself cry out. Not a sound. The heavy boots moved on and quickly made their way throughout the house while the sergeant and his two officers searched the other rooms for any signs of life.

How could these men have no idea what they had just seen? But the sergeant ordered the men out of the house, shouting that the fires were coming, this house was done for. There were still three more homes on the block to be searched.

The boots stomped away. No one bothered to close the front door.

Silence returned. The smell of smoke was becoming strong now. Overpowering. The fire was nearly upon the place. It was the awful feeling of choking on smoke that finally roused Shane. His arms were nearly useless and his legs felt full of lead, but somehow the pantry doors opened for him. He rolled out and onto the floor. The change was instant and powerful—as soon as he left his little shelter, the heat coming from the advancing fire was blistering hot.

Without meaning to, he glanced over at the three bodies. He quickly turned away, but that one glimpse was enough to show him why the police failed to realize what they were seeing. Mrs. Nightingale was almost completely covered by the dish cupboard. It might have been knocked onto her during the killer's frenzy with her daughter, or perhaps deliberately placed over her later. Only her lower legs protruded; she looked like a casualty of the earthquake.

Amy lay under the overturned kitchen table, mostly concealed by it. The parts of her that could be seen gave no sign of the horrors she endured. And although little Carolyn was more bruised and bloody than the others, within all the wreckage and chaos she was also mistaken for an earthquake victim, battered by the violent shaking. These dead could speak nothing of the evil they had seen, certainly not to men hastily conducting a hunt for survivors. And now, with the fires nearly upon the house, Shane realized he was going to be the only witness. There would soon be nothing left to see.

He closed his eyes against the horror show and crawled out of the kitchen, muscles numb, pulling himself along on all fours until he reached the front of the house. At the entrance, he grasped the doorsill and hauled himself to his feet. Then he turned to face the daylight world for the first time since the Great Earthquake struck the city.

The whole planet seemed to be on fire. Even the sky.

He blinked into the reddening artificial dusk to see a shattered and smoking landscape stretching in all directions. Brick buildings were nothing but shells. Most of the wooden buildings were ablaze. The streets were full of rubble. And everywhere, refugees stumbled along. Some carried mounds of belongings, others pulled carts by hand. A small few had managed to find draft horses somewhere and put them to work pulling wagons loaded down with hasty piles. Everyone was retreating before a wall of flame and smoke.

He stumbled out into the road and stood among them. The sun was mostly blocked out by the massive columns of smoke and their message of ruin. He gazed into one giant swirling cloud, and for an instant his burning eyes told him that he caught a glimpse of a face, twisted and horrible.

He noticed something hard and small clutched in his fist and opened his hand to see his pocket watch. He had grabbed it off the hook and carried it away with no idea he was doing so.

A hand grabbed his shoulder and spun him, nearly stopping his heart. Before him stood a woman who resembled Mrs. Nightingale so much that a cold rush shot through him. The woman spoke to him in a coarse whisper.

"Are you going through Chinatown?" "Why?" Shane asked.

But to his surprise, the word "why" didn't fully emerge. It stuck halfway across his lips and hung there like a toothpick that he couldn't spit out. "Whuuh...whuuh..." The sensation was so foreign that at first, he forgot to be embarrassed.

The woman ignored him and continued, "Somebody said there's only one working telegraph left in the whole city! At Post and Montgomery. *Chinatown!* Do you hear me?"

"Yes," Shane answered.

But "yes" didn't come out, either. All that came out was, 'Yehhh... yehhh..." And this time he felt the distinct sensation of words sticking in his throat.

She went on. "I walked all the way out to Ocean Beach because there was a rumor that the Atlantic cable is still working, but it only goes overseas. My family's in Oklahoma! What are we supposed to do if our families are here in *this* country?"

Shane barely heard her. Why wasn't his mouth working? "Chinatown is just a few blocks that way," was what he meant to say, instead of "Ch-Chi-Chinatow, tow, town is juhh, juhhh." And by now he was disturbed enough that the woman noticed it on his face.

"Are you all right?" she softly inquired. "Because I could sure be glad for somebody to walk me through Chinatown. You know, in case the Coolies want to get back at us. Now that everything..."

Now her voice trailed off. She looked more closely at him and seemed to regard him as less than likely to represent a solution.

"Nnnn-nnnn-no. I—I'm not guh-guh-going tt-tt—"

She spun on her heel and walked off before he could finish the sentence.

His stutter took away any small desire he might have had for communicating with her or anyone else. Now he wanted nothing so much as to dissolve into the landscape. When he looked around to get his bearings, he noticed that most people seemed to be migrating generally southeast, toward the open expanse of Golden Gate Park. It was opposite the direction the woman took, which seemed reason enough for him to go that way. Some small part of him hoped if he kept quiet for a while, his speech problem would magically disappear. He fell in step with a loose crowd of wanderers moving in defeat toward the bay.

To his relief, no one took notice of him. People bumped into him without seeing him, without even slowing down. Everyone stared with hollow eyes. Their expressions seemed to confirm what that faceless, solitary demon of the kitchen said over and over while he destroyed the Nightingale family.

This was surely the end.

Shane allowed himself to be swept along with the others moving away down the street. Even within the chaos all around, he was eager to be gone, just in case Father Nightingale returned to see what Shane allowed to happen. When he turned for one last look at the house, falling sparks had already set the roof on fire. The place would burn down fast. He was glad for that much. He would never have to see the awful remains of his adoptive family.

With that, he realized that of course Mr. Nightingale was dead. No matter what kind of difficulties he might have had with his store, he was not the sort of man who would leave his family alone for a day and a half while the shattered city burned to the ground.

Shane decided it was good that the anonymous crowd could swallow him. He didn't want anyone, not a soul, to recognize him for what he knew himself to be: He was a contemptible creature. He was a failure as a young man, even as a human being. His rightful place was in the grave.

*Just don't look them in the eye.* He learned the lesson so fast it seemed to arrive complete, a gift of instinct. *Move along quietly, keep it smooth, no jumpy motion. Nobody ever thinks a twelve-year-old is doing anything important. Be invisible.*

And in that fashion, Shane Nightingale moved undetected among the living, seized by the overpowering impression of being a dead thing trapped inside someone else's moving body. It was a mystery to him that no one seemed to notice it.

# 3

SAN FRANCISCO'S CHINATOWN
Day Two

RANDALL BLACKBURN HAD LOST all track of time. He guessed it was pre-sunset on Thursday afternoon. But he couldn't be more specific than that. After nearly a day and a half of fighting the Chinatown fires whenever he wasn't filling temporary graves. He was dangling from the point of collapse. All he knew for certain was that his mission was blessedly close to ending.

There was no longer enough emergency work to justify the extra risk of inmate labor, so he finally sent his exhausted workers off to the Army holding pens across the bay in Oakland. He knew that truthfully, the battle against the fires was now lost. In spite of everyone's best efforts, the conflagration was burning its way all around Portsmouth Square and throughout Chinatown. For many blocks in every direction, nearly everything that hadn't been laid to waste soon would be.

At first, most of the residents had stayed around to fight the fires. Even after all was lost, quite a few remained and took to makeshift shelters erected in the open areas of the Square. It was only when a squad of soldiers showed up to reinforce the police gravediggers that the refugees were finally swept off to less crucial areas.

Blackburn deliberately worked beside two whining underlings, Officers Gibbon and Mummery, trying to control their potential damage to morale. *They're doing everything wrong for new recruits with careers to consider*, he thought with disdain.

Gibbon and Mummery were nearly ten years junior to Blackburn and should have both had more energy for the task. But they allowed their work to make them sullen, and that was something rare in the lower ranks. Most young cops appreciated police work as a respectable and secure livelihood and kept their attitudes in line. Such things were especially important for a young family man, as nearly all new cops happened to be. But these two dolts were behaving like men who had gotten their jobs easy, from relatives, perhaps, or through bribes.

They clearly failed to see any reason to adopt Blackburn's dedication. And there was no practical way to punish them under the circumstances, something that these two had already figured out. It left a bitter taste in his mouth that all he could do was to give firm orders, then make sure to set an example so they saw him going about each of his own jobs in the way it was supposed to be done.

He employed the most careful efforts with the remains of victims but still held to his central order and refused to permit anyone on his squad to quit before all the bodies pulled from the rubble were safely interred and protected from the rats, or until all of the park's available ground was filled.

There was still open grave space left when the delivery system broke down. It happened somewhere back along the way, no one knew where. With a fraction of the city's officials still living, and with the city's physical resources hardly functional, the remaining workers' growing fatigue was now causing the work process to decompose faster than the corpses they hoped to save. He lost count after burying fifty.

All of them were planted deep.

Fatigue settled in on Blackburn and all the workers. It was natural for anyone who had ridden out the Great Earthquake, as it was already being called, to function on fear and adrenaline for the first few hours. Many were too traumatized to sleep at all. But halfway through the second day, the healthiest and strongest also felt their physical resources depleted. Even humble tasks became confusing.

Blackburn could see anarchy snapping at their heels, and he could only hope the rest of the city's dead were being reduced to ash in the unchecked fires. Protected in that fashion, at least, from the final indignity of feeding the rats roaming as free as domestic animals. The fires, in the end, were proving to be good for that much.

No one could know how many San Franciscans and hapless travelers died across the city with all trace of their existence wiped away. Human remains joined thousands of abandoned pets and even large draft animals in mass cremation. Thankfully, uncountable swarms of rat populations were converted to ash and bone as well.

But since rats were always the first to run and the last to get caught, the rats would be at the fresh graves the next day if he and his men failed to go deep enough. And yet he was nearly delirious with exhaustion. If only his bosses would let him get some sleep. He had managed to snag a few catnaps here and there, but with waves of uncontrolled flames rampaging through the city and raining hot embers, there was never time for anything more.

Only when the last of the bodies were taken care of did he manage to spend a couple of hours sound asleep, facedown under the nearest tree, before some lieutenant shook him awake and ordered him to form up a detail. He was to lead a top-speed, house-to-house search for survivors in any of the neighborhoods standing in the path of the advancing flames. He and his crew would have to keep themselves moving just ahead of the wall of fire in a final pass through the homes before they were consumed.

His stomach was already twisted with hunger; his bones ached. He wondered how the two soft recruits were going to take to another difficult assignment. But he was pleasantly surprised to see Gibbon and Mummery actually perk up a bit under the challenge. The necessity of it was plain, even to them.

Unfortunately, there weren't many victories there. Most of what he saw within the masses of tilting wreckage was an endless repetition of mangled bodies, long dead. A small few were still alive but trapped beyond saving in the few moments before the flames found them. Most of the living victims wanted to be left alone to tug at their restraints. But three of them, strangers trapped together, all begged to be shot, just as the young man had done on the first morning. He took a deep breath and obliged every one of the three in the same way his father taught him to dispatch game—shoot quick, take them by surprise if you can, and show mercy by getting it right the first time.

Before another hour passed, Blackburn realized he was at that strange house where he and his men had heard the woman's terrible screams during their long march to the Square. He sent his men in but then decided to join them and check for clues about the source of the screams.

It turned out there was nothing there, only more of the endless dead, beaten by the quake. He got his men out of there with scant minutes to spare. There wasn't even time to examine the bodies. His team had done all that they could, and it was no longer possible to keep ahead of the fires. He sent the men back to Portsmouth Square to get some rest.

As for himself, he doubted there was a place to return to; his apartment building had stood inside the previous day's burn area. At the moment, he felt more upset about not knowing where to go to get some uninterrupted rest than over the loss of his home. As far as his apartment was concerned, there wasn't much to lose. The place itself had merely been somewhere to store clothing and to sleep between stretches of overtime. The only possessions holding any grip on his affection pertained to his work, and those were still safe inside his sergeant-sized police locker in the more fortunate part of the station.

Despite his efforts, he realized that the earthquake had taken a much smaller toll on him than the majority of the people he was paid to protect. Something about that felt right to him, since he lived in such simplicity and diverted nearly all of his energy to his career. But there were days, now that he was over thirty, when he found that the world had little patience for a single man, a widower (how he hated the word) who had been alone for nearly ten years without ever coming close to remarrying. Society in general tended to dismiss him as a confirmed bachelor and a social stand-off. In his bleakest moments of reflection, Blackburn found that the idea of close friendship between men, or of romances with women, somehow seemed more like the performance of an exotic play than like something he might actually find in daily life. But now with the fires continuing to eat up the city, he couldn't let go of the desire to rush home and try to retrieve something, anything, and join the treasure hunters sifting the rubble.

His lieutenant was not a fool and could judge how close to exhaustion all his men were, so he ordered Blackburn and a few of the others to crawl into the nearby police command tent. They were advised to get a few hours of rest but then stay put until needed. The lieutenant reminded him there was no point in trying to go home, anyway. Everything was gone.

Blackburn was too drained to argue, especially now with the chance to sleep. He found himself lying on a blanket pad in the police tent without remembering how he got there. The instant he closed his eyes he fell into a deep slumber filled with sensations of physical torment and images of disaster. As awful as these things were, they barely raised his pulse. There was nothing in the realm of nightmares that hadn't already been exceeded by the waking world.

***

Shane Nightingale stayed with the same crowd of refugees that he had joined in front of his house, even after they turned northward and trailed along in front of the dynamited mansions on Van Ness Avenue. Within an hour, maybe two, his band of wanderers made it all the way up to the boat docks at the top end of the city. Their journey was made in silence over the rubbled streets and through the smoky air, in silence broken by nothing but the scuffing of the relentless footsteps. If anyone spoke at all, it was almost always in a whisper.

He understood that. A sense of shame tends to keep one quiet. After the last three days, his own sense of shame was so strong that it attuned him to the same sort of things in others. He could see the signs of it all over them. To him, the crowd of wanderers resembled children who had just been severely scolded. Back at St. Adrian's, the other boys in his dormitory used to look like that after they had all been subjected to severe whippings, convinced by the friars that they deserved it.

So did the city deserve destruction? After all, everyone in San Francisco was aware that their town had a reputation for providing easy access to sins of every stripe. Throughout the seaport city, even people who never partook of the temptations offered by the sin trades nevertheless benefited from the money that sin brought to the local economy. The city's prosperity was related in countless ways to the infamous solicitations and brothels of the Barbary Coast's dark corners and to the hidden dens of Chinatown.

These wanderers around Shane had all been among the lucky citizens living off of the surplus prosperity boosted by such things, up until that very morning when all of them bore witness to the destruction of their world. Even as his impromptu band of companions searched for ways to escape the relentless firestorms, it seemed apparent to Shane that they all wondered how much personal stock they might hold in the city's collective guilt.

*And how can this city's guilt be doubted?* Look at what had befallen them. It stretched in every direction. For all he knew, for all that any of them could know, the entire planet was being shaken to pieces and burned to ashes, and there was nothing to do but watch. What difference would it make if they ran in one direction or another?

He overheard a couple of new arrivals to the crowd telling others there was something of a refugee camp in nearby Golden Gate Park. The messengers claimed that a few church groups had formed soup lines there.

Hardly anybody turned to head for the park, though.

Shane understood. A refugee camp would be a place full of victims. The emanations in such a place are strong, like the fouled air inside a damp hospital. No one had any desire to stay in smoke-stained tents among others who could only remind them of their broken condition. What they all wanted, as if thinking it with a single brain, was to escape the crumbling city.

The crowd passed squads of military men posted in front of certain mansions to fend off looters. The mansions seemed cruel and arrogant amid the destruction. It was hard not to hate whoever lived in such places; some of these guards were looting the homes themselves. Shane just looked away and said nothing, so ashamed over his failure to stop the Nightingale murders that he couldn't feel superior to anybody. Twice, he and a few of the other young men found themselves pulled from the crowd by Army unit commanders and conscripted to help move rubble off of stranded victims. It wasn't necessary to talk in order to do the work, and he liked the feeling of being good for something. Still, every time they released him, he ran ahead to catch up with his shambling group of familiar strangers.

The crowd reached the marina at around three in the morning. There was no one to help them. Any sort of seaworthy vessel had already sailed out. Rumors spread about a couple of ferries that would come and take anyone across the bay who could afford to pay profiteers' rates. A few of the refugees decided to wait for that uncertain rescue, but the rest of them began to drift. Within a couple of miles, they came to the Pacific shoreline at the western edge of the Presidio Military Reservation, but the soldiers on duty there didn't look happy to see the crowd. They ordered them all away, telling them every vessel had already been conscripted to help carry soldiers in from nearby Fort Baker on Horseshoe Bay.

The crowd had no choice but to cooperate—the soldiers raised their rifles and announced that Mayor Schmitz and Commanding General Funston had declared the city under full martial law. Any citizen who disobeyed a soldier's orders was to be shot. No prisoners would be taken because there was no place to put them.

Nobody made any strong objections. Everyone moved on. They kept up their slow pace until sometime around four a.m., when they came to the flats of Ocean Beach. Predictably, everything resembling a boat had already disappeared from there, too. People began circulating the same rumor Shane had heard before: something about an intact telegraph cable in the area. Some of them wanted to send messages out, but Shane couldn't picture sending a message to anybody. He wondered what could possibly be said about any of this, even if there was anyone out there to hear it.

A small group peeled off to search for the rumored telegraph station while Shane and the others walked away. This place had been their last hope of finding a boat, a ferry, even a raft to get them away from fires that appeared poised to burn all the way out to both horizons. Now there was nothing else to do but begin a walk of many miles, all the way off the San Francisco peninsula. Most of the group seemed determined to go.

Just when Shane decided to make the long hike with them, half a dozen mounted soldiers rode up at full speed. They reined in long enough to call out for able-bodied help. One of them spotted Shane, who found himself yanked up onto the horse and plopped down behind the saddle before he could object. The soldiers all wheeled their mounts and headed directly back toward the center of the city.

He was drafted onto a cleanup crew in the Mission District, the oldest part of the city. His particular group was sent off to the famous old Mission Dolores to do brick and stone repair. At that moment, the prospect of labor seemed like good news to him—he had no idea of where to go anyway. As long as he worked hard, nobody seemed to care that he didn't want to talk, so it seemed that the Mission Dolores work crew could be a good place to lose himself for a while.

He knew a little about the Mission, having learned from the friars back at the orphanage. It was the oldest Christian church in the city, dating back to the 1700s. He had even seen pictures of the Mission in a history book at the Nightingale house. As soon as his crew arrived, he recognized the famous lines of the Mission walls. It felt good to be in a place that seemed familiar, even if the feeling only came from someone else's photographs.

One of the soldiers told Shane there was a list of sites inside the city which were to be restored right away. The list was written by a so-called "Committee of Fifty," made up of the town's most prominent citizens, and this Mission Dolores was right near the top of that list.

The news got better. The "Committee" apparently realized that good labor depended upon a decent food supply, and so a bread and soup kitchen was in full swing outside the Mission doorway. The aromas reminded Shane that he hadn't eaten since the night before the earthquake. Suddenly it was all he could do to stay on his feet long enough to get through the line. He ate until he became sick out on the street, then he went back through and ate a second time.

By the time the sun was all the way up, Shane was full and the food was staying down. The hours began melting by while he worked in a hand-to-hand brick line, helping to carry away fallen bits of the newer church built next to the old Mission. He tried to give the appearance of confidence by doing an impression of a man who knows how to work. Even when he smashed his fingers, he didn't allow himself any more reaction than to gasp at the pain. The second time it happened, when he couldn't keep the tears from rolling, he managed to wipe them off with his shoulders while he kept on working.

The task got him all the way to lunchtime before the work ran out. He took another helping of bread and soup and had just enough time to choke it down before being drafted into another small crew. They were to reset the gravestones around the Mission's old cemetery, a small plot of land packed full of San Francisco's earliest settlers. It was relatively easy work, so the crew alternated their graveyard labor with spells of firefighter duty within the surrounding neighborhood. However, Shane saw there wasn't much to be accomplished against the fires. Somebody said there was a rumor about hoses that were going to pump ocean water all the way up from the pier, but there weren't any to be seen.

It seemed as if they were only there to witness the destruction. There was no way to do battle with it, other than helping to pull trapped people out of the fire's way, or by helping to move important belongings. The thick adobe walls of the Mission and its clay-shingled roof were easy enough to save from the fires, however, and while the city founders' gravesites had taken some damage, the cemetery portion struck Shane as basically unscathed and beautifully peaceful. He immediately understood why the "Committee of Fifty" included this place on their list.

The physical work was perfect for him, easing his tightened muscles and numbing his scrambled emotions. Meanwhile, the food line stayed active, and a few more trips carried him through the rest of the day. By evening, the little cemetery almost looked as if nothing had happened there.

Shane's team of exhausted conscripts finished for the day just as thick rain finally began to blow in off the sea. The workers sent up a spontaneous cheer. Shane even felt the gnawing ache lift off his chest for a few seconds, borne up by the sound.

Most of the drafted workers were allowed to leave at that point, but Shane dawdled around. He hated the thought of leaving the food line before they took it down. One of the grateful Mission friars noticed that Shane was making it a point not to leave, and asked if he wanted to lie down on a sleeping blanket there under the Mission's strong roof. The simple generosity of the question caught Shane so off guard his throat seized up. He couldn't bring himself to risk an answer without breaking down, and he was grateful when the friar accepted that Shane could only nod. The man handed him a sleeping roll and pointed to an isolated corner.

Shane eagerly rolled out the mat and lay down. The padding was just thick enough to soften the floor; he could still feel the cold stone beneath, but that didn't matter. It was a kingly luxury to remain sheltered in that dry and quiet place, while outside the Mission a forgiving rain gradually began to quench the city's smoldering ruins.

---

Blackburn smelled the thick char in the air before he heard the words. "Sergeant. You awake? Come on, now, Sergeant—you awake?"

He opened his eyes and looked up into the face of another young SFPD lieutenant. The lieutenant's face glowed orange and yellow in the light of his field lantern. He repeatedly jabbed Blackburn's bare foot with his boot heel.

"I'm up!" Blackburn groused.

"You sure, now?"

"Wide awake."

"You don't *look* wide awake, Sergeant. You know what day it is? It's Saturday evening, almost seven o'clock. You been out cold, all day long!"

"God's sake, Lieutenant! I went straight from digging graves the first day to fighting the fires when they came through here."

"Are you being insubordinate, Sergeant?" the lieutenant asked with a sneer.

"No. Sir. I am trying to say a man has to have some rest."

The lieutenant clucked his tongue in the way he reserved for men of lesser rank. "Now, them volunteer ladies over there got a coffee wagon set up. Go get yourself some and stay awake. I'm gonna have orders for you."

The lieutenant turned away to check a sheaf of notes in a leather-bound notebook and walked off muttering, "And then by God, I'm gonna get some sleep myself. Somebody else can try to shovel their way through this shit pile."

Alone now, Blackburn strained to see out into the night. Countless points of orange glow marked the horizon in all directions. They were the deep fires that hadn't succumbed to the rain yet, even though the surface fires were mostly extinguished. After hours of light drizzle, thick trails of steam rose from the downed buildings all around the edge of Portsmouth Square. The stench of burning things drifted everywhere.

The scene was how his boyhood pastors had described Hell to him. He rose to his feet, painfully stiff, and headed for the coffee wagon.

Before he took three steps, the young lieutenant called out, "All right, then, Sergeant! The next thing on this list is the Mission Dolores. Their messenger said it's *muy importante, comprendo?* Take your coffee and hike over to Sixteenth Street. Check up on the Mission's cleanup progress. The town bigwigs want to make sure our civic heritage is protected."

The lieutenant stepped close to Blackburn for emphasis and went on, "Offer them police assistance to guard the place, but listen to me: *Convince them they don't need it.* Truth is, we couldn't get around to helping them for days, and we don't need word about police weakness getting around."

"I'll try, sir."

"Don't *try*, Sergeant, accomplish your task! Encourage them. Flatter them if you have to. Slather them with bullshit if that works. Just convince them they can handle it on their own. People congregate at a famous old church like that, they trade gossip, you get it? If the city realizes how badly overwhelmed we are—"

That one set off Blackburn in spite of himself. "Well, goddamn it, Lieutenant, is there some mysterious reason we can't draft civilians and maybe make some real progress?"

The lieutenant glared at him and raised the lantern to include Blackburn in the glow. "Your problem is your mouth, Sergeant. Now, I know what an outstanding job you did here, but your mouth could be the one thing that winds up holding you back. Get your coffee and get going. When you complete your task at the Mission, take a few hours off. Rest up. Check the ruins at your apartment, though you'll likely be wasting your time."

"Thank you for the advice, sir!" Blackburn said with too much enthusiasm. He saluted, waited for the return, never got one. The lieutenant was gone. Blackburn lowered his arm, turned around, and headed for the coffee table. Coffee. That was something, anyway.

---

Shane heard boot steps along with the scraping of a pair of sandals. Instinct told him if he wanted to avoid talking to anyone, to lie still on the Mission floor and do his best to fake being sound asleep. Through squinted eyes, he watched the same kindly friar who had given Shane his blanket roll. Now the priest shuffled along beside a police sergeant and—*oh, my God!*—it was the same man who had just been in Shane's dream, the one who was actually in the Nightingale house.

How could that be?

He was too stunned to react while the footsteps came close…the footsteps paused…Shane could hear the big man's breathing.

"So that's it, then?" the sergeant's voice boomed. He stepped into view, just a few feet away.

The Mission assistant quickly drew close to the sergeant and raised a finger to his lips, then pointed down to Shane's makeshift bed. Shane dropped his eyelids closed the rest of the way and heard the sergeant mutter, "Oh," then lower his voice before continuing. "So you haven't really had any other problems here, right?"

"Sergeant Blackburn, I get the distinct impression that you don't want to hear what I've been telling you."

"Oh, now, don't say that. You just don't realize how much clever work your volunteers already accomplished here. Maybe they helped keep thieves away, just being here! Amazing teamwork! No outbreaks of trouble, no fistfights, no need for a police presence at all."

"Sergeant, this Mission is a valuable part of the city's historical—"

"All right! All right, listen, Padre, my head is splitting open. Tell you what; let me get a couple hours of shut-eye here, and after that we'll talk."

"You should tell your commanders at City Hall that my position will not change. We need a sizeable labor crew here, and that will require police presence. Just because we've had no trouble yet is no reason to—"

"Some *rest*, Padre," Blackburn interrupted. "It's what I really need. Then we'll talk. Aren't you always more cheerful after you've had some sleep?"

There was a pause. Shane couldn't tell what it meant, until the padre's quiet voice replied, "I'll get you a bedroll. Take the corner opposite the young man over there."

Shane bit his lip in frustration. The big sergeant—an unknowing witness to the Nightingale family murder scene—was going to lie down and sleep no more than ten feet from Shane's spot on the floor. The whole situation mocked him. Surely the Devil was in control of his life now.

While he listened to the padre's sandals scuffing out of the room, his heartbeat hammered until it felt like it could create echoes off the stone floor. Irrational fears flooded him. What if this sergeant could simply take a good look at Shane and somehow see his whole dreadful story written on him? What if, with a single glance, the big man somehow realized the two of them had been inches from one another inside a now-vanished crime scene?

Shane could hear the big man breathing, almost sighing. He sounded tired. The sergeant yawned and stretched, popping his joints, until the padre finally returned with the bedroll. The two men exchanged a few pleasantries, then the friar disappeared and left the sergeant alone there with Shane, trapped as surely as those unfortunates under the rubble.

All he could do at the moment was to keep faking sleep while he listened to the sergeant spread out his roll, slip off his boots, and lie down. After a minute, the sergeant's breathing became deep and even.

At least he never said anything.

It seemed safe enough to assume the big man didn't have any sense of who Shane was. That offered some comfort, but he still had to wonder how anyone could fail to see the guilt boiling inside of him. Strangely, nobody had so far. How long could that last? He wanted nothing more than to remain as a bundle of rags sleeping in the corner, lost among thousands of faceless refugees.

He gradually drifted back to sleep, resolved that if this Sergeant Blackburn of the City Hall precinct was still around when he woke up, he would slip away without giving the man a chance to ask him anything.

# 4

FIVE DAYS AFTER THE GREAT EARTHQUAKE
Monday, April 23

TOMMIE SIPPED A STEAMING MIX of oolong tea, honeycomb, and three teaspoons of whiskey while he stood nude but for his slippers before the large window of his top-floor study. Glorious. His Victorian house atop fabulous Russian Hill stood unscathed by the earthquake and the fires. He received a rush of affirmation at this evidence of his value compared to the city's ruffian public, to the point that while he took in the sight of the ruined city, he found the rest of its scrambling victims mildly disgusting, like the panhandler who stumbled into his favorite restaurant the other evening and disrupted the *amuse-bouche* with his pitiful sob story and a plea for free money.

Outside his home, the path of destruction stretched in all directions, a true godsend. In spite of heroic efforts from the surviving firefighters and police, almost nothing done by human beings to fight the leaping firestorms had done any good. The only evidence left in the city was that of Nature's indifference to suffering. Everything else went up in smoke.

Death was everywhere. For uncountable numbers of terrified residents who thought that the earthquake and fires signified the end of the world, it turned out to be precisely that. Rats now roamed the city with impunity. Tommie was astonished by how many of the rodents found their way out of burning buildings. *Only five days*, he marveled, *and they've already learned not to fear us.*

He struck a graceful pose before a full-length mirror: deep feminine contemplation. *So then*, he asked himself, *how do I move in harmony with this turn of events?* Tommie knew the mayor's office was doing its best to crank out information to the newspapers and wire services regarding the numbers of the injured and dead. But the simple truth was nobody could offer anything better than a well-intended guess, and estimates would be held down to minimal levels. It struck Tommie that the authorities were providing valuable aid in covering his tracks.

He was aware of all these things because just the day before, he ventured out in male clothing to catch up on general gossip. Although he kept to himself while strolling through the refugee camps, he frequently paused just long enough to eavesdrop. By the time he returned home, he had a good general knowledge of the state of things.

It struck Tommie that the writings of history seldom included reliable information about the ways things smelled and the impact of stench upon human behavior. If one day he were to write a tome about this disaster, he would write thousands of words about the sense of smell in human beings, and the massive capacity for assault upon a person using nothing more than elements of stench and their impact upon human reaction. Despite the onshore breezes, the city continued to reek of rotting and burned flesh and human droppings among the rubble. Nearly every person he passed on the streets looked as if Life had just smacked them in the face, hard. You could close your eyes to it all, but everybody has to breathe...

For him, those facts merely added to the same self-evident truth he had seen demonstrated by the advancing wall of flames when the majestic conflagration advancing upon his home split in two. The two sections each proceeded *around the sides* of Tommie's lovely hilltop neighborhood— completely sparing his house, his birthright, the only home he knew. And as for the earthquake itself, his own recovery required little more than throwing out a few broken lamps and rehanging some art. Now, all it took was a simmered potpourri of cinnamon and allspice to conceal the charcoal smells from blackened ruins only a few blocks away.

He stepped out of the slippers. Now stark naked, Tommie set aside his empty glass and began to roll his new, electrically powered vacuum cleaner gracefully across the floor. The diesel generator down in the basement chugged up more than enough power while Tommie guided the machine back and forth, back and forth, using the same slow and sweeping motions displayed by the lady in the magazine advertisement. He carefully kept his free hand out to the side, arm raised halfway between the hip and the shoulder, fingertips extended. The invention itself had only been on the market for a few years. *Pricy!* The best people all had them. He practically danced with the machine.

And so the Great Earthquake had vaulted Tommie into his dream, granting him the power of an avenging angel who rises up to mete out justice. From the first moment, Tommie had known where to start: that arrogant bag of skin, Mr. Nightingale, the dry goods man and one of Tommie's most unhappy creditors.

For years, Nightingale had allowed Tommie to pay off his tab whenever he got around to it. So what if he neglected payment for a year or so? Money was not an issue. Tommie could write out a bank check for just about anything he wanted. It was his reward for choosing the right parents and patiently awaiting the day of their aided demise. He would have forgotten the whole Nightingale thing by now, never feeling a hint of difference in his daily life.

The issue was how much it pained him to pay out money at all. It seriously pained him, and it made no difference that he had so much. Each time he paid a bill, it felt like swallowing a tiny dose of poison. As far as Tommie could see it, every price tag, every line of credit, every invoice that came in the mail, they were all nothing more than coded and toxic messages from a world that wanted to take and take and take until everything Tommie had was gone. He had to wonder, where would that leave a creature such as him?

His adoptive parents made good on their promise to educate him and set up a wonderfully generous endowment plan for his future, which was helpful of course, but their supposed generosity made them look stupid in his eyes. For the last few years of their lives, it mostly hurt to look at them.

He knew and they knew and he knew they knew he knew that they had willed everything in their opulent life to him, waiting only upon their eventual demise. No, of course he did not help Mother Nature along with that. But he appreciated their choice to have so many rhododendron plants on the grounds all around the house. He had no part in those choices, and the doctor speculated they appeared to have accidentally consumed homemade honey taken from bees who harvested pollen from the rhododendron blooms, right there on the grounds. After all, there was a sizeable spike in blooms that year, plenty of sunshine, and the boost in rhododendron pollen in their homemade honey had reached deadly levels.

As a devout student of Irony, Tommie found the tangy flavor of their demise delightful.

He cried and cried over their deaths for public consumption, but he kept the plants. Sentimental value and all.

He struck another lovely and graceful pose before the mirror, arching one eyebrow while he cast his gaze to the floor and back to eye level. His reflection looked like it wanted to bend him over a trunk.

It had never been necessary for Nightingale to take him to court and win a judgment against him. Everyone knew Tommie was good for it. *They ought to know, anyway.* All of them. They had no excuse for not knowing. Nightingale had shown no appreciation, no respect at all for Tommie's point of view. First the greedy man put a lien on Tommie's house. Then, the day before the earthquake, the fool actually showed up at Tommie's door to dun him for payment. Unannounced and uninvited. All this over a few thousand dollars.

Nearly catching Tommie inappropriately attired, writhing on the floor in private personal amusement.

And so it made no difference that Nightingale had been out tending to his store, right after the quakes died down. His presence at home would have accomplished nothing for the rest of the family. Tommie would have just killed him, first thing. The result for the others would have been the same.

A house full of females, in a time of general civic emergency, when everybody's full attention was focused on the earthquake and fires. What a perfect situation. What an ideal set of victims they proved to be for Tommie's next adventure and for the true Savoring of his work. It was all the better, since none of the Nightingales had any idea who he was or why he was there.

The memories swept over him in a wave of ecstasy. Tommie felt good, all the way down into his bones. The thought struck him, *there's a poem in this.* A fine poem: short, romantic, musical. He picked up a notepad and his silver writing pen, to put his calligraphy studies to use.

*Your horror was so pure,*
*Rays of terror flashed from your eyes*
*Like the breath of a dying angel.*

Those three lines were all it needed. Something about it made him crave a sexual release. Within moments, satisfaction filled him like warm and soapy bathwater. With it came an inspiration—from that moment forward, each of Tommie's deserving ones would get an original poem left behind with them. Yes indeed! To commemorate their contribution to the Savored experience.

As soon as darkness fell, he got into full costume and makeup, then headed for the Barbary Coast. A brief step backward, for old times' sake. A quick knife kill and an easy escape. The drunks were sure to be back down there, feeding their habits again, earthquake or not. Who among them didn't deserve it? *The poem's the thing.* What Tommie needed most of all was a deserving corpse to pin one on.

# 5

THREE WEEKS AFTER THE GREAT EARTHQUAKE
Early May

SHANE'S DOGGED WORK HABITS quickly endeared him to the padres. He became all the more valuable after it dawned on the holy men that neither the San Francisco Police Department nor the United States Army could supply the labor to repair and guard the Mission, regardless of the good intentions of the Committee of Fifty. The priests already realized Shane was homeless, so now they asked about his family. All he was able to tell them was they had been lost to the Great Earthquake. Beyond that, his throat locked up on him when he tried to explain.

Once they understood what he was trying to say, they offered him a position there at the Mission. There was need of a grave tender and night watchman for the Mission cemetery, because there was a real danger that some of the more desperate earthquake victims might decide to raid the city founders' resting places for buried gold and jewelry. Shane's compensation for the job was only a few pennies per day, but meals were included at the friars' table and they offered to let him set up a permanent living space in an empty toolshed without realizing he was already sleeping there.

He snatched at the opportunity. All he had to do to move in was hang his watch on one of the nails protruding from the rough wooden walls, and he was there.

A grave tender. A fitting job for someone as dead as he felt inside. But it did what mattered most and gave him a place to exist, a reason to be. The core of his days formed around a welcome routine of work, meals, and rest.

He quickly learned that the padres at the Mission were generally not like the friars at the orphanage at all; they left him alone to his chores and his daily life. One or two of them came sniffing around, but he refused to respond and instead hit them with his practiced blank stare. It worked because it gave them the opportunity to dismiss him as crazy and keep their dignity while they walked away.

Shane hardly felt the slip of time. On the outside, he buried himself in his new life at Mission Dolores. Inside, he survived private turmoil with a simple grim march through days of routine and repetition, each more or less the same as the next while he moved through them like a sleepwalker. Before the quake, a demeanor such as his would have called attention to itself, perhaps gotten him in trouble. Now everybody on the streets seemed preoccupied with their own stock of primal fear. Many carried a lingering sense of doom approaching just over the horizon. It was true, there was no way to know if this was over.

In the nights that followed, the natural human tendency to feel rage over the betrayal of the ground beneath their feet gave everyone plenty of cause to wake up screaming. *Night criers.* He wondered if he was one of them. Living alone out in the toolshed as he was, how would he know?

Even the quiet ones slept without truly resting, those who silently swallowed their nightmares and never spoke of them. They clenched their jaws hard enough to crack their teeth and then minimized their suffering by denying its existence. Among people in such a state, Shane had no trouble passing unnoticed.

His state of mind was perfect for the job of tending to a graveyard. He craved the isolation. Inside of those first days and weeks, his method of disguise was to do his best to act normally, but without attempting to speak, and to avoid drawing anyone's special attention until he could get clear of them. He took examples from the non-English-speaking Chinese and Mexican laborers after he realized they could get through most situations with a combination of shrugs and hand gestures. It was a minor revelation.

His reputation as a good worker soon began to protect him. He found that he was able to do a good enough job at his assigned tasks to make others appreciative of his presence and less inclined to get suspicious about him. He was living among those who considered repeated reliability and honest labor to be a powerful statement of personal character if it was combined with a quiet and humble demeanor. By and large, people left him alone.

Once the friars demonstrated how they wanted the repair work to be done—the careful mixing of fine mortar, the precise fitting and gluing of broken tombstones and statuary—he discovered that he could sometimes escape the grip of his despair for a good hour or two while he was absorbed in his work. There was a small sense of peace and satisfaction to be coaxed from the results, even if the relief never lasted for long. He was grateful to do the jobs right there where he was living, and to spend both the nights and the days among his newly repaired handiworks.

His first serious solo job assignment was to repair the split gravestone of one Catherine Hoban, who died in 1854 at the age of twenty-six. Shane's mind filled with images from the woman's time, because the strict monks at St. Adrian's had made sure he knew all about the Gold Rush era. The stone's inscription told of Catherine Hoban, who lived through the great gold strike of 1849, and later through the following massive surge in the city population, plus the huge influx of young Chinese men imported as labor. Catherine Hoban was alive when San Francisco exploded into an international presence as a seaport. She died just as the city was emerging, when she and San Francisco were both still young.

Shane carefully daubed the fine mortar all along the two edges of her broken headstone, and while he worked, he tried to feel for a presence in her grave. He wondered, was there something that would indicate whether or not Catherine Hoban had died a peaceful death, or was hers violent and terrible? The tombstone markings told him nothing.

He fit the two pieces together and made sure there was a complete bond all the way along the break, then held them in place by hand while the mortar dried. He could accomplish the task easier by propping the two pieces in place, but he wanted to give respect to the repaired stone and set it with perfect balance by hand.

The city was enjoying a brief break in the pounding rain of the past few days, and he was comfortable enough while he held the two stone pieces together that he drifted away in memories of peaceful days at St. Adrian's. The monks there had always told Shane he was left at their door with nothing more than a piece of paper which only said, "Shane, 4, born January 1." No last name. No other information.

He had always found it hard to accept that he was already four years old when he arrived at St. Adrian's. If that was true, it seemed like he ought to be able to remember something of his life before the orphanage. But his memory of anything prior to being there was blank.

Inside St. Adrian of Canterbury's Home for Delinquents and Orphans, his daily life always reminded him of the life of an ant, the place itself a busy anthill: life there was a relentless pace of endless chores, one after another after another. He was rarely able to leave the orphanage, so whenever he had free time, he explored the world through the books that the friars taught him to read. And although the friars and their Helpers gave plenty of reason to fear their discipline, they employed that fear against their young charges by enforcing the proposition that ignorance was deadly.

His unwavering focus came from the friars' conviction that knowledge might actually make a difference in the lives of these children, who were otherwise guaranteed an existence as social throwaways. They could survive a childhood without ever being adopted, but the friars often promised them that without education, they could choose between growing up to be prostitutes or thieves. And then they could take their natural places among the other denizens of the Barbary Coast district, down by the shrouded waterfront.

So Shane made it a never-ending point to absorb all of the friars' lessons and to score well enough on their tests so they saved their worst torments for thicker heads. The way he looked at it, the constant access to books saved his life in that place.

As for the more intimate arts of family existence, it was only over the past year in the Nightingale house that he ever witnessed and participated in the daily life of an actual family. The most awkward part at first, for a boy of eleven, was the unaccustomed closeness of two "sisters" who were so highly attractive to him. He came to hate his penis for being untrustworthy and made it a habit around the house to always carry something he could swing around in front of himself if the need arose.

Amy's sense of music filled his heart from the day he arrived. Her voice expressed a light and feminine energy that seemed to just soar up from her, free of self-consciousness. By the time his first two weeks in the Nightingale house passed, Shane was convinced he was lucky to be able to live so close to her. He could never allow himself to forget that there was to be nothing more; life slapped him flat to the ground every day. The worst of it was the simple fact that he was still only twelve, and a sixteen-year-old girl was older by a lifetime. Even if he had come up in the proper social class, she never would have welcomed his affection.

It was Carolyn, most of all, who always saw him as nothing more than what he was: a house servant. But sometimes she let him hold her hand to steady her while she practiced standing on the tips of her toes. She was so light and graceful, as if her bones were hollow like those of a bird. Delicate and full of quiet mischief, she dreamed of being a ballerina. Carolyn ignored parental objections to her dancing and spent about half of every day flying through the air. For one crazed instant, Shane wondered how the killer knew Carolyn was the dancer in the family. For a long time, Shane had heard the madman swinging her body, dashing her against the walls.

It was during the final weeks prior to the earthquake that Shane felt himself sinking into the family unit and beginning to perceive them in new ways. The constant combination of civilized discourse and household intimacy forced him to learn to work within a family relationship. The little routines of it came to feel good, reassuring.

Now his torment included a palpable sense of loss over this new way of being with others—and the guilt of having done nothing but lie in his hidden pantry bed, soaking his pants, unable to move or cry out while the family was systematically slaughtered. No matter how he reasoned his way through it, in the end, Shane knew his present-day circumstances were the direct result of his inability to fight against the killer. What if he could have won, somehow, through sheer luck? Or what if his display of boldness and bravery could have *forced* God to grant him a miracle? It was clear that his new curse of stuttering kicked in because some part of himself wanted to stop in the middle of whatever else he was saying and instead scream out that he was a coward.

When his muscles began to ache from holding the tombstone pieces in place, he realized a good amount of time had passed while he held the mortared stones, so he gently tested the glue and confirmed that the bond was strong enough. He stood up and looked at Catherine Hoban's head-stone: a tall, thin flag of granite. The balance between the two rejoined sections was as perfect as he could make it.

When he stepped back to admire his handiwork on the gravestone, he felt the simple pleasure of taking pride in the work of his hands.

---

Randall Blackburn stood alone in the darkened shadows of a garbage-fouled back alley near the Barbary Coast district. He stared down at the dead man's body, which was not that of an ordinary waterfront drunk. This one was a handsome fellow in the prime of his life. He was perfectly dressed, a well-heeled gentleman in an expensive wool suit, groomed down to the details. This was a victim who would certainly be missed by somebody.

There was a note on the body which, along with the telltale *modus operandi*, assured Blackburn that The Surgeon had struck for the second time in nine days. The wound from the heavy-bladed throwing knife was visible at the base of the man's skull. While the wound itself didn't prove the knife was thrown, the obvious depth and angle of entry practically guaranteed that there was no other way to cause that exact injury. And tonight's victim was the second to have a fancy note attached. That first note had been a crude attempt to use humor to further debase the victim. Blackburn clearly recalled its swirling, feminine hand and the preposterous message:

*Worthlessness is purity, Making me a diamond Among the rejected.*

Blackburn didn't believe he was seeing the work of some deranged copycat in tonight's victim. The specific method of brutality, the skill at silent killing, the lack of interest in robbery—these things were more than clues, they were trademarks. No, this Surgeon character was evolving herself a new style. Her tastes were changing.

That single fact was so promising that it made Blackburn feel hopeful. Newness equals unfamiliarity, and unfamiliarity could keep The Surgeon off balance just long enough for her to make a mistake.

For the past several days, the authorities had managed to keep news of that first note away from the newspapers, hoping that by retaining some of the details they might gain leverage in interviewing suspects. Up to this point, secrecy hadn't been much of a challenge; the victims had all been broken men, barely noticed in life and ignored in death. But on this night, with a victim who looked like a gentleman, it was plain that silence from the police would not suffice.

Once again, the crime had happened inside Blackburn's beat during his midnight shift. An involuntary shiver ran up his back when he briefly wondered if the killer was deliberately doing this to him, sending some sort of message. But he decided there was no reason to think anything like that. Yet.

After all, the persistent rumor was still that the killer was one of the street whores, and long-term planning didn't exist in their world. And the worst he had ever done was to arrest them and pull them in off of the streets for a night, where they could safely sleep it off and then have a hot meal the next day. For some, jail was the best accommodation they visited all week.

*But who, then?* The question taunted him.

The nicely dressed dead fellow at Blackburn's feet was going to be the spoiler of certain ambitions held by Mayor Schmitz and Chief Dinan. Now with this high-class victim, they couldn't possibly keep the new trend of notes a secret and then employ that secret in tricking a suspect into confession, which would have allowed the mayor and the chief to come off as heroes for the newspapers. A major public relations event such as the capture of a wanton killer would have served both men well.

Blackburn felt a sinking sensation as he acknowledged that another brazen murder on his watch was a guarantee of more "punishment" with continual midnight assignments on the Barbary Coast. It tormented him to know that this time he was going to be in such a deep trench with the brass that he might never dig his career back out.

He bent close enough to read the handwriting on the small paper note. This one was neatly placed in one of the body's fists. The delicate slip of paper was perfectly smooth and unwrinkled, tucked between two of the dead fist's fingers.

*The world has loved me, made me welcome everywhere I stayed*
*But I left my wife to disgrace myself on women who are paid*
*And nothing could have stopped me but The Blade.*

"At least this one rhymes," Blackburn muttered. So The Surgeon wanted everyone to know this victim was a man who deserved harsh justice. At that moment the body expelled gas, as if to confirm that this one wasn't going to keep itself away from the newspapers. The Surgeon's new trademark doggerel "poems" would be public knowledge before long, making the department brass unhappy in the extreme. Although the sun wasn't going to come up for another two hours, Blackburn already sensed that the day was going nowhere but downhill.

He whistled down a mounted officer and told him to hurry back to the station house for a body recovery wagon. The officer cantered away, and then there was nothing left to do but stand guard over the scene.

---

Shane's new job carried a lot of free time, especially during late night hours. So within his first couple of weeks at the Mission Dolores cemetery, he began trying to undo his maddening stammer by reading out loud, after he accidentally discovered he could still speak clearly if he was reading. He had been silently going over an announcement on the church bulletin board when he began to mumble the words under his breath. It went on for a while before he realized what he was doing—something about having the words to read and follow allowed him to bypass his stutter. Not only did he speak clearly when reading aloud, it was effortless. With that realization, he began to practice reading in earnest. He generally did it at night, but he would take time out for it anytime he was alone. It soothed him to be able to hear the sound of his own voice speaking clearly once again. It gave him a form of hope.

Besides, he was seldom ready to go to sleep before sunrise, ever since the unthinkable thing. It felt safer to sleep in the daytime—harder for anybody to sneak up on him. Daylight also helped him to wake up faster whenever the familiar nightmares returned.

But at night, alone and safe in the cemetery, Shane wrapped himself in darkness like a warm blanket. It never occurred to him to think of the place as frightening. Instead, he paced among worn tombstones and practiced his reading by lantern light. While the words on the pages flowed easily from his mouth, he concentrated on impressing his brain with the sensation of speaking freely, hoping the practice would eventually keep his speech from seizing up as soon as he went off of the page and tried to talk.

Most of the time, he read without any real regard for the content of the article. Once in a while, though, a story captured his imagination. Especially the society pages, adorned as they were with pen-and-ink sketches, sometimes even daguerreotype photographs of successful men and women. The shots accompanied articles about high-society weddings, births, graduations, and charity balls. The images stuck to his brain like flypaper. It wasn't the idea of money and power that was so captivating; it was the impression of contentedness. They all looked so satisfied. How could it be otherwise for such people, living such lives?

He tried to envision what it must be like to live each day feeling assured that they were a desired presence anywhere they went, always knowing just how to behave and what to do. These people had the world's stamp of approval. Unlike Shane, their conduct brought credit to their families. No doubt, any one of them would have known what to do in the Nightingale house. They would have been able to take action where he could do nothing more than lie paralyzed.

The Nightingale family had given Shane their last name and saved him from his life as a foundling, showing him a house where there was decency and discipline for everyone, even if he was little more than a glorified servant. It wasn't an unhappy household; happiness simply wasn't part of the daily roster. Mr. and Mrs. Nightingale were both vocal supporters of hot baths, cool tempers, and cold routines. It felt sterile to Shane, even though he couldn't imagine what he would actually do differently, given the chance.

He only knew that despite his respect and fondness for the people he lived to serve, he never felt any desire to emulate their way of life. That was even truer now that being reminded of the Nightingale house made his mouth taste of ashes.

Shane became consumed by the urge to study the happy people of the world and discover the secret to living their lives. Most of all, he wondered what they might know that might have given him the power to take action back in the Nightingale house, if only he had known it too. Could learning the answers to that guarantee such a thing would never happen again? That question, especially, began to haunt him.

Now while he read the society pages and practiced his speaking, he was also searching for a *particular example*—somebody who might teach him, by personal demonstration, the secret of how to live. But since Shane also knew that privileged people have authority—his experience in life so far had shown him that too much authority tends to turn nice people into mean ones and to make nasty people just plain evil—his plan was to select his subjects, then hang back and observe them from a distance. Let them teach him without realizing it. That seemed safer than confessing his weakness and asking for help, exposing himself to scorn and perhaps earning himself a ticket back to St. Adrian's, where children could sometimes be heard making those same yelps of surprise and fear that he now knew far too well.

Surely these society people were the antithesis of nearly everything he had absorbed with the hardscrabble survival skills learned in the orphanage, or the grim and gray discipline of the Nightingale house. He would practice. He would do more than practice; he would study them, copy them any way he could. There was no choice. Until he did, he felt certain he was missing too many pieces inside to be able to hold his own out there among the fast-talkers. With lives such as these society people seemed to have, surely they knew how to avoid going through their days feeling like garbage. Surely there was something he could learn from them.

"What a thing," Shane said under his breath, "that anyone can actually live like that." His mind sank into the fantasy images while his body exhaled so deeply that the muscles rattled in his shoulders and his legs. "What a thing," he said again, just because it seemed to need saying. He was too preoccupied to notice that he was speaking without any sort of stammer at all.

# 6

ONE MONTH AFTER THE GREAT EARTHQUAKE AND FIRES

LIEUTENANT GREGORY MOSES could not believe his good fortune when he was given the job of Acting Station Chief at the City Hall precinct house. It was only a temporary position, and he never let himself forget that. The job literally fell into his lap with the Great Earthquake, and it had somehow remained there throughout the four weeks since. Nearly everything about the job still felt new, and virtually none of it was comfortable. Moses's decades of experience as the department's Keeper of Records never gave him any reason to expect to find himself as a station chief. And since Moses had never tasted the curse of political ambition, the personality traits necessary for leadership were baffling to him. After so many quiet years in the Record Keeping Department, padding back and forth among the stacks and files, the instant promotion and its never-ending urgencies felt about as natural as a suit of needles.

There was no avoiding it. Moses was promoted at the direct order of Police Chief Dinan on the very day of the quake, after Station Chief Winkle took a fatal brick to the skull. Somebody pulled one of the precinct's old command-succession charts from the City Hall ruins to see who was next in line for the job, but it turned out every individual on the list was either dead or missing. Chief Dinan read farther down the list than anybody ever expected circumstances to actually require and came to: *Number 7: Head of the Record Keeping Department.* That would be one Gregory Moses.

Moses's rank of lieutenant had always been a simple perquisite grafted onto his job, a reminder that confidentiality was of the essence. For many years, the first order of secrecy down at City Hall had fallen to him. Because of Moses, all the friends and relatives of the "Committee of Fifty," plus the city's other backroom organizations, were able to conduct their lives inside a zone of official silence. No matter how nasty certain personal events might be, Moses always saw to it all of the appropriate sensitive facts were reliably covered over. While it was true that Moses's line of work made him the custodian of a world of secrets, rather like a father confessor, the secrets he held were not the kinds of things that were helpful in running a police station and the precinct it served.

Accordingly, each one of these thirty days since the Great Earthquake had felt like a long trudge through knee-deep water. Every moment was impossibly hard. Not only was Moses inexperienced with command, but while he called the morning roll and handed out the daily assignments, his brain burned with a pervasive sense that when it came to acceptance by the rank and file, he was in dangerous territory.

Back when the news of his fateful promotion first reached him, Moses experienced it as some sort of dark anti-miracle, as if sent by demons— every pound of fat on his body quivered with the realization that this uncanny opportunity had come to him at precisely the wrong moment in his life. He was a good hundred and fifty pounds overweight, having long since passed "portly" and landed firmly in the territory of the morbidly obese. Back in the Record Keeping Department, nobody ever called him to task about it. There was an unspoken agreement that Moses was to be tolerated so long as he did solid and reliable work, never betrayed any secrets, and stayed out of sight among the stacks.

And until the Great Earthquake, he was safe in his humble ambition of efficiently running the Record Keeping Department and knowing he would be left in peace to slowly die inside his expanding carcass. He had discovered that the relief of giving up on life had provided a strange form of comfort to his depressed condition. Moses was otherwise loath to be the center of attention anywhere, especially in a command position as he was now, responsible for dozens of officers who could see at a glance that he was unfit for the job.

He missed the quiet anonymity of the stacks. Now he couldn't get the eyeballs off of him. For the last four weeks, his bizarre turn of fortune had forced him to stay on the job as much as eighteen hours a day, seven days a week. He took no time off, hoping to use his sheer level of work effort to compensate for his obvious lack of worth. And since he had survived all that time on little more than soups and cigars, the weight was falling off of him. If he could keep that up, in a year or so he might look normal again.

But it was hopeless and he knew it. Without the nearly supernatural level of motivation he experienced in the wake of the Great Earthquake and Fires, as they were now being called, he would never be able to suppress his appetite for long enough.

For now, at least, it was easy to endure hunger. His hunger pains helped to confirm that at least he was doing what he could about himself, knowing he couldn't possibly have the respect of the other officers, most of whom kept themselves in fine condition. He was lucky the men listened to him at all. After all, what was he going to do in the event of a general mutiny, break down in tears?

Most of the time, Moses sealed himself inside his work routines to insulate himself from the hot sensation of people's stares and the implications in their eyes. He stayed so busy with one task after another, hour to hour, day to day, that the business rituals became unseen armor. For a while, the armor helped him to keep away from certain other, more difficult aspects of his job. These job aspects were the ones that made it necessary to have an approved line of succession for Station Chief in the first place—they were the reasons you couldn't possibly fill the position by placing an ad.

Thus it wasn't the labor of the job that challenged him, it was the question of what to do about his predecessor's complex web of favors and punishments. He already knew quite a bit about the predecessor's private agenda: men who were owed favors, payoffs, or reprimands by the precinct. His knowledge of secret things was a clear and convincing sign that he carried a larger than average nightstick, but how long could that intimidation last? If there was any hope at all of staying on in this position—an impossibility it embarrassed him to consider—much would be required of him.

Most importantly, Moses knew it was vital to begin sending out a steady stream of authoritative signs to the rank and file. He needed to act as if he would always be the Station Chief, even if the idea was absurd. So far, he had only been able to put off fulfilling the former job holder's political obligations because of all the chaos in the recovering city. But his honeymoon period in the new job was now stretched to the maximum, and human nature was kicking back in. If Moses planned to hang onto this awful blessing for even a little bit longer, then he needed to make himself known as a man of action. He had to send all the right signals to the brass and to the men.

The thing that galled him was that political favors were to be done for people to whom he owned no gratitude, while the punishments were for those he regarded with no malice. No doubt the people on the receiving end of those things, good or bad, were wringing their hands while they waited for a sign as to what to expect from the new management down at the precinct station. The department brass, no doubt, expected him to willingly participate in their ongoing patterns of petty evils, all in the name of the greater good.

No one was looking, so he allowed himself to sneer and mutter under his breath, "For the greater good: follow the Devil's map to Heaven. Trust what the Devil tells you and ignore your own senses."

He glanced down at the notation for the name of his next appointment and saw a perfect example of it all: Sergeant Randall Blackburn. Moses was aware that his predecessor had habitually handed out the contemptible assignments of the Barbary Coast district to Sergeant Blackburn, in spite of the man's excellent police work. Blackburn was a sacrifice, also for the "greater good," which Moses saw as a pitiful sop to the officers who resented Blackburn's do-or-die attitude. So instead of slapping the lazy and envious bastards back into discipline, somebody up in the department brass figured it was easier to make a show out of Blackburn's stalled career. They left the sergeant permanently on the least desired and most dangerous walking beat in order to set him up as a thing of ridicule, thereby defusing the growls and whines of a bunch of jealous little boy cops. Moses figured they should wear knee britches if they were that fragile.

Moses also knew about Gibbon and Mummery, the two recruits who bought their way onto the force because their fathers were on the City Council. They drew the best assignments, turned in the worst performances, and suffered no consequence beyond an occasional verbal reprimand, and even the reprimand was performed entirely for show. They sneered their way through most of their assignments and produced results that a child could beat. And proof that there was a Devil: they both survived the earthquakes.

There was a dozen examples, no doubt with more to come. The real job of Station Chief wasn't roll call and paperwork, it was Lord High Executioner. It was precisely that sort of power Gregory Moses had always loathed and avoided, the power that brought out aspects of people's personalities he never cared for at all. It was painfully ironic to him that the constant drumbeat of such cynical petty evils was part of why he effectively retreated from the dangerous human race in the first place, making it hard for him to work in that arena now. Such things had combined to make it easy for him to give up on the outside world in the first place, to surrender to the private joys of chewing and swallowing.

On the horns of this dilemma, Moses wondered what the surviving officers *actually expected* of him. Were they looking for a signal that the status quo would go on, or did they want him to break out in some new direction? Was he supposed to be an agent of change?

Worst of all, if Moses tried to make a peace gesture—say, just wipe the slate clean of political obligations and let it all go—could it backfire on him and send a message of weakness? If that happened, then once they removed him and sent him back to Record Keeping, everyone would know Moses had failed his golden opportunity. He would have to continue coming to work every day, to a place where contempt for Gregory Moses would be the standard rule from then on, with the safety of his retirement still years away.

He concluded that no matter what lay ahead, his only hope of enduring in this position was to carry out the roster of petty evils which had been willed to him. If he did, perhaps these minor concessions to a hungry demon might be enough to let him hold onto this job, this windfall, this unexpected and undeserved boon, for just a little while longer. Because it felt so champagne smooth in those isolated moments, whenever he was alone in a room without eyeballs on him, to look into a mirror and regard himself as a worthy man. How fine would it be, to actually hold onto that identity?

For now it was time to deal with this business about Sergeant Blackburn. Once he did, his position would soon be widely known, travelling at the speed of gossip. Moses stepped to the door of his office and leaned out to take a look; Randall Blackburn was waiting on the long bench that lined the hallway.

Moments later, Moses leaned against his desk, making elaborate business out of lighting a cigar while Blackburn stood quietly, waiting. Moses sat and got settled before speaking. He cleared his throat twice.

"The problem, Sergeant—as I see it, at least—is that the United States Army has done an exemplary job in helping to restore order here. And I mean they did it to the point that they made us all look bad. Let us salute the Army," he added in a voice dry enough to cure meat.

"I think you'll have to salute them for me, Lieutenant. There were soldiers openly looting some of the same houses they were sent to protect in the first damn place."

"Mm. And how do you know this?"

"I saw them."

"Did you stop them?" "No."

"Did you try?"

"No. I shot over the heads of some civilian looters. Didn't do much good."

"You didn't try to stop the soldiers?"

"I said no. Sir."

"Sergeant! I am *not* in the Record Keeping Department anymore, in case you forgot."

"What do you mean?"

"Your tone of voice! Regardless of how anyone feels about it, my rank is now Acting Station Chief. You need to reflect that in your attitude!"

Blackburn calmly stared back at Moses for three or four more heartbeats. It was just long enough for Moses to decide that he needed to retake control.

"The fact is, Sergeant Blackburn," Moses began, "the thought among our commanders is that this unrestrained behavior by US soldiers—on our turf—is a blow to the reputation of the San Francisco Police Department. Publicly, we are forced to thank the Army for the help. Privately, we'd love to shoot them all in the head. And just between us, the brass have decided that we're going to get even with the Army by outshining them."

"...Outshining?"

"I told you about your tone of voice, Sergeant."

"Sir. How would it help us, to 'outshine' the Army?"

"It doesn't! It helps the department brass. The politicians. Maybe they're the ones we ought to shoot in the head, eh?" He looked up at Blackburn with a hopeful smile.

Blackburn kept his face blank. "Yes, you could do that, but there is that other thing about hanging for it."

Moses let out a tired sigh. "My God, Blackburn. You're as tiresome as your reputation, I'll say that." He sat up in his chair. "Now, they appreciate that you were instrumental in keeping down the threat of disease right after all hell broke loose and everything. But they also figure that in times like these, a month is too long for Sergeant Hero to go without doing something else impressive. Especially in the wake of your allowing the soldiers to run riot, and all."

"What? I was under *strict* orders from Chief Dinan not to stop for any—"

"What you need to do is solve a big case for the department. Something flashy. Say, an important murder."

"All right, look. Sir. I know The Surgeon stepped up from killing drunk sailors with this so-called gentleman victim, but every street source I have is looking for—"

"No! You are *not* going to stick that tired old case into this discussion. We don't know for sure if the new bodies are really The Surgeon's work. Personally, I think she died in the quakes or the fires. This new one isn't doing the castrations, and I've assured the brass that the last one was faked."

"Faked? Oh no, sir, I don't—"

"It's a copycat."

Moses pushed a paper-thin case file across the desk at Blackburn. "And here's your lucky break, Sergeant—this case is solved already! All you have to do is bring back everything the District Attorney's office needs to guarantee a conviction on *this* case, in less than twenty-four hours."

Blackburn opened the file. There were only two pages inside. Most of what was there had already been in the afternoon paper: A local society gentleman, the former Navy Captain Harlan Sullivan, was killed by his mistress the night before, when she invaded his home and shot him in the upstairs bath. His nude body was found collapsed across an industrial-sized scale standing near the large, claw-foot bathtub. The captain sustained a single gunshot wound to the back of the head. Witness testimony from wife Elsie Sullivan described how she came home just in time to see the mistress flee out the back. The victim was already dead when she arrived.

To the responding officers, she revealed that she and her husband had an "arrangement," and that his mistresses were tolerated by her, so long as he kept it all out of her life. She assured the officer that her husband had always followed the arrangement. All she could confirm was that he had somehow lost interest in this latest one and tried to break it off with her. But unlike other mistresses in the past, this latest one apparently refused to be left behind.

The head butler finally caved in under strong questioning. As the majordomo, he knew everything about the house, and they pressed him hard. He was a strapping man, barely of middle age, but he proved easy to frighten. After a few solid kidney punches, he admitted knowing all about this mistress, and that the husband had recently broken it off with her. When police asked him if it was possible that the wife somehow did it out of jealousy, he laughed out loud; the couple's living arrangement was an open secret. Elsie Sullivan loved the daily banquet of her privileged life. She would never, the majordomo assured them, risk prison for the likes of Mr. Sullivan.

"We arrested the mistress this morning," Moses broke in on Blackburn's reading. "Her name's Marietta Pairo, twenty-nine, very nice looking. They found the murder weapon under her mattress. Not your usual whore, I should think."

"Was he paying her?" Blackburn asked.

"I don't know."

"If she's a prostitute, she has to get paid."

"Sergeant, I don't happen to know *or* care if she—"

"I just mean that a mistress isn't necessarily a prostitute. She might be blamed for participating in adultery, but sometimes the other woman isn't paid anything at all and sometimes she really does love—"

"And at twenty-nine," Moses rode over him, "she seems a bit long in the tooth for this sort of work, eh? Anyway, we had to take her in. She killed one of our most prominent citizens and got herself spotted by his equally prominent wife. So now we have her, we've got the murder weapon, and we know she did it. But since we can only hold her for three days, we've got to get her charged. The brass wants to bring in an unbeatable case."

Moses had decided to look directly at Blackburn while he delivered his order, instead of casting his eyes downward the way he usually did. He squinted to get his focus, then used his most direct and authoritative voice. "This case has all the elements of an open-and-shut deal: important society people, wife pressing for a conviction. Naturally, the suspect claims innocence. You need to return with a solid piece of evidence or some great witness testimony by tomorrow at noon. Something that will put the story in a nice box for the prosecution. That's all."

Blackburn stared at the little file, incredulous. There was no official statement from the suspect, no testimony from anyone besides the wife. So they had a pistol and one witness, but they "knew" the mistress did it?

"Lieutenant," Randall Blackburn spoke in low tones. "Do you mind telling me where this order is coming from?"

Ordinarily, Moses would have dropped his gaze under such a direct challenge. Nothing in the life of the department's official Record Keeper prepared him to go man-to-man with a cop who boxed ten rounds with the local toughs on nearly every shift. But this time Moses returned the gaze. He even leaned forward while he replied, "Much higher up than either of *us*, you can bet on that."

Lying so boldly felt good to Moses. The sense of power was wonderful.

In that moment he became aware of the warmth of his penis lying against his thigh. He continued with added energy.

"You know, Blackburn, it seems like you take some kind of pride in being a so-called 'lone wolf.' Except I think you forget that *nobody likes* the lone wolf! Understand?"

Moses realized this last line was dangerously close to how he felt about himself, so he didn't wait for an answer. "You get away with it because you turn in good results. But since it *has* been a month since your last big moment, you need to bring this one home, and fast." He ended in feigned innocence. "At least, that's how the word comes down to me. So just go ahead and walk the Barbary Coast beat tonight, but follow any leads you develop, then stay on to work this case until noon. Put in for the overtime."

Moses deliberately capped the order with a shrug, but somehow it didn't feel right. Easy gestures of casual authority were a form of arrogance he had yet to master. With a rush of self-consciousness, he realized his fake shrug most likely resembled the involuntary spasm of a man who just sat down on a cold toilet.

It didn't matter, he told himself. The course was set. Moses looked up at Sergeant Blackburn and smiled. The smile came easily to him and went unchallenged, surprisingly enough. Under any other circumstances, Moses would expect a man like Blackburn to wipe the expression right back off of him.

But not today. Probably not tomorrow. And certainly not until that inevitable moment when they removed him from this marvelous position. Until then—

His smile broadened. He couldn't help it. Fat Gregory Moses hadn't truly smiled in a long time. It felt good. Oh, it felt good.

# 7

THAT AFTERNOON

BLACKBURN SAT AT A thick wooden table in a clammy little
interrogation room while the jailer escorted murder suspect Marietta Pairo
back to her cell. He had gone straight to the jail to have Miss Pairo brought
up to the interview room as soon as he left Lieutenant Moses. He was
surprised to discover that the retired captain's girlfriend was remarkably
stupid and inarticulate. He wondered how the captain had been able to
stand her company whenever they weren't between the sheets.

Over the course of the long interview, Miss Pairo tried out a range of
attitudes on him and ran herself through a gamut of emotions, but her fear
and anxiety were as plain as her protests of innocence. She could not
explain how the gun got into her locked apartment. It was certainly the
murder weapon: handmade five-shot revolver, firing a distinct .35-caliber
forged lead slug. The barrel still smelled of freshly burned powder, and the
chamber was minus a round; Miss Pairo's denials added just enough to the
case to make his job hard and guarantee the need for fieldwork. The rest of
her interview was worthless. The poor woman would eagerly swear to
seeing pigs fly if she thought that it would get her off the hook.

It went no better at the home of the late Captain Sullivan. Elsie Sullivan

was a self-possessed and well-spoken woman in her forties, a product of a
social class that prided itself on tightly controlled emotion. She was heavier
than most women, but Blackburn noted that she still presented herself
well, with a series of girdles and corsets that held her in an hourglass shape
beneath her outer clothing.

She was able to tell her story with relative poise until she got to the part
about finding Captain Sullivan sprawled across the big floor scale. Her
voice broke and her face went pale while she described the scene.

None of it did Blackburn any good. Her story fit all the known facts. As
a potential suspect, what motive did she have? The family money was hers
as well as his. Her closest staff members backed up her story about the
terms of her marriage. They all scoffed at the idea of Elsie Sullivan having a
fit of jealousy over one of her husband's passing flings. Furthermore, Mrs.
Sullivan was fully cooperative with the police. She proclaimed herself eager
to have the guilty party tried and convicted.

And Blackburn didn't believe her at all.

Even when he set aside his natural resentment of smug complacency,
he still didn't believe her. Her pretty face and polished mannerisms gave
her a pleasant veneer, but her eyes left him cold. They reminded him of an
animal who knows nothing but hunger and fear.

Experience had taught him authority stinks because first, orders are
easy, and second, so is ducking responsibility for those orders. He was in a
pigsty of a situation, a hopeless assignment. The brass wanted evidence
before noon the next day, but he had nothing. Orders are easy.

So it looked as if today was another in which he would be questioning
his life in police work. Asking himself why he took all this horse flop and
tried to call it a career. The only consistency he found in police politics was
the unavoidable hypocrisy. The same superior officers who refused to grant
him promotion nevertheless referred to him as a "born police officer."
What the hell did that mean?

He was still strong, relatively young, but his body ached in every joint
whenever he awoke. Maybe he was too young to be moving like an old
man, but every morning until he had his coffee and stretched out the kinks,
he was stiff with the aftereffects of countless violent encounters. The
constant pain of aging joints was guaranteed to be with him sooner than it

would come for the guys with the desk jobs. But he was "born for" the work.

Who is born for such a thing? He hated the question and the way it made him feel.

---

Shane lay on his back, sound asleep, protected in the cool darkness of the little toolshed at the rear of the cemetery. The society pages were draped across him like a blanket. In that day's newspaper, even the usually decorative Society section was given over to crime reporting, elaborating on the scandalous story of Captain Sullivan's murder by his enraged mistress. The drama was deep—she was arrested with the murder weapon in her possession.

The article took care to acknowledge the widow Sullivan's lack of involvement. And while no reputable newspaper stooped to printing a sketch of Captain Sullivan's body, sprawled wide across the big scale, the scene was described in sufficient detail to create the same effect.

Shane had grabbed up the newspaper as soon as it hit the corner stand that morning, eager to practice reading out loud as soon as he got the chance. But when he came across the Sullivan murder story, it hit him hard, wiping away all the other trivial items. Everything about the case struck him the wrong way, though at first he didn't understand why.

For an instant he wondered if it was because he felt his hope fading for finding a livable life, a life where he could build something. But the thought quickly faded. Not even that unspeakable thing could explain his feelings. The only thing clear to him was that he was to blame for his position in the graveyard toolshed. He dug the hole with his cowardice during the long night and day of murder.

What if he could have stopped it? What if God or some sort of angel appeared and gave him the power to stop it? The question had the power to crush his skull. He pushed it away just in time and distracted himself with the news article.

Something about the story made Shane remember a time when he accidentally spied Mrs. Nightingale while she examined herself in a large mirror. A coincidence of geometry and a passing moment placed him so he caught her reflection through a carelessly closed door. And in that ambushed moment she presented her full self to him, unknowing, while he stood nailed to the floor and stared from the darkness, watching her turn this way and that.

Within moments, the novelty of her nudity was overcome and his attention riveted itself to her troubled face and frustrated breathing while she struggled to get a view of herself that gave her whatever she was seeking.

Mrs. Nightingale was a full-bodied woman, by any standard. Shane knew how much she loved to eat, also that she considered any form of physical exercise the antithesis of refined living. She always dressed well and walked with such stiff pride, it never occurred to him that she was anything but delighted with herself. And yet at that private moment, her principal traits were vulnerability and distress over her appearance. It opened his eyes to the depths of effort a woman can expend for her appearance, since appearance had a great deal to do with how well they lived. It suddenly seemed clear to Shane that if a woman suffered this hard over the shape of her body, she must be in a constant state of torment in the presence of other women. The younger ones, the prettier ones, the ones with ideal figures—what else could they be to Mrs. Nightingale except constant jabs, reminders of her own failings? Self-criticism was something Shane knew too well.

She stepped to the mirror and tossed a robe over it, completely blocking all reflection, and turned away in disgust. *The reminder is too much*, he heard himself say out loud, and in the next instant he realized she had heard him, too.

She gasped in alarm, spun to face him, and locked her eyes with his. His stomach dropped.

She had all the power. For a single moment that felt like an hour, they simply stared in silence. He would not have been surprised if she screamed at him, perhaps struck him with her fists, then called for him to be taken away. The only clear thought in his head during that time was the realization that she didn't appear angry.

At last she simply nodded and simply said, "*Yes*." She spoke the word softly, gentle and kind in her tone. She continued to hold his gaze while she slowly closed the door.

Then it was over. The memory dissolved, and sleep carried him away.

---

Shane woke up to a throbbing headache, with pains so sharp that he had to move slowly while he sat up. He pulled the newspaper blanket off of himself. The paper was open to the Society section, and as he glanced down, his eye caught the realistic pen-and-ink sketch of Mrs. Elsie Sullivan. She was bigger, much bigger than Mrs. Nightingale had ever been.

*So that's it.* Apparently the news article had prompted that strange memory as he fell asleep.

He looked at it again. Yes, the accompanying sketch of Mrs. Sullivan showed that with regard to her appearance, she had far more to be concerned about than Mrs. Nightingale ever did.

He wondered, what was Mrs. Sullivan's stance in front of the mirror? Could she stand the view? Or did she cover her mirror too?

That's when the key seemed to jump off the page at him. The large scale in the bathroom, the one where the body was discovered—it was too much for the job. More like something you might find in a meatpacking house. The scale was a heavy-duty item meant to take a lot of use. Mrs. Sullivan would never have brought something like that into the house. What woman would? The whole idea felt wrong.

No. *Of course it was brought in by Captain Sullivan himself.*

And why would he do that? Sullivan was a fit man, hardly in need of a heavy-duty scale.

Shane felt the answer before he had time to think it—the scale wasn't there for Captain Sullivan. It was there for the lady of the house. The only other adult in the place, in fact. He brought it home, but for her.

Shane knew all about being the object of taunting, and now the same familiar feeling was here. What else could that big scale be, he asked himself, besides some sort of goad from Sullivan to his wife? The scale's mere presence in the house presented an ongoing insult. The contraption might as well have been screaming, *This is what it takes to weigh you!* In its power to inflict pain, it could laugh at her in a cruel voice no one else heard.

Shane wondered how long the big scale had been in the house. Surely every single one of those days held some special new humiliation for Elsie Sullivan. Each one was delivered by the sight of the scale itself, possibly along with the occasional verbal barb from her husband. Like straws on the camel's back, they built up, one after another after another, into a boiling mass of resentment and perhaps a murderous rage.

What if she shot him at an angle to guarantee he would fall more or less across the thing? And then she left him there on purpose. *This is for your oversized scale, bastard!*

Shane couldn't explain the gun, but he felt certain now that Sullivan's mistress was innocent. It hurt him to think of how terrified she had to be, locked up for this crime. The memory of Mrs. Nightingale's final screams of terror and desperation were stuck in his brain like bullet fragments, and he had to wonder if the Pairo woman's fear was any less. He found himself overwhelmed with the urge to help her, but the force of it didn't keep him from being baffled as to what he could actually do. Was he supposed to go to the police with all this?

And tell them what, exactly?

Why should they believe anything he told them? Worst of all, what if somebody recognized him for what he was? What if somehow these men who dealt with criminals every day could look at him and see his horrible guilt?

Still, the picture was now burned into his brain; Marietta Pairo's pain was linked to the final agonies of Mrs. Nightingale, and there was nobody to help her now but him. He had to ask himself if he was ready to abandon another innocent one, ready to lie quiet and piss himself instead of taking the necessary risk. Back in the kitchen pantry, his legs were paralyzed and his throat sealed shut. But if he kept silent about his suspicion now, just to keep himself safe, what would his excuse be this time?

What good was his life under that kind of guilt burden?

Shane picked up his newspaper and opened it to a full-page advertisement that left a good portion of the page blank. He tore off the blank part to use for notepaper and went to get a pencil from the Mission schoolroom.

There, he addressed the note to the head police officer named in the newspaper article: Sergeant Randall Blackburn.

His handwriting was perfect, the result of learning at the hands of friars who tolerated no error. He began to record his suspicions as if writing out the answer to an important classroom test.

---

The freshly minted Widow Elsie Sullivan spent her entire ride to the City Hall Station fuming in outrage and plotting her ultimate revenge against that arrogant police officer, Blackman or Blackheart or whatever his name was. The man had not only committed the outrage of summoning her down to the station house, he sent hirelings in uniform to arrest her like some petty criminal. Fortunately, none of her friends were in attendance. Still, plenty of servants observed the spectacle of a grieving widow being escorted from her home and driven away.

The few moments it took to walk with the officers from her doorway to the police car felt more like half an hour. Her blood boiled inside of her all the while. She thought of French royalty being hauled to the guillotine in death wagons.

*Fine enough, gentlemen*, she seethed. The policeman would play his little game of hauling her in, flexing his great authority. She would toy with him in his bad joke of an "interview" until he tired of bothering her and "allowed" her to leave. And with that, his power over her would be exhausted. At that moment, he would have concluded his little fishing trip with nothing.

Then it would be time for her to demonstrate her power over him. Not the petty, niggling power of a common street bureaucrat with minimal education and excessive brawn, but that of an intelligent, college-educated, ambitious woman with access to half the people in the SFPD who ranked over him. Several were within her active social circle. Thus the more subtle but far more lethal power of her social influence was about to bear down upon this bastard sergeant, and from every direction. A plague of locusts.

Elsie rode along in the police cart enduring simultaneous levels of discomfort. The officers had arrested her *just* before she was to begin her bath. The clothes they made her put on were the same soiled garments she had just discarded.

At first she was so taken aback, it was almost funny to her. It felt unbelievable, the sight of these two officers blithely destroying their futures by treating her this way. They wouldn't even allow her to dress in private, insisting instead that they guard her in plain sight while she went from bathrobe to fully dressed and all phases in between. The officers also refused to allow her to don her usual array of support garments. Instead the men barely gave her time to put on her outer clothing.

With her flesh unsupported, Elsie Sullivan's naked body usually felt, to her, like a moist travesty. But once she was safely ensconced in her lifts and wraps and girdles, she transformed into a formidable warrior woman. Men were respectful and a little shy in her presence, and most women didn't even try to give her any sort of trouble.

Today, however, without the needed strength that should have been supplied by her fabric exoskeleton, she found herself arriving at the station feeling like a glob of overlapping rubbery bags. Fear painted the air around her in a sour animal stench. Her own odor was excruciating to her. Several times, the assault on her senses caused her to shiver uncontrollably.

By the time they pulled into the station and escorted her inside, she was only able to maintain composure by concentrating on her breathing and avoiding all eye contact. *They have no idea what they are doing*, she kept reminding herself. *They have no knowledge of the sort of strings that I can pull.*

She didn't take their actions personally, as compared to those of the sergeant. Elsie Sullivan held a complete grasp on the appropriate care and feeding of servants, and of the delight which their proper use delivers. But she was convinced something was wrong with this Blackbeard fellow. His clumsiness in dealing with her begged for retaliation so loudly that she felt a wave of pity for the foolish man—not that it lessened her craving for his violent destruction. That was a foregone conclusion.

Elsie Sullivan had never entered City Hall through the police doors before, and she was shocked at how primitive and nasty things were below the station. The inner offices looked like they had been carved out of a cave, dimly lit, clouded by fresh cigar smoke, sour with the residue of old tobacco. The two officers who did not yet realize their careers were dead escorted her into a small and bare office. There was nothing more than one large wooden table in the center of the room, with two hardwood chairs. The professionally doomed men sat her down at the table with a few polite, empty words, then walked out and left her there alone. She heard a key turn the door's lock.

Elsie could only stare around the bare room in silence. Soon a powerful knot of dread appeared inside of her, inviting her to panic. She vowed not to give in to it. Instead, she committed herself to turning its energy toward fueling her anger and to focusing her mind while she waited for a weakness to appear in the situation. An opportunity. Then Elsie Sullivan, a grieving widow who had entertained most of the city's powerful citizens right inside of her home, would finally have her opportunity to turn the tables on this puffed-up little policeman. She would guarantee herself the opportunity to calmly observe him while he stood broken and publicly humiliated, all out in the open, for anyone to see. She would stand aside, coolly watching, dressed in something especially fine.

*Why do men have to kill their enemies? It's so much better to let them live while you torment them from a distance and prolong their suffering.*

She needed to urinate badly enough to feel concerned about it. This situation had to be taken care of before she was forced to put herself in the vulnerable position of asking to use the facilities. She tried to estimate when that would be. Thirty minutes? An hour? Say an hour, then. That single hour more or less defined her timetable for this encounter. No matter why they had dragged her here, it was crucial for her to get back out within that much time.

Keys jingled on the other side of the door. Then came the clicks in the lock. When it opened, Elsie watched the doomed police officer walk in. He was by himself. She quickly checked his name tag. *Blackburn, then. Sergeant Randall Blackburn.* She silently repeated it to herself to set it good and solid in her memory while she kept her face impassive.

He closed the door, stepped to the table, and pulled up a chair to sit down across from her. But she decided not to give him any satisfaction by speaking first. *Let him make the overture.*

The sergeant simply pulled out a torn scrap of paper with some careful handwriting penciled across it. He appeared to run his eyes over the lines again, then he set the paper down on the table and looked up at Elsie, studying her face. She felt his gaze moving around on her. Still, she fixed her eyes on the door, raised her chin, and said nothing.

But the sergeant, instead of speaking, just picked up the scrap of paper and read it over again before he finally lowered it back to the table and returned his gaze to her face, still reading her in some fashion. She cursed herself when she felt the old hot rash blushing its way across her upper chest and throat.

That was it. The business with the paper scrap appeared to be some sort of attempt on his part to provoke her. Elsie decided not to let him toy with her. She would speak first after all. So what? It meant nothing, to speak first. She set ironclad control on her voice and prepared herself to lash out with quiet power. Then she turned to face him.

"Sergeant Blackburn, I am trying to imagine what possible circumstance could arise that would cause you to have me arrested and brought here like a common criminal, when all you had to do was to send word that you wanted a meeting. *What* could be so compelling to you that your men would deny me the right to get properly dressed before leaving my home?" She held her voice down, perfectly pitched to show calm control and absolute determination.

"It doesn't matter what you have on," the sergeant quietly replied. "Think of Miss Pairo, sitting alone in a cell right now. What do you think she's wearing?" His voice was even softer than hers.

*Don't take the bait!* Elsie matched his technique and lowered her voice even further. "Sir, perhaps a male who wears a uniform every day cannot appreciate the social expectations placed upon a woman's manner of dress, *especially* when she mixes with the city's most powerful and influential people. On a daily basis." She wondered if that was blatant enough for this plebeian.

But he murmured his reply, absently tapping the scrap of paper against the tabletop. "None of that matters anymore."

"I beg your pardon? Perhaps none of it matters to *you...*"

She had yelled. A real slip. But another moment passed and the sergeant didn't make any reaction. He just kept reading over that godforsaken piece of paper. Elsie felt the air going stale. Could the man smell her? Her skin crawled with the feeling of self-consciousness.

Blackburn nearly whispered, without even looking at her. "Mrs. Sullivan, I've been informed your husband wanted the prestige of a wife with a youthful figure. He chided you about losing weight until it became a major issue in your home."

Elsie's blood ran cold. The hot rash on her chest and throat turned to flame.

"He bought an industrial-sized scale and brought it home as an insult to you. He probably claimed that it was to 'remind' you to lose weight or something, but that doesn't matter. You knew it was actually there to mock you."

Elsie tried to recapture her confidence, or even a reasonable imitation of it. She squeezed her brain for some fiery retort that would shut Blackburn up. But her mind seemed gripped in solid ice. What was happening to her?

*How does he know these things?* And still he kept talking.

"It was a good thing that you had the, ah, 'arrangement' with your husband about his mistresses. Since you were aware of when they were planning to see each other next, you knew just when to shoot him, then run to her apartment while she was still on her way to meet him. You took his key to open her door and then planted the gun inside." He focused his gaze directly into her eyes, but she was primed for combat and did not turn away.

"I am impressed, Sergeant Blackburn. Did you get this information by reading my mind? If so, I think you need a few more lessons."

The big sergeant just sighed. He seemed to make up his mind about something before he finally spoke. "Mrs. Sullivan, have you heard of the science of reading human fingerprints to determine someone's identity?"

"Yes. I've heard of it." Elsie felt a brief flicker of triumph. She had indeed read about fingerprinting in a recent magazine from Great Britain. She was careful not to smile too much. "As it happens, I know there are scientists who say it is valuable for identification, but that no police departments are using it. Too cumbersome, I think they called it."

"Oh, it can be a bit messy, I suppose, what with the black powder and all. But in fact the English detectives at Scotland Yard are beginning to use it, and we've been considering it here in San Francisco. Yours is one of a dozen test cases we're running."

She watched Sergeant Blackburn pause, probably for dramatic effect, before he added, "And your fingerprints are all over the gun we retrieved from Miss Pairo's apartment."

All of the fine hairs on Elsie's body stood up. She knew better than to speak. *A nervous mouth will betray you every time*, she could hear her mother's voice saying, giving her valuable lessons in how to lie to boys. *Keep quiet and let them wonder what you're thinking.*

She took another look at Sergeant Blackburn. He really was quite handsome, with a lovely, strong voice. She briefly wondered if she could still seduce a man like him, but immediately felt foolish for thinking about it. She forced the thought out of her mind and tried to reclaim confidence where suddenly there was none.

Several awkward moments went by. The two of them were alone there, after all. No windows. The door was made of solid wood. No one could see.

She knelt down in front of him and started to undo his pants.

Blackburn slipped both of his hands under her arms and lifted her to her feet. He was almost gentle, but not quite. "Use the writing tablet, there, Mrs. Sullivan," he told her in a voice that did not invite a response. "You need to write out a full confession. Put all of it down, and don't leave anything out." He regarded her for a moment, then added, "I promise you, it's for the best."

"Do you mean that?" She asked in the voice of a timid little girl, a voice she found tremendously effective in the bedroom. It compelled a man to show her that he wasn't angry with her.

"What I mean is, you're under arrest for murder and you won't be leaving this place for quite a while. Which is why it doesn't matter whether you are well dressed today or not."

"I can afford to post a very high bond."

"There is no bail for murder." He went on to explain that as soon as she finished her confession, she was going to be dressed in the muslin coveralls of a jailhouse inmate. Free of charge.

As much as his words frightened her, Elsie felt sure that she caught a flash of reassurance in Sergeant Blackburn's eyes. It puzzled her for just a moment, then she realized that yes—he seemed to be saying he could help her, if only she did as she was told. She sensed that her charms were working as well as ever, even in her degraded condition.

Feeling better now, she sat down to the writing tablet and picked up a pencil. When she looked up at Sergeant Blackburn and smiled, she caught him almost smiling right back, plain as anything. She began to write, then, in her studied and elegant hand, determined to please him enough to gain every possible advantage over him.

She wrote out everything: how the captain tormented her so cruelly and for so long. She emphasized that Marietta Pairo was not the subject of her malice. Rather, the younger woman was simply the natural scapegoat. The captain, of course, was the problem—a man who was simply too nasty to live. The deservedly late captain. Elsie did not doubt that she could make any reasonable person see that.

Mind over matter, the way she had always done it. So she ignored her current state of appearance and projected the idea of herself as a woman in distress. Within moments, she was transformed. While her physical appearance remained deplorable, she could tell that her presence itself was sweet as blueberry pie. She knew that when she was like this, no man would do anything to harm her.

She concentrated on writing out her confession just as instructed, making sure to use her best penmanship. The things she was committing to the page were too scary to think about. Somehow the fears tightened her muscles and twisted her stomach. So she kept them at bay by focusing on the challenge of writing with perfectly even letters. This served to show the policeman that she obeyed the rules, while her handwriting was still decorated with enough feminine swirls to be sexy.

Elsie Sullivan trusted that she would soon have this Sergeant Randall Blackburn curled up in the palm of her hand.

# 8

THAT EVENING

BLACKBURN WAS THE HERO of the hour. The Sullivan widow was in the city jail, huddled with her attorney and sending out scores of frantic missives to her highly connected friends. Lieutenant Moses rewarded him by allowing him to nap in an empty cell until it was time for his night beat. He got four hours of near-death slumber, then half a pot of tar-like coffee and check-in time for another full shift.

The moment he stepped outside into the darkness and cool night air, an unexpected pulse of energy swept him up. On the crest of it, his sense of possibilities expanded. He felt the fatigue, he just didn't respect it anymore. What he really wanted to do was ignore the unstoppable avalanche of crime on the Barbary Coast and do a little investigative work instead.

The very idea picked up his pulse. He was wide awake now. Hunting down a good mystery was far more compelling than spending the night arresting small-time criminals. So in silent retaliation for the brutal treatment by his supervisor, he decided to give the street denizens a few hours off and pursue the mystery instead. He turned away from City Hall's temporary station. The distinct advantage to walking the Barbary Coast beat was that his supervisors seldom found cause to risk themselves by going down there to check on him.

He headed in the opposite direction of the Barbary Coast district and took a walk toward the Mission Dolores, several long blocks away.

The day before, when a boy walked into the station bearing an urgent note for Sergeant Blackburn, the desk sergeant on duty declined acceptance unless the boy provided a return address. For some reason, the boy refused to leave his name but did say he was living down at the old Mission Dolores. He claimed that he worked there at night, guarding the place from looters.

Blackburn smiled and exhaled. This was a solid footing. If the boy really was at the Mission, he would be easy enough to identify. The desk sergeant also noted that the boy had a pronounced stutter. Such a thing could cut right through the ordinary interview process.

Blackburn still felt a pleasant buzz of surprise that the ruse about fingerprints had actually worked on Mrs. Sullivan. With the science being so new, she failed to realize that nobody ever took sample fingerprints from her before her arrest. The technology seemed to meld science and magic, and since most new inventions of the day seemed to be half miracle, anyway, maybe she just thought there was some capacity to it that she didn't comprehend. By the time her lawyer arrived and she began to feel buyer's remorse, she had a long, detailed confession written down and signed in front of several witnesses.

It would never work to back away from her confession. The current state of criminal law in San Francisco was to lean toward the harsh side. The beleaguered population was in no mood for sob stories. There was no social climate permitting anyone to cry out for sympathy because everyone who heard a tragic story also had a few of their own.

Blackburn had gone into the case knowing the city needed to take a close look at the wife, despite not having enough to charge her. The rush to nail Marietta Pairo felt wrong to him, as well. And as far as Mrs. Sullivan's vow of putting out appeals to high-powered friends went, well, many of those same people were also friends of Captain Harlan Sullivan—shot through the head while defenseless. Mrs. Sullivan would have to get used to eating prison food.

The kid with the note, though. The boy: he was more interesting than some pitiful self-made widow. What was his connection to that woman? What would make him so eerily intuitive about her? How was it that he could be dead right about all of it?

This mystery somehow fit into the strange aura hovering over the city ever since disaster struck. With that first shock wave, everything about the physical world came under an unstoppable destructive force. So had the more ethereal things, such as one's view of the way the world functions. In the aftermath, the strangeness of a magical clue being delivered by some ragged and anonymous boy somehow fit into the post-quake picture, right along with the ubiquitous piles of rubble. The land down near the bay shore had turned to quicksand from the sheer intensity of the great vibrations. Now everybody in the region understood the ground itself could not be trusted to hold still or to remain solid.

So why not a boy with a magic note?

It was a fairly short walk but he made slow time, stepping among the makeshift shelters that now served as homes and businesses for the die-hard populace. Block after block, pale stalks of smoke twisted up from countless cooking fires. He cringed at the thought of another conflagration. Meanwhile, grim and determined faces peered out at him from swaths of stained blankets and ragged clothing. The city was surviving, but the eyes of its people were universally dark and hollow.

Everyone in the region shared the same invisible wound. Blackburn kept his own shoved far down, but he imagined others could see the effects on his face as clearly as he saw it in theirs. The worst of the temblor's shaking took place inside the people themselves. For many, despair reigned and left them with the question: If nothing outside of you is to be trusted, how far inside yourself do you have to retreat to find grounds for your life?

Blackburn was stuck with that challenge as much as anybody else, and he felt moved to stand up for these people. This part of town was mostly a stalwart population, immigrant pioneers of hardy stock. He could see in their behavior that they remained honorable and clung to their families. No one was gambling or lying around drunk. Everybody in sight was either doing some sort of business or tending to their makeshift homes, with all but the smallest of children occupied by one handy task or another.

In spite of his admiration, Blackburn moved among them as an audience member, seldom a player. While walking his beat he was still only an observer unless action was necessary. The act of constant observation commanded a certain distance, grimly effective insulation against human warmth; walking past these tightly knit families filled him with a lonely ache. If he were off duty, it would be a perfect moment for a whiskey or two and to maybe lose count. Instead he left the hunger hanging and moved on.

When a rat the size of a house cat darted in front of him, he kicked at it without coming close. The rat disappeared in a flash of matted fur. It was finally becoming more rare to see them. With the return of daily human life, damaged though it was, the swarms that had roamed the streets with impunity right after the earthquake were fading back into the broken sewer lines and scattered rubble piles. Since confrontations with humans frequently ended in death for the rats, they were discovering it easier to hide in daylight and forage in darkness. He wondered if any of them really carried the plague. If there were any plague victims in the city, it seemed strange that he had heard nothing about it.

He reached the Mission Dolores well after midnight, so he bypassed the church and went straight to where the little graveyard fronted onto the road. The place was dark, with silhouettes of the larger tombstones and funerary statues defined by faint moonlight. At first the whole cemetery appeared deserted. But he stood for a moment to let his eyes adjust to the thicker darkness and bottomless shadows. Beneath the old trees, smudges emerged and began to sharpen in form.

Then...there it was. Emerging in the very back, the outline of a toolshed. Within it, a bright candle or lantern was burning.

He silently entered the graveyard and made his way back toward the shed. Once he got within a few yards, he could see a pale rectangle of light on the ground outside the shed's door. A boy's skinny and distorted shadow passed back and forth in front of it, and a faint muttering sound drifted up from the shed. The boy seemed to be reciting or chanting, but Blackburn couldn't hear the words.

He glided forward a few more feet until he could get a good look. The kid was lanky, nearly skin and bone, but didn't look sickly. Twelve or thirteen years old, probably. Not shaving yet. His thick, tousled hair looked like he cut it himself and his work clothes were cut for someone else. His shoes and socks looked right for his size but the leather was worn through, enough to notice at this distance. All in all, he gave the impression of being a coiled spring wrapped in skin and hair.

He was reading aloud by the light of the single oil lamp, pacing back and forth while holding a newspaper open in front of him. His voice was soft and clear, and he seldom stumbled over the bigger words or odd pronunciations. Blackburn was struck by the sight. He knew in this time and place, illiteracy was common as the fog. Yet somebody had seen to it that this scrappy kid learned his ABCs.

At that point Blackburn finally realized what he was hearing—for some reason, the boy was reading from the newspaper's society pages, those fluffy stories telling all about the parties and celebrations and glittering lives of the town's noted citizens. He read carefully, pronouncing each word as if they were all equally important. He was so caught up in his pursuit that Blackburn got within a few feet of him without being detected.

---

The fog outside of Shane's toolshed had grown thick enough to slip in through the open door in low wisps, but he was too engrossed in his reading to notice the cold. When he read aloud, he was somehow able to send the words straight from the page through his mouth. He spoke with confidence. His goal was almost fingertip close. *Burn the sensation of uninterrupted speech into your brain until you speak just as well without the pages!*

Blackburn spoke in a soft voice, "Is that how you heard about the case? Reading the newspaper out loud?"

Shane dropped the paper. A gust of wind swept it away from his feet and out into the darkness. He whirled to face the speaker and saw the police sergeant, Randall Blackburn, the recipient of his note.

Blackburn was also, Shane now realized, the last one besides him to see the murdered Nightingale women. Now he caught himself staring at the ground. So he forced his eyes to look up and meet Blackburn's gaze.

His mouth wouldn't move. The best he could do was offer a wan smile and nod. It took the big sergeant a moment to catch on, then he realized this was all the response he would get. He smiled and also nodded.

And then Sergeant Blackburn just stood there, sizing Shane up with an unreadable expression. Shane thought the sergeant seemed to be waiting for him to say something, but what?

He stepped over to an upturned flowerpot and sat on it. Sergeant Blackburn seemed to smile a bit. He reached into the shed and pulled a large pot of his own out through the doorway. He stopped outside the door, leaving the interior for Shane. That was a surprise. The gesture felt respectful. Or was the cop just guarding the doorway?

Blackburn flipped the big pot over and sat where they could see each other. Shane knew the thick ceramic planter weighed more than he did, and here the sergeant handled it like a tin washtub. It made him feel like he was made of paper himself.

That sense of fragility hung Shane halfway inside the moment and halfway back in the pantry at the Nightingale house, the last place where he had felt so much physical power emanating from a single person. In the Nightingale house, the madman radiated a presence which also left no doubt; *you are in the company of chaos and doom.*

Shane's instincts told him the cop had the strength to easily kill him, but he was just as sure there was no such danger.

The sergeant seemed to decide something. He shook his head, then spoke up. "Well, I already know it was you who left me the note, and ordinarily I wouldn't bother you about it, except that you solved a case. Not just solved it, actually. You stopped it cold in its tracks when it was running away from me. So you can see how I might be curious."

He smiled as if he just remembered he knew how.

Shane tried to breathe slowly. Was the sergeant's expression a real smile or a trick? *Don't think about the Nightingale house. Don't even picture it.*

"All right, then. Always start with the basics. My name is Randall Blackburn. Sergeant, SFPD...And you are?"

"Shane Nightingale," he attempted to respond, except that it came out "Shh-Sha-Sha-Shane Ni-Ni-Night-Nighting-ga-ga-gale."

"Shane Nightingale, you say?" Shane nodded.

"All right, then, Shane. Now ordinarily you could address me as Sergeant Blackburn and that would be that. But I'm thinking that the practical thing to do is stick with something easy. It's going to be a mouthful to use my rank, so let's just drop that and assume you know how wildly important I am. That leaves either Randall or Blackburn. I'm guessing that 'Blackburn' is not a good combination of sounds for you, so what about Randall? Can you just sort of slide into that one? 'Randall'?"

Shane tried. "Raaand-Rand-Raaa..."

"All right. Back up a bit. Let's try 'Sergeant.' What do you say?"

"Se-Ser-Ser-Se-Serg..."

"I might have been too hasty discarding 'Blackburn.' Maybe you should at least try it once or twice."

"Black-Black-Blackie...Blackie."

The big cop laughed out loud. "Blackie? Surely not!"

"N-n-no! No. I meant-mean-meant Black-Blackie..." He sighed in frustration.

"There you go! Winner by default! So you're Shane and I'm Blackie." He laughed again. "It's still Blackburn when you can manage it, but we'll settle for Blackie to save time, fair enough? And the reason I'm here right now, Shane, is because your note, well, it was a powerful thing today. Once you explained Mrs. Sullivan's way of thinking, I was able to go in and trick her with a phony story about a new science called fingerprinting. She caved in and confessed it all."

Shane's heartbeat refused to slow down. At any instant, the other shoe was sure to drop.

"So you see," Blackburn went on, "you broke the case."

*There it was!* Panic flashed through him. Somehow or other, he had broken the case! Blackburn's case was broken and it was all Shane's fault. That's why the big police officer was here! Now there would be trouble.

He was an idiot to send that note.

Blackburn seemed to catch his concern. "Breaking a case is a good thing, you see." He grinned. "Really good. You can do it all you want."

The bigger man paused for a few more heartbeats, then went on, "But it does leave me with a mystery. How does a young fellow like you, working over here at night in the cemetery, figure out what's going on inside the mind of a grown woman you've never met? I don't see any flying broomsticks around here, or a crystal ball. Did you find out by magic? No? Did a little bird tell you?"

"My family!" He got it out all at once. "Wa-wa-watching."

"Wait...You learned why Mrs. Sullivan shot her husband by watching your family?"

Shane sighed and shook his head.

"All right, we won't get impatient. Just have a go at it a little at a time. I've got a sandwich we can split, if it gets late." He smiled, then folded his arms and waited.

Shane realized he had to attempt an answer despite having far too much to say. His first sentence had already promised no easy task ahead. "If you, you, you, be sti-still and wa-wa-watch a woman in fro-fro-frrr-front, front of a mi-mi-mirror, you'll see."

He glanced over at Blackburn, but the sergeant was gazing straight at him, patiently waiting for him to form his words. He wasn't glazing over yet, the way other people did when he tried to talk.

So Shane went on, sentence after painful sentence. Torturing himself with the effort and no doubt tormenting his listener with the time it took. But whenever he looked at Blackburn, the sergeant was attentively listening with no trace of impatience or exasperation. Not since the night Shane escaped the burning house had anyone allowed him to speak more than a few words without interrupting him or simply walking away.

Before long, he was able to concentrate on the story he wanted to tell. Shane let the struggle for the words take care of itself.

He spent five minutes explaining his background as a foundling orphan raised by the friars of St. Adrian's Home for Delinquents and Orphans—quick to stress that he was an orphan and not a delinquent. He hated this part of the story and kept his eyes half closed while he pushed through it. He practically chanted the details. About a year prior to the earthquake, he was adopted into the Nightingale family. English immigrants who had no extra family in the region.

Shane spent at least ten minutes getting across that he was more of a servant than a family member, despite taking their last name. He often came and went unnoticed in the home, and he had seen Mrs. Nightingale agonize in front of the mirror about the fit of her clothing, about the body that constantly betrayed her. The failings she perceived in the mirror were a real source of pain. Her husband was kind to her and never made any complaints about her figure that Shane overheard. Even so, her frustration with herself was there for Shane to see.

The lessons stuck.

Then the other day, while he practiced reading out loud, he came across the Sullivan story. Nothing about it seemed strange to him, until he read about the big scale in the house. Instantly, he could recall Mrs. Nightingale howling in frustration over her body. He couldn't actually remember what she sounded like in front of the mirror anymore. Now, all he recalled were the noises she made while death approached her. But the pain for both women was real. If Mrs. Nightingale had been inclined to sum up the cause of her anguish in the form of her own husband, she might have turned on him, too.

The wife was taunted into a state of anguish by the damning presence of the heavyweight meat scale. Surely it took days, weeks, perhaps months for the effect to take hold. But like a dull arthritic ache that blossoms into fiery pain, the daily humiliation became unendurable. By the time she pulled the trigger, all she knew was *make it stop*.

---

Over an hour went by while Shane battled with the words to tell his story. The night was shifting into the chill of the deep late hours. The smell of damp bushes and grass drifted over the cemetery.

He had never spoken nonstop for that long, even when he was reading out loud. Yet to his surprise, throughout his story this Sergeant Randall Blackburn seemed to be in no hurry at all, as if waiting for five minutes to get a sentence or two was something he did every day.

Shane was finished with his story before he realized he had gradually grown comfortable enough that his stutter was greatly reduced. Otherwise it might have taken him another half an hour.

Blackburn stood up and stretched, cracking his joints, so Shane took the opportunity to do the same.

"All right, then, Shane. I appreciate what you've told me about this woman's special sensitivity and all. And I see you were able to sort of be a fly on the wall around your adopted house. But I have to tell you, this leap you made from one to the other, from your own experience to a murder scene in some stranger's house—I've never seen it before. Not even among adults, or among other cops. But you used it to solve this case."

"You s-s-solved it. You told her about finger-pri-prints. You did it."

Blackburn looked at him and smiled. "Not much of a glory hog, are you? You know, Shane, I think you ought to take more satisfaction in this. You did a good thing. Without your help, an innocent woman would have had her life destroyed."

Shane didn't have an answer for that. Obviously the sergeant had no idea what a foul creature he was.

"So what do you say, then, if I come back sometime soon? Maybe we can talk over another case or two. Just to get your point of view. There's a café just reopened, not too far off. I can buy you dinner."

Shane wondered if he heard right. This police sergeant who did not realize that he and Shane were together in the Nightingale house now wanted to come around to discuss police cases? He felt like a pawn in somebody else's chess game. "I don-don-don't know."

"Won't trouble you at all. We don't have to go off anywhere, if you're busy and all. I could be here and gone in a few minutes. What do you say?"

Shane made himself smile and nod. Anything to get Blackburn out of there. Things had happened much too fast. When Blackburn turned to go, Shane felt himself speak without even thinking about it. "I'm glad you— glad that you—I'm—"

Blackburn just smiled and waved. In another heartbeat he was gone.

By that time Shane was so exhausted, he couldn't even replay the events of the night. All he knew for sure was for the first time since the earthquake, he had spoken to someone about his former family. That person was the man who had led his team into the Nightingale house. And Shane had come far too close to revealing his dreadful secret.

For the rest of the night hours, his body paced quietly while his thoughts boiled. It was only after the predawn light began to rise that he headed over to a spot next to the Mission chapel and lay down on the ground, spent. He had no desire to return to the darkness of the shed. Even though daylight was beginning to spread across the graveyard, sleep rolled over him like a shadow.

# 9

**HOURS LATER**

TOMMIE IGNORED THE KNOCKING at his front door while he stood up on the top floor of his lovely Victorian home and gazed out over the crumbled and blackened city. The cast-iron door knocker could fairly rattle the entire house, but most people only gave it one or two raps; Tommie had made sure the heavy swivel was poorly lubricated and uncomfortable to use.

He trusted that whoever was down there would go away soon. No doubt a stranger or strangers. There was no family left, hallelujah, and those who were once friends of his parents had long since gotten the idea that they were not friends of his, no matter how much they admired his inheritance. To safeguard privacy, he always kept his ground-floor windows so well covered that there was no way to tell from the outside whether he was home or not. It was a reliable way of getting people to leave him alone without making them too angry. Angry people get suspicious. Suspicious people intrude upon one's various pastimes.

And yet ever since the quake, these pests were often at his door. Religious witnessing teams, people canvassing for volunteers to take in displaced citizens, beggars knocking for food, for medicine, for money.

Naturally, if desperate and foolish enough, somebody could always break in. So far, nobody had been rash enough to dare. Unfortunately. That would be real icing on the cake, Tommie was certain. Still, he reminded himself that he had no need for any discontent. Because ever since the earthquake and the bizarre energies involved in the upheaval of the earth, the messages from each and every moment gave him repeated assurances that he was on the right track. He was doing Good Work, even though this rotting world was unlikely to ever acknowledge that or show the slightest appreciation for it. And yet his Good Work was vital. Everywhere he looked, there were more signs to reassure him and urge him on.

It was a sure sign that he had just made up his mind to elevate his work to an entirely new level only a few minutes before the earth heaved and citywide chaos gave him the power to kill at random, undetected.

It was a sign that on the same morning when he decided to switch to female victims, he should find the family of store owner Nightingale while the bastard was out.

It was a sign that the wall of flame split in two and passed his neighborhood on either side.

And it was a sign that each of his other killings since the morning of the quake was effortless to perform and easy to disguise.

He felt contented, down deep, like a cat that has just polished off a dish of cream. Over the past few days he had actually had enough appetite to eat several of Mrs. Allison's meals, and he even made himself take a few little naps, almost like real sleep.

There was that one problem bothering him, though. Shock and death still came too quickly for Tommie's taste. Even when he had no intention of killing right away, sometimes his victims just laid themselves right down and gave up the ghost. Or they dove for the escape of death like swimmers leaping off of an ocean cliff. After a little introductory knife work, most victims became incapable of following his train of thought while he explained things to them.

*There!* he thought with relief. The infernal knocking finally stopped. Another victory for patience. Let the self-righteous sisters of mercy troll for handouts somewhere else. As if he cared to interfere with the thinning of the herd, the very process to which he was dedicated?

He turned back to the sweeping view, northeast toward the wharves at the tip of the peninsula, and straight west out to the Pacific Ocean. Slowly, he brought his gaze downward, bringing his line of sight away from the horizon and closer to his own neighborhood. Most of the panorama was still a tableau of destruction, even though the broom-and-shovel crews were working around the clock. And then, only seven houses away from his own property, the magical ring of untouched homes began. With Tommie Kimbrough's place smack in the middle of the safe zone.

His satisfaction was only spoiled by the sight of a giant rat waddling—waddling—along the sidewalk like somebody's pet. It galled him to see his neighborhood invaded by vermin. Every other living thing in the area seemed to instinctively realize that if you didn't belong in Tommie's untouched neighborhood, you should stay the hell out. These seaport rodents cared nothing for any of that. *Rats may be foul, but they're smart,* Tommie thought with grudging admiration. *A rat can survive most of the things that will kill a human being. Only a fool thinks a rat is stupid.*

A cold shiver ran up his spine and rattled his shoulders. It occurred to him that he had something in common with these marauding rats. Like him, a rat was a remarkable killing machine. But by carrying the Black Plague, rats wielded a far greater power of death. An entire army of human soldiers might lay siege to a powerful city for many months without success, but a few infected rats could take out most of its citizens in weeks.

He felt a pang of jealousy over such power. What could be greater than the thrill of savoring his time with a victim? Answer: savoring the power to cause death from a distance. Death for dozens, death for hundreds, death that took days or weeks to arrive. Death that spread like a black fog. All at his bidding, and damn them all for everything.

A realization struck like a church bell: *When you cannot conquer a source of power, harness it!*

"Of course," he finally spoke out loud. "Of course!" he said again, louder this time.

Now Tommie's eyes were open wide. He could see the next step in his vital work as clearly as he saw the red afternoon sun, way out there, dipping into the sea at that fateful moment. Bowing to the coming darkness, just for him.

The entire time Blackburn sat in the headmaster's office at St. Adrian's, he felt utterly confused as to just what sort of place he was in. The name made it sound like a formal religious institution, but the place claimed no specific church or affiliation. He looked for anything he might have missed. There was a cloistered feel to the grounds and the buildings, but no visible religious symbols other than plain Christian crosses placed here and there.

The man behind the headmaster's desk was introduced only as "Friar John." His outfit made plain his priorities; the attire was that of a monk despite the secular job title. The headmaster droned on, accompanied by a wet swishing sound coming from a corner in the background, where a young girl of perhaps ten years studiously mopped the floor. She had close-cropped flaming red hair and a spray of freckles across her face, and her girlish energy radiated even in the act of pushing a mop.

Blackburn wondered why men who were not Catholic would call themselves "friars." Or were they some new kind of Catholic? Nobody offered an explanation. He decided not to mention it, rather to wait and see if the topic arose on its own.

He had to admit that Friar John spoke in such measured tones that serenity and gentleness appeared to radiate from him. Nevertheless, Blackburn felt a wave of vaguely unpleasant sensations wash through his intuition. At least the man was cooperative and expressed no hesitation in telling all about the boy, Shane. Blackburn listened to every detail of the story, how Shane was adopted by the Nightingale family a little more than a year ago. It all matched the few details that the boy gave him.

It seemed clear that the central mystery of Shane's extraordinary ability was not going to be solved in this place. Friar John explained that the records told nothing of Shane's origin or anything at all of his life prior to arrival. He was said to be about four years old when he was admitted, along with a scrap of paper that only gave his first name, age, and birth date. Friar John assured him that Shane was remembered as smart and quiet, and liked well enough by the other children even though he often seemed to work at being invisible.

Blackburn gave Friar John the sad news that the entire Nightingale family was killed in the earthquake and that now Shane was living on his own. He avoided giving an address to see if the headmaster would press him for the information, but Friar John just nodded and explained that unless Shane got into trouble, he wouldn't be forced or even asked to return. With the new influx of orphaned children from the quakes and fires, nobody was pressing for more juvenile wards. The boy had no need to fear that anyone from St. Adrian's was going to come looking for him, he said, and smiled.

Blackburn noticed that the swishing sound had stopped. He instinctively glanced over toward the girl. She was staring straight at them.

Friar John spoke in a vaguely annoyed tone, "Sergeant, this is young Mary Kathleen, with us since her crib days. Spends most of her time on punitive work assignments and never seems to learn a thing from them." He raised his voice to make sure she heard him. "I hope you never have cause to arrest her and take her downtown!"

Mary Kathleen stifled a good-natured laugh, unperturbed.

Blackburn liked her smile, so full of swagger. The kid looked like she could box a kangaroo. "Did you know Shane?" he asked her.

"He's older," she answered. "Was he hurt in the quake?"

"Mary Kathleen," Friar John interrupted, "you are free to go for now. You can finish this up in the morning." He gave her a wan smile that Blackburn recognized as trouble when it made her expression go dark.

She nodded to herself, then set the mop against the wall and walked out.

"Nice meeting you," Blackburn called after her.

She turned and flashed him a smile just for an instant, and then she was gone.

---

For Mary Kathleen, St. Adrian's policy of not allowing children off of the grounds without supervision was the same as a ball and chain. It could never be tolerable to her. The only meaningful answer to such an awful restriction was to take solo field trips in spite of it. Secret excursions into the world denied to her.

She could only use the few assets available to her. So while she was certain if she told Friar John one of the Helpers was sneaking around to watch her bathing, she could get the man in trouble, she also knew this particular Helper would do anything to keep her silent. That was highly useful in expanding her horizons, from time to time. On this occasion, the cooperative Helper covered for her while she darted out the back way and scrambled over the fence. She circled the grounds at a dead run to reach the front entrance before Sergeant Blackburn got too far away. She was determined to follow him all the way back to wherever Shane was staying, no matter how long it took.

So he was called Shane "Nightingale," then. She wasn't used to thinking of him that way. At St. Adrian's, neither of them had a last name. It was supposed to make it easier for people to picture having you in their family. Then they could stick their last name on you without feeling guilty, since you didn't have one in the first place. If the Nightingale family was all dead, though, she wondered if Shane still wanted to use their unusual last name. Was he really Shane "Nightingale" anymore?

When Sergeant Blackburn finally emerged from the front gate, she was delighted to see he wasn't climbing onto a horse or buggy. He just stretched his legs and headed off at a fast walk. She went after him, following from behind and moving at a brisk trot to keep up with his stride. The chase quickly took a toll on her. Mary Kathleen could bound like a rabbit, but she usually only needed such speed for a block or two, just enough to evade a pursuer. For the past couple of years, anytime she sneaked out there were always a few older boys or grown men who pawed at her from shadows, pulled at her from doorways, tried to follow her into secluded places. Then, a brief explosion of speed was the only power necessary. Now with this endurance test on the hilly streets, block after block behind the big policeman, she fought for breath.

But she had clearly heard the cop tell Friar John he just finished his night shift. Surely that meant he would be on his way home now, didn't it? And before he went home for the day, he would stop and see Shane, wouldn't he? If the cop was so interested in him, why wouldn't he go visit him? She kept telling that to herself while she labored to keep up with the sergeant's long strides. Her overall plan was good enough to make her feel inspired.

She was a hunter and a spy: a spy disguised as a silly tomboy girl. She needed a name for herself, therefore. Something better than "Mary Kathleen." Something to fit the adventure.

"Mary Kathleen" was a false name given to her at St. Adrian's, back when she was too young to remember. And since "Mary Kathleen" was a disguise that she had to wear at St. Adrian's in order to get from day to day, it made perfect sense for her to cast it aside in favor of one she chose herself.

She sorted through her best words for one that might capture the feeling of this person she wanted to become. Well, a spy and a hunter were both dramatic roles, so why not use a dramatic word? For example, her little field trip today was like a scene from a magical play, a sneak-away adventure inserted into an ordinary humdrum day. The adventure itself, she realized, was a vignette: a separate scene in a larger play. Her life was a vignette all its own.

That's when it hit her. "Vignette" was perfect as a new name for her, a name so special, nobody else even knew it. She said it to herself a few times. It was right. It was done. So Vignette, then.

Vignette willed herself to safely travel the streets by being an invisible and unimportant little girl nobody would particularly notice or remember. In that fashion, she kept from being detected by the sergeant while she tracked him. Luckily, he seemed to feel no concerns at all that there could be a small female hunter on his tail, following him up and down all these fragmented city streets.

It only took around two hours for her faith to manifest, but by then her legs were getting wobbly. During that time, the big sergeant walked all the way to the office of a newspaper called the *California Star*, and while she spied from outside the building's brand-new picture window, he stood inside for a long time talking with a couple of other men. The men seemed to listen carefully to him, and one of them even brought out a notebook and wrote down what the sergeant was saying.

After that, Sergeant Blackburn left and walked a few more blocks to a ruined restaurant that was trying to get back into business. He bought a thick sandwich of some kind and walked away with it wrapped up and tucked under his arm. It looked like such a good idea that she spent the few coins in her pocket for one of her own before hurrying off to catch up to him.

Preparation protected her again. The only reason she had anything at all to spend was because Friar John was careless about loose change. She would never have any money if she didn't keep making trouble and getting herself assigned the extra work duty. She had yet to come across anything outside of the orphanage that a ten-year-old girl could do to make money except for things that made her skin crawl. The creepy Helper was bad enough.

It consumed all Vignette's energy to take the two steps necessary for every one of the sergeant's long strides, not only keeping pace with his speed but also darting from the cover of one object to the next. Fortunately for her, there was always something handy. All of the makeshift structures people were putting up to live and work in made the streets look like campgrounds and offered plenty of obstructions.

When she saw the sergeant eventually turn into a big adobe church called Mission Dolores, only to walk out two minutes later without the big sandwich, she knew the day's hunt was successful. This time when the sergeant walked away, she remained behind.

Minutes later, she was at the front gate to the cemetery, peering through the vines growing over it. There was a skinny boy sitting under a tree near the back, hungrily polishing off the same sandwich. A breeze shifted the nearby tree branches, and sunlight flashed over the boy's face so clearly that she finally recognized him. It was Shane, all right.

Whether he would remember her or not, she recalled him well enough, even as she realized she had now taken her endeavor as far as she could. Because even after the spying, the hunting, the adventure, Vignette still had no skills for confronting a boy who felt important to her.

Before she knew it, she became Mary Kathleen again. Dreaming is one thing, but there is always the real world waiting. She had been gone for too long; her absence would soon be noticed. She backed away from the gate and turned toward home. If she wanted to continue having adventures, she could hardly start turning up missing at roll call, drawing concern about her whereabouts. No. Let the friars go on thinking that her only form of rebellion was to talk out loud in class.

She needed the work details to collect coins for moving around the city.

───────────

Blackburn sat in the living room of his new little basement apartment, located in one of the few standing areas of town. Evening was just settling in. The restored gaslights along that particular street were already burning, playing their yellow and gold illumination in through his ground-level windows. It was an odd view, and he had not yet gotten used to it. Tonight was his first night off since the week before the Great Earthquake struck.

He tried to let himself melt into the only comfortable chair he had obtained so far, but he could feel his body habitually gearing up for a long night shift.

His stomach gnawed with hunger pangs. He wished he had thought to get a sandwich for himself along with the one for Shane. But back then it had been close enough to breakfast that he didn't think about it. Now he was too tired to even bother opening a can, so he let himself sink deeper into the chair. Sleep came to claim him, sweeping his hunger aside. Warm relaxation enveloped him. The boy was far more interesting than food, anyway. Blackburn closed his eyes and let the mental notes play through his thickening thoughts.

So Shane more or less grew up in an orphanage but lived with the Nightingale family for a year, until they died in the quake somehow. Officially, he would be a suspect if there was any evidence left unburned. But all Blackburn's intuition and experience told him the boy was incapable of such crimes.

Next the boy takes refuge in a live-in job at Mission Dolores. While reading the paper aloud one day, trying to cure his stutter, he comes across an article about Captain Sullivan's murder—and right then he just "knows" Elsie Sullivan is not the innocent widow but actually the perpetrator. The boy then sends a note so bizarre, Blackburn would never have considered except he was desperate for some break in the challenge Lieutenant Moses threw down to him.

Then, when he used the information to break Sullivan and get a full confession, the boy explained his knowledge with a story that would have been long even if he could speak clearly. Something about a married woman's combination of insecurity and vanity about her appearance, when she is of an age where many other women are more attractive than she is, everywhere she goes. Something about realizing that the detail about the industrial scale was a clear clue regarding subtle mental torture in the Sullivan household. About seeing the body sprawled across the scale as being much more than mere coincidence, but a staged comment, a work of sculpture done in flesh and blood.

At the age of twelve, this Shane Nightingale fellow described the human capacity for levels of pain and rage that most civilized people know nothing about, no matter how old they are. It made for a good story, and the boy deserved a little recognition. That day, the boys at the *California Star* agreed; they wrote down everything Blackburn told them. The next afternoon's paper was going to run a human interest article about how Shane Nightingale, the sole survivor of his family, offered insights that solved the Sullivan case.

And so maybe this newspaper's acknowledgment would go some distance toward giving the kid back some spirit. So far, Blackburn regarded Shane as a young fellow with a unique combination of confidence in his vision and an utter lack of confidence in himself. Just listening to him try to get a sentence out was painful. If a boost in self-confidence could smooth out his speech, that would make a pretty fine reward for the kid's act as a good citizen. Once the article was out, maybe somebody at City Hall would even want to grab onto the story for political reasons and give the boy some kind of city award. Although the way Shane's eyes lit up at the sight of that big sandwich today, a decent lunch might do the trick.

The last thing Blackburn did before falling into a deep sleep was to make a mental note to take a copy of the next day's paper over to the Mission as soon as it came out. It would be great to see some pride on the kid's face.

# 10

MEANWHILE...

"T-O-M-M-Y..." Lieutenant Moses carefully printed the name.

"No, Lieutenant, it's spelled with an 'i-e,'" Tommie corrected from his place on the other side of the giant Police Roll Call Book.

Lieutenant Moses exhaled and focused a hooded glare. "You could have told me that before I started writing." He reached for his big gum eraser and stroked the end of the line clean. Then he chanted along with himself while he formed each letter: "T-O-M-M-I-E..."

"Good." Tommie smiled.

Moses observed how closely Tommie Kimbrough leaned in over the book. It made the much bigger man feel a passing desire to squash the bony upstart, just to get a spot of amusement going on an otherwise stressful day. As if it were not bad enough that he was already having to guard his own backside from every political angle, Moses had to struggle with attempting to form key relationships with arrogant peacocks like this: one of the city's trust fund babies, *buying* his way into police business so he could play copper. Probably to impress his latest crush.

However that might be, after donating enough to cover the cost of completely rebuilding the city's primary morgue, this civic-minded little fellow with strange tastes asked for nothing more than to be allowed to volunteer his time at the temporary morgue facility, where they were strapped for labor anyway. He claimed that in his free time at the morgue, he planned to draw medical sketches of anatomical parts for use in textbooks. The eager fellow had appeared in front of Moses wearing several thin layers of clothing, as recommended for sloppy body work, clutching a generously sized lunch bucket with a tight-fitting lid to keep odors out of the food. Clearly, thought Moses, Mr. Kimbrough had done a little such work in the past.

"Have you brought any eucalyptus oil?" Moses inquired. "Peppermint oil, or like that?"

The visitor offered a modest smile and pulled out a small vial. "Eucalyptus."

"Good enough, then." So all right, maybe the guy wouldn't fall down and faint over the first mushy body. With a city broken into a million pieces, who was going to refuse his offer to help?

"And it's K-I-M-B-R-O-U-G-H, yes?"

"Correct. Excellent, Lieutenant." Tommie smiled again.

For an instant, Moses felt a flash of concern that Kimbrough might have been planted there, perhaps to secretly evaluate Moses on the job. Moses had to admit he would use a spy himself to keep this position, if he could. Countless other men wanted the job. So why wouldn't someone higher up, maybe someone with a friend who needs work, use a spy to watch Moses and to look for dirt? For weeks, rumors floated all over the city about various plots to take over the government amid the chaos of the city's long recovery.

Moses wrote in "K-I-M-B-R-O-U-G-H," then noted the time and date. He closed the book. That was it, then. He would just have to see to it that little Mr. Kimbrough never got the chance to observe anything that could be used against Moses. "Before you go..."

"Yes?" Kimbrough turned back with a pleasant expression.

"Whenever you come in, you are to go only to the morgue. There's too much traffic here in the station house, so don't dally around the place. I signed you in here, today, but from now on there will be a sign-in book for you over there. No offense, but my time is pulled in other directions."

"Yes, that's fine, Lieutenant. Just as well. No need to trouble you."

"Right. And while we're talking about not troubling me, you'll make sure to keep your head down and don't bring me back any difficulties. Agreed?"

"My conduct in the morgue will be appropriate every time I go in, sir!" Kimbrough said, imitating a recruit in a drill. "My head will be down at all times. Because neither of us wants any trouble. Sir." He grinned and saluted, clever as hell.

Moses studied Kimbrough's face for sarcasm and felt sure it was in there somewhere, but decided to let it pass this time. The size of Kimbrough's donation made him practically bulletproof so long as he didn't rob anybody important.

Like a well-trained physician, Moses considered his first obligation as Acting Station Chief to be that of doing no harm. Therefore, the safest thing to be done about this Tommie Kimbrough fellow was to push him out the door and make it plain to him that he could only keep Lieutenant Moses off of his back by staying out of the station. Then let him make all the strange drawings he wants.

Moses waved the eager artist off toward the morgue area, adding a look meant to remind Kimbrough not to make any mistakes. He observed with satisfaction that the little guy was so intimidated, he not only hurried to obey, but he even made a point of looking like he was glad to agree that yes, he would keep himself scarce.

Satisfied, Moses lumbered off in uniform pants that were now several sizes too large for his shrinking portage. Time to see what else his people were stepping into around his partially reclaimed station. Endless little problems to fix. "Acting, hell," he dared to grumble out loud. "I *am* the Station Chief."

---

The temporary morgue was less than a block from the station, set up in a fresh clearing bulldozed out of the rubble. Workers had used fallen stones to construct a giant single room with walls two feet thick and a sloping canvas roof. Tommie stopped just outside the morgue's large doorway, which was simply a set of thick canvas curtains reaching all the way to the ground. Nobody was inside at the moment.

He noted a worn set of wagon tracks in the ground just outside the door, indicating that the morgue team was probably out fetching more guests. He clutched his sealed lunch bucket, pushed the thick curtain aside, and stepped in without bothering to look around to see if anyone was observing him.

The instant that the curtain closed behind him, the great room plunged into darkness. A thick stench exploded in his nose and mouth, then slid down his throat like fetid syrup. The buzzing of thousands of flies filled his hearing. Tommie stood perfectly still for a few seconds, struggling to control his gag reflex and to slow his breathing. He groped for his vial of eucalyptus oil and streaked a thick smear under his nose and into his nostrils. The room's sickening smell remained, but its power was dimmed just enough to be tolerable. He pulled several loose wooden matches from his pocket and struck one with his thumbnail.

A flare of yellow and red filled the area around him, revealing just enough to confirm the place was perfect. A demon's toy shop with everything he needed, just waiting to be used.

A dozen or so crude stone body basins lined the walls like oversized bathtubs. Each one was large enough to place a body inside and still leave room to line the body with ice. The ice water was efficiently drained away through small holes and down along thin troughs made of hastily thrown mortar. The troughs ran down both sides of each basin into another gutter leading outside under the wall. It was an efficient, if basic attempt at public hygiene.

"Damn it all!" He cried out without meaning to when the flame burned him. Biting his lip, he lit another match with throbbing fingers and began to move along the wall, checking each of the bodies, just in case. During his wanderings around San Francisco's back alleys, he had heard rumors about the Black Plague turning up, but while most other people laughed off the stories, he knew they might be true. Why, every single day Chinatown received crates unloaded from ships that brought their cargo *and* their stowaway rats. Sooner or later, a few of them were bound to carry plague.

And yet the city's Guiding Lights would be loath to allow it to affect business in their burgeoning port city. And unless a real contagion broke out, something too big to hide, the chaos of Chinatown could be handy to conceal all sort of bizarre death with the city's willing assistance.

Meaning if there was no plague victim in storage right now, Tommie was confident there would be one soon. He used up the rest of his wooden matches trying to find any Chinese faces—even one—but every festering body was either white, black, or one of the natives. The most decomposed and truly disfigured ones didn't look much like human beings at all. Hardly worth burying. It amazed him that in the midst of this citywide crisis, people were still expending time and effort on the likes of them. *Let the flies have 'em.* There was nothing for him here, yet. He passed by the last body just as his last match burned low. By the time the flame went out, he was on his way back outside.

*Wait...just wait*, some inner voice assured him. *It's coming. Wait for it.*

In every direction, the city was an anthill of activity and reconstruction, but the pall that hung over the morgue's grim presence kept a bubble of avoidance for a good twenty yards in all directions. Few travelled there. It suited him to stand comfortably inside that dead zone, completely unnoticed by the scurrying creatures who swarmed the broken city.

Within a few minutes, his wait was rewarded. The body wagon pulled back up to the morgue with another sad stack. Tommie introduced himself and showed his letter of permission from the Committee of Fifty, at which the corporal in charge threw up his hands and told Tommie to do whatever the hell he wanted except get in the way. Tommie made a show of helping them unload the bodies, enough to get a close look at each corpse. These were all white, as it turned out, probably a family. He was quickly aroused at the thought of the Nightingales, and of the time spent with them that was over all too soon.

Four more wagonloads came that morning, but with nothing more interesting than decayed remains. It was not until midafternoon when the corporal and his private drove up again, looking much different than the slumped, exhausted men they had been all morning. Tommie was passing the time by smoking a thin cigarillo and practicing his smoke rings when noises of fast hooves and squeaky wagon springs caught his attention. He looked up in time to see the body wagon driving in hard and fast. The men pulled to a halt and jumped down, both looking tense. They immediately huddled in animated conversation.

Tommie felt his boredom leave him, and while the two officers debated next to the wagon, he walked around to look into the back.

There was only one body. It was adult sized, but completely covered in layers and layers of cloth wrapping. The whole bundle was so thick, it looked like the corpse was swaddled inside of a heavy winter sleeping bag, bound together by an intricately tied network of knotted ropes. Somebody had gone to extraordinary effort.

At that moment, the corporal hurried over. His face was coated in a light sweat, and he spoke in anxious tones. "Mr. Kimbrough, I understand that you got clearance and all. And you know we been letting you alone so far, right?"

"Yes, Corporal. That's quite true. Is there a problem now?"

"Oh, there's a problem for sure, sir, but not with you. I've got to ask you not to even think about opening up that body's wrappings, there. Not to draw sketches or nothing. We're about to put it under every scrap of ice we got left. There's doctors from Sacramento coming in here to look it over. Until they get here, we got to let it be. Can you promise me you're gonna leave this feller alone?"

"It's a man, then?"

"Makes no difference. If you can't agree, then we're gonna go talk to somebody with more rank than I got."

"Certainly, Corporal. Certainly. I completely apologize. You do such important work. Want me to help carry him in?"

The corporal shook his head. "We already had to put the thing in there. No reason for you to get any closer to it."

The other man, Private Something-or-Other, stepped up to help, and the two men lifted the body with exaggerated care, making sure not to touch it with anything other than their thick leather gloves. Tommie ducked inside ahead of them to light an extra lantern for the task, and they placed the body in the stone basin farthest from the others. They covered it with several half-melted blocks of ice and pulled a thick tarpaulin over the entire mass.

He followed the men back outside and watched while they shook their leather gloves into a small fire pit. The corporal poured a generous helping of lamp oil onto the gloves and threw a match onto the pile. All three men stepped back while the flames leaped up amid an inky trail of smoke.

"Corporal," Tommie asked in his best casual voice, "where did you say that body came from?"

The corporal studied him for a moment before he took a breath and shrugged. "Chinatown."

Randall Blackburn sat across from Shane Nightingale at a little table in the partially restored café. He had waited until they were done eating their filling lunch of heavy soup and bread before he presented Shane with the afternoon paper. Then he listened with satisfaction while the boy followed his request to read the article out loud. The story was accompanied by a generic pencil sketch of a twelve-year-old male that nobody would recognize as Shane, but his name was mentioned several times. Blackburn's acquaintance at the paper had pulled every heartstring his editors would allow.

The writer repeated Blackburn's story about a young man adopted out of a local orphanage by the Nightingale family, of the well-regarded Nightingale Dry Goods Emporium, and who was now the family's sole survivor. Instead of dwelling on how the Nightingales were killed, it celebrated the fact that even while Shane worked for his keep at a local church, he read the *California Star* with such regularity that he noticed the article about the murder of Captain Harlan Sullivan. And based upon Shane Nightingale's astounding insight and the reporting of the *California Star*, an important clue was delivered to Sergeant Randall Blackburn of the SFPD, and a gross injustice was prevented. The true culprit was arrested and an innocent woman, wrongfully accused, set free.

"'And now,'" Shane finished the last line in a strong voice, "'the true perpetrator sits in police custody after a full confession.'" He sat and stared at the page for a moment, then slowly lowered the paper to the table.

Blackburn grinned. "Now I see what you're doing with this thing of reading newspapers out loud! It's impressive. You never missed a beat."

Shane nodded and looked up long enough to show a timid smile, then quickly lowered his eyes again.

"Don't worry," Blackburn went on. "I didn't tell them which church you're working at. Otherwise all the young ladies would be sneaking down here to meet up with you."

Shane nodded a little, but this time he didn't look up at all. The boy was so clearly lacking in self-confidence that Blackburn hoped a little celebration in the newspaper would be a great way to buck up his spirits. But even though Shane was able to read every word of the article and surely understood that he was being publicly applauded, he wasn't making any reaction at all.

Blackburn suddenly felt like a complete fool. Obviously, he misjudged the boy's depth of grief over losing his new family. Had he managed to somehow make this boy feel worse?

"Well, Shane," he went on. "It's just a story. Tomorrow they'll have another one. I just thought you might like for people to know how you helped me out. You deserve it. Take some pride in it." He smiled and clapped the boy on the shoulder. "Brag on yourself a little bit. No harm in letting people know you've done something good for this city."

Shane took a deep breath and finally raised his eyes to meet Blackburn's. "Thank—thank you. I kno-kno-know you tried to he-he-help. But I juh-juh-just...I just..." He stopped and shook his head in frustration.

"That's all right," Blackburn hastened. "No need to go on about it. I should have talked to you first." He grinned. "Guess I thought the surprise might lighten your day." He handed the waiter the money for their meal and stood up. "Anyway, you keep that copy. If you want to practice reading, it sure can't hurt you to read about yourself." He pointed at the paper. "Save it for your kids."

He walked away and let Shane have some time to think of himself as a hero. For Blackburn, it was uncomfortable to be alone with another male who was emotionally overwhelmed. And while it was less disturbing to be with a very young person in such a state, Shane was close enough to manhood that his pain was awkward to witness, even though it also seemed unfair to expect him to show a man's stoicism and put up a strong face.

*What an age to be*, Blackburn mused, *old enough to see things as they are and too young to do anything about it.* In comparison, his own boyhood up among the California giant redwoods was fairly idyllic, all things considered.

He now realized that to offer that little news story as some sort of reward, expecting it to help this troubled boy, had been optimistic to the point of ignorance. He mistakenly thought he might fill in a deep well by pouring in a bucket of water.

        ———

As soon as the big sergeant was gone, Shane lowered himself back into his seat at the table. He felt certain his wobbly knees nearly gave him away. He had been so horrified by the sergeant's news article that he nearly blurted out his dismay half a dozen times. For once, the blessed, goddamned stutter saved him.

He began a slow, staggering journey back to the Mission. The cool green isolation of the Mission cemetery seemed to be the only place in the world where he could find any safety. The holy men there seldom concerned themselves with daily newspapers, and many of the city's residents could not read at all. Once he made it back to his toolshed, he could lose himself there, which was as close as he could come to crawling into a hole.

# 11

―――――――

**THE FOLLOWING DAY**

SHANE'S ARTICLE CAME OUT in the *California Star*, and a copy found its way into the makeshift morgue near the City Hall Station. It was carried under the arm of the same private from the day before, who sat down and finished reading it while sipping coffee brewed over the fire pit. Instead of tossing the used newspaper into the flames, he pulled it into sections and then used them to protect his hands from the cold while he carried the day's delivery of ice blocks inside. He left each section of the paper with each ice block, piling the ice with the newsprint sandwiched between them to help keep the blocks from freezing together.

He left the pile under layers of burlap to distribute over the corpses as needed. The ice was never to be allowed to melt off of the mummy-wrapped body located in the back. That particular guest got fresh ice first, no matter what. Tommie worked in earnest, and soon the stench of decay infiltrated the pores of his exposed skin and every fiber of his clothing.

*No worse than a public outhouse*, he cheerfully pointed out to himself. He hated those places. Human zoos.

Now, on Tommie's second day in the morgue, he was even permitted to make himself at home in that grim place whether or not any of the other men were around. Just him and the quiet ones. And since this was the first time he had found himself alone, he immediately got down to the only thing he was actually there to accomplish.

He stepped outside into the sunlight and carefully checked his clothing. He had on full body underwear beneath a light pair of pants with his legs cinched tightly with twine at the cuffs. His waistline was tied with more of the twine where his shirt met his belt. Over that, he wore another full outfit of long pants and long sleeves sufficient to pass for normal among that day's audience members.

Just as he stepped back into the darkness of the morgue, he pulled a rolled-up piece of fabric from his pocket and shook out a fine silk cloth stitched into the shape of a large cone. He pulled the cone over his head and down to his shoulders, forming a hood thin enough to see through without eye holes. He tugged a pair of thin leather gloves onto his hands, and when he pushed aside the heavy canvas curtains, he carried nothing else with him but the sealed lunch bucket. He moved quickly to complete his task.

He removed his outer layer of clothing and set it next to the ice pile, while remaining inside his sealed suit. Then he plucked an oil lantern from a peg near the door and headed straight back to the special body basin holding an icy-cool corpse somebody in Chinatown wrapped in far too much covering as a message for those with eyes to see.

Tommie was certain whoever was inside of the layered shrouds fell to the Plague. He would know the truth soon enough.

When he reached the rearmost body basin, he set down the lantern and went straight to work, pulling the heavy-bladed knife from his rigged pocket and unsheathing the blade. He had spent hours sharpening it to an edge far thinner than necessary, and now as he sliced away the bottom of the body's fabric cocoon, the blade passed through the thick layers of cloth with almost no effort. He made a perfect cut five or six inches long, separating layer after layer while he worked toward the corpse itself.

His moves were well studied. In Tommie's judgment, the best thing about independent wealth was the time it gave one for reading and reflection. Such things provided bits of knowledge more powerful than a sidearm. He now knew, for instance, that while a rat bite could infect a human if the rat carried the plague, the devil in the disease was that fleas from an infected rat could also carry the plague. And not only are fleas practically invisible, they can jump several feet. It might be possible to avoid the rats once plague is on the loose, but avoiding contact with fleas was far more difficult without the sort of protection he wore.

To accomplish his goal, he only needed a minute of contact with the body. Perhaps less. By now, any fleas that might still be on the cadaver should be stunned by the cold. Research had shown him how the Chinese Oriental Rat Flea thrived on the hides of black rats but became *inactive in cold temperatures and was easily destroyed by fire.* Thus he felt confident that with only a few seconds of exposure, and with the immediate burning of his clothing afterward, he could dodge the disease.

As for any remaining danger, what was life without risk?

The sliced wraps finally parted to reveal the corpse's lower leg. Tommie picked up the lantern and shined it close to the opening to get a good look. *Perfect!* The purplish, blackened skin was also covered with red-and-brown circles. It made no difference if there were any fleas to carry this disease. Here, the tissue itself was infectious.

He set the lantern aside, picked up his lunch bucket, unsealed the lid, and reached in. From the box, he pulled a small black rat by the tail, then took the animal firmly in his other hand. In a single, swift move, he stuffed the rat into the corpse's thick wrappings, carefully pushing it all the way down to the flesh, then yanked his arm out and pinched the opening shut. All he needed to do now was to place another large block of ice directly over the opening so the rat could not escape. He picked up the largest remaining ice block and set it in place to cover the slit in the shrouds.

Between the rat's frenzy of fear and desire to escape, it would gnaw on the body. It would draw the plague into itself. An hour or two, he thought, should be plenty. In the meantime, he would lug more fresh ice over and completely cover the corpse, making certain the rat had nowhere else to go but into the body, which would be warmer than the ice surrounding it.

Tommie walked back toward the spot where the fresh ice sat waiting for him, stopping halfway between it and the body to set the lantern on the floor. He stepped over to the pile of ice and picked up the top block, using the same section of newspaper left behind with it. It was the financial section, full of grim indicators that Tommie didn't bother to read. He carried the block back to the body and rested it against the one that already covered the slit. There were a few half-melted blocks still in place, but he thought the corpse could use four or five more.

He went back to the ice and picked up another block, this one covered by the section of the paper showing Shane's article. He didn't bother to look at it, just used the paper to make it easier to lift the block and carry it back to the body. When he was finished, he collected the papers, with Shane's article on the top, still not noticing the story. He carried them out to the fire pit to burn them along with his clothing after the entire job was done. He tossed a few of the papers into the pit after wadding each one. Just as he reached for the page with Shane's article, the name "Nightingale" caught his eye.

Tommie became utterly still, as unmoving as the surrounding corpses.

*No...*

His denial began its automatic responses—there were others with that name, unrelated others. He had seen the name before. Unfortunately, the question could be answered in an instant; all he had to do was pick up the page and read the article.

Finally, with a slow and deep breath, he broke the spell holding him and reached forward to pick up the damp page. He held it close. There was the name, and there was the article containing it, along with the drawing of a twelve-year-old boy, captioned "Shane Nightingale." The first name of "Shane" sent up another red flag. Tommie's hands grew shaky while he began to decipher the smeared words on the page.

Something about the boy helping the police to solve a high-society murder. Police Sergeant Randall Blackburn tells all about this amazing boy, blah, blah...

Then there it was.

It hit him like a nail to the forehead.

"Shane Nightingale" was some throwaway kid. He wasn't really a Nightingale; he only took the name of the family who adopted him. A year earlier, he was taken in by the Nightingale family of the renowned *Nightingale Dry Goods Emporium,* all of whom had perished in the earthquake and fires, except for Shane.

*"...except for Shane."*

There was one Nightingale still left. Tommie missed one.

*"...except for Shane."*

Shane. The human bad penny. Tommie silently screamed in frustration, wondering how such a thing could have happened. Although even as he asked himself, he knew the only possible answer: Friar John. Somehow, for some inexplicable reason, the headmaster had not only sold out Tommie's patronage, but he had set Tommie up for an inevitable encounter between him and the boy. Another Nightingale was out there. And because of that, *incompleteness* now marred the memory of Tommie's special work.

He took a quick look around to confirm that the body wagon was still nowhere in sight, then hustled off to the station to ask a few casual questions about this Sergeant Randall Blackburn and his special little friend.

---

Blackburn decided to pay a second visit to the orphanage, this time unannounced. He went in uniform to avoid misunderstandings, but gave no other consideration to the friars. The thing he gained from reading the article about Shane was the realization of the huge hole in Shane's background. Whatever clue to the boy's insightful ability there might be, surely some evidence must have been left at the orphanage during the years he spent there. Blackburn needed to get a closer look at the place itself.

He closed the distance of the last block before the back gate to the grounds of St. Adrian's. A familiar sense of danger manifested beneath his stomach and across his shoulders.

He challenged himself over that. *What danger? It's a place full of kids!* There were some unusual people taking care of those kids, but it was necessary work, and it was something few others wanted to do. So then, what danger?

It had to come from whatever it was preventing a twelve-year-old boy, twice orphaned, from being interested in returning to the familiarity of St. Adrian's. Why would he not want to come back, instead of taking his chances alone on the street? It seemed the danger came from whatever persuaded that boy to prefer living all by himself in a toolshed at the back of a cemetery.

He reached the gate and saw it was both unlocked and unguarded. That made walking in easy enough, but it seemed strange. An orphan might not desire a life alone on the street, but most delinquents would prefer it. So how were they kept from running off?

He moved quietly, but made no effort to sneak around. The grounds were nicely kept and all outdoor traces of the earthquake damage had been eliminated. The brick buildings showed a few cracks, but nothing of real concern. Either the place was solidly constructed or the shock wave spared this part of town, leaving it as another of those strangely untouched pockets of land that existed here and there.

A cool breeze ran across the manicured grass. There was a quiet dignity about the place, but his anxiety kicked in with a snap of instinct when he moved toward the main building, a long and low two-story structure. The place was supposed to be full of kids, over a hundred according to Friar John. Yet even in this close proximity, Blackburn heard nothing. The loudest sound to reach him was the rustle of the breeze in the foliage and bird calls from the upper branches.

He opened the door and stepped inside, quietly pulling it closed behind him. Everything remained quiet. He stood still for a moment, letting his ears adjust to the room the same way his eyes adjusted to a drop in the light. Faint background sounds reached him: a scraping of a chair, a quiet set of footsteps, an indistinguishable voice. Somebody had recently vomited in there.

The bare floorboards squeaked under his weight when he moved along the hallway, passing several classrooms. A small window in each classroom door revealed young students bent low over their desks, silently reading or writing. In one class, a middle-aged male was delivering an arithmetic lesson and writing on the blackboard. Every student paid strict attention.

He was still watching the class and wondering how the teachers kept such perfect order when he flinched at the sharp sound of a mop handle falling onto the floor. He turned to see the same young girl who was cleaning Friar John's office on his last visit. She stared at him as if he were a ghost.

He started to apologize for startling her, but before he got the first word out, she spun on her heels and ran. Her speed was impressive.

Blackburn made one more pass down the hallway, focusing on the classes on the opposite side this time, but learned nothing else. He was just starting up the stairs to the second floor when he was stopped by a sharp voice coming from behind him.

"Hello, Sergeant."

There was no sound of welcome to it. Blackburn turned to see Friar John, who had managed to get close enough to breathe down his neck without giving himself away. Blackburn was equally surprised by and suspicious of the man's sneak-skills.

Moments later they were back at the door to Friar John's office. The friar had managed to whisk Blackburn there so quickly, he saw little else along the way.

"Thank you, Mary Kathleen." The friar spoke without bothering to turn around and confirm she was following them. "You may go back to class now."

"Can't, Friar. I'm kicked out for talking again. Supposed to mop the hall."

"All right, all right, just go back to it, then."

She hurried back to her mop and pail without ever looking at Blackburn, which seemed a little odd, given her surprise on encountering him. But nothing about the place quite came into full focus for him.

He followed Friar John into the office.

---

Vignette sneaked up to Friar John's door carrying the mop and bucket as props. She sidled up close enough to listen in without being seen. Then she silently placed the bucket and mop in position so it might look like she had been working there if anybody spotted her. Curiosity owned her at that moment and drove all her actions, The surprise sight of the same policeman initially frightened her, encountering him as she did in the middle of a hallway she had just been sentenced to clean.

For her, the policeman's appearance at St. Adrian's was clearly a sign, fate of some sort. She knew these were the kinds of things she was supposed to leave up to the Lord, but she had been finding herself feeling less and less certain about the Lord's reliability, given her life experience so far.

She listened to the two men talk.

"Sergeant Blackburn, if I had anything else to tell you, I certainly would."

"I don't doubt that, sir—" "Friar John."

"I don't doubt that, Friar John, but—"

"I even looked through his permanent file after your first visit, just in case. But there's just nothing there. Nothing useful."

"Right, but I'm here because sometimes people remember things after a few days of thinking it over, so I generally like to—"

"Wander onto their premises without notice?"

There was a silent pause while both men regarded one another.

"If I need to," Blackburn replied in a soft and even tone. He held Friar John's gaze until the headmaster dropped it.

"Now, sir," Blackburn continued, "here's the—"

"Friar John."

"...Here's the thing, Friar John, this boy knows too much about certain kinds of very dark things."

"I hope you are not implying he was mistreated here!"

"I don't deal in implications, sir. The fact is, he knows so much about the dark side of human nature that besides helping me to solve a crime, he has attracted my concern. I want to know where he comes from. Something happened to him. I want to know what it is."

"Since he left, I haven't the slightest—"

"Something happened. Why is his stammer so bad?"

"His stammer? Are we talking about the same boy? The Shane Nightingale I know speaks with a perfectly clear voice."

"Well, that's funny, then, isn't it? Now he has a stutter so bad it almost shuts him up entirely."

"Your guess is as good as mine, Sergeant," Friar John quietly replied. He added the smile that made him look Holy.

Vignette wanted to shout and kick the wall. Friar John's nice-guy act made her furious. Couldn't the policeman see through it? Surely this big cop was too smart to *fall* for it, wasn't he?

Friar John continued smiling. "I don't mean to sound harsh, Sergeant, but I have over a hundred children of all ages here, and so I simply cannot concern myself with them after they go. Of the ones here, some are violent, some are skilled criminals, some are little angels who've been thrown away for one terrible reason or another. Once an orphan is adopted out, we never take them back unless they want to come. Or perhaps if they get arrested."

The sergeant then sat very still for a long minute, with Friar John waiting. Finally the sergeant sighed and stood up. "All right, then. But something's wrong here, and I believe I'll have to follow it up until it's all sorted out."

Friar John stood, too. Vignette could tell he looked relieved. She wondered if the sergeant noticed it. The scene held her attention so well, she nearly forgot to grab her mop and look busy when Friar John escorted the sergeant back into the hall. Friar John absently waved her away, then walked the sergeant in the opposite direction.

As soon as they rounded the corner, Vignette dropped her mop and bucket, ran into an empty classroom, and scrambled out through an open window. She had no way of telling where this was going, but every inch of her tingled with anticipation. She was certain Fate had her in its grip.

She sprinted across the grounds and crawled over a side fence while Sergeant Blackburn left by the front door. She knew she could catch him, and this time she intended to follow him until he went home. She needed to know where the big man lived because she could feel events pulling her out of St. Adrian's for good. Maybe she could sneak back and pick up a few of her things after nightfall, but she could never tolerate living there again. She was certain of nothing more than that the life of Mary Kathleen had become a suit of clothing several sizes too small.

Tommie was only at the station for a few minutes, being careful to keep out of Lieutenant Moses's way while he pretended to search for promising angles for sketches of the building. He explained that he would need to sketch something of the station house to accompany the cadaver illustrations. He was there just long enough to learn Sergeant Blackburn was not expected until sometime before midnight. Nobody else seemed to know anything about this Shane Nightingale creature, either.

He arrived back at the morgue to see the body wagon parked out front, so he hot-footed it. He hurried to the canvas door and called inside, "Hello?"

A muffled reply came from somewhere in the back. He lifted the canvas and squinted into the darkness to see the private standing with a lantern—right beside the infected body. Tommie felt an icy blast hit him.

The private waved to Tommie. "Corporal told me to come back here and work with you, make sure everybody gets properly chilled."

"You're not serious."

"That's what I would have said if I outranked him. Anyhow, I been checking over here to see how you're doing with it."

Tommie felt his heart speed up. "Uh, well, I've been working slowly. Got a spasm in my back. Makes it hard, lifting."

The private grinned. "Yeah, my back gets that way every time I lift something, too."

Tommie hurried over to him, as if to inspect his own work. His heartbeat was not slowing down.

The private gave him a leer that was half conspiratorial and half evil. "You ain't been in here having your way with the females, have you?"

Tommie gasped in shock at the thought before he could stop himself. He felt the blood drain from his face.

The private burst out laughing. "Relax, mister! I'm just playin' around. All right, so what do we got here?" The private muttered to himself for a moment while he looked over the body. Then he nodded and turned to Tommie. "I guess I can tell the corporal that you're slow, but thorough!" He laughed.

Tommie laughed.

A small squeaking sound came from the basin. The private's laugh drowned it out.

Tommie snatched the private by the arm to turn him toward the entrance, as if to usher him outside to talk. But it didn't keep them both from hearing the second set of squeaks.

The private briefly glanced at Tommie, as if he might be the one who made the noise, but just as quickly rejected that and turned to the body instead.

Tommie laughed in terror, realized it was inappropriate, stopped himself, and adopted his most polite and charming tone of voice: "Um, Private, can you come outside to the fire pit?"

The private ignored him. "You hear that just now?" He fetched the lantern and began to look all around the body basin.

He strengthened his grip on Private What's-His-Name. "I was having trouble getting the paper to catch flame, and maybe you could—"

Loud sounds of squeaking filled the silence of the morgue.

The private made a show of pulling his arm free while he stared at Tommie. He leaned in closer to the body, studying the shrouds. "Almost sounds like it's coming from in there... Jesus! Some critter's got trapped in there! Did you see it move, just then? Just a little?"

"No. Of course not! It's too cold. You know that as well as I do. But if you could come outside for just a minute—"

This time the squeaking went on for several seconds at double the volume. Both men clearly saw tiny movements beneath the shrouds.

"See?" hollered the triumphant private. He began quickly lifting ice blocks away from the basin.

"No, Private!" cried Tommie. "There's nothing—"

"There is! It's something, all right...What the...?" He saw the sliced cloth. "Some idiot done cut into this thing! Who in hell would do that?" He tossed a suspicious glance at Tommie.

The private leaned in closer to peer into the opening, just in time to see a tiny pair of rodent eyes reflecting the oil flame. It was the last thing he saw in this life before Tommie bashed in his skull with a solid stone brick.

The private dropped dead in a heap.

Tommie stood inside the pale yellow circle of lantern light, staring down at this new and interesting problem. Finally, he broke the spell that bound him by taking a sharp breath and telling himself *first things first*. He picked up his lunch bucket and set it ready with the top open, then reopened the deep cut into the thick shroud. With his gloves still protecting his hands, he quickly reached in and grabbed the rodent behind the head so that it couldn't bite, then pulled it out, dropped it back into the pail, and resealed the top.

With the rat safely captive, he again held the lantern close to the slice in the shrouds and peered inside. The satisfaction brought by the sight that greeted his eyes was almost as good as an orgasm. The body had been stripped of several ounces of flesh by the rat; teeth and claw marks were plain to see. Living death was now his.

But his heart was still beating fast. The private. The body. *This is a police morgue.* Police. Oh yes. What to do about the private's body?

The genius of desperation filled Tommie. He folded the slit in the cloth under itself so that it wasn't visible, then pulled the private's body back and lay it against the basin directly behind him. He placed the private's body face up, as if he had landed there after falling backward and hitting his head on the basin's edge. To complete the picture, Tommie placed a large block of ice on top of him, as if it were in the private's arms when he fell.

He swung the lantern back and forth over the scene a few times, making sure the improvised accident scene was convincing to the eye. It was dark in there now, but it wouldn't be later. This all had to look good in daylight.

Satisfied with that much, he carried the lantern back to the peg by the door and stepped outside. All clear for now. Nobody there, nobody approaching. So the last thing on his list was to do a bit of acting. Another role to play, and that was fine with him. He looked forward to it in earnest. The emotional flatness of the average adult male was so restrictive and frustrating for him that containing himself in public was like trying to hold back the need to vomit.

His hunger for an audience rose and began to pull at him while he took off toward the City Hall Station. He spent his time working on his expression of shock, ready to shout to any and all that the private lost his balance while showing Tommie how to handle the ice blocks, and that he had suffered a fatal fall. He tried to recall the soldier's name and got nothing, but assured himself that such a lapse would be accepted under the circumstances.

*It's the worst thing I've ever seen!* Tommie reminded himself to say. There was probably something else, but what? Then he got it—*Does the poor man have a wife and children?* Oh yes. People ask that. The rest was simply a matter of reciting his story so thoroughly that nobody could do anything else but believe it.

After the charade was through, he would consider what to do about Shane Nightingale, whose very existence had rudely converted Tommie's three-day triumph into nothing more than an incomplete aspiration. It galled him to have accidentally left a Nightingale to walk around free. Every moment this boy continued to exist was a wrenching affront.

Suddenly Tommie realized what that little thing was, tapping at the back of his brain like a relentless woodpecker. It was the memory of Mrs. Nightingale calling out, "Shane! Shane!" He ought to have realized old man Nightingale wasn't called "Shane." It was right there in front of him from the first moment of his assault on her, but he allowed the ecstasy of the experience to overwhelm him.

Because of course she wasn't calling to her husband; she knew he was not there.

She called out to the boy. If she did that because she knew Shane could somehow hear her, it meant Shane must have been inside the house. He might have somehow concealed himself, silent and unmoving, while he listened to Tommie slaughter them all. Listened while Tommie gave of himself so freely during that entire time, explaining his reasons for each and every stabbing jab, every swiping slice, every twist of the garrote. Young Shane Nightingale had gotten himself a formal education.

The boy was an intruder, an uninvited witness to Tommie's deepest secrets.

The smear on Tommie's work had to be removed. It was a galling mistake and it called out for correction. Most important, the correction had to be done in an artful fashion, in some manner that went far beyond the mere expedience of getting away with homicide. This situation, Tommie acknowledged, was one that required his most worthy effort.

A long, screaming poem of a murder.

# 12

LIEUTENANT MOSES WAS STANDING next to the duty sergeant's desk when he saw Blackburn walk into the station. It was only midafternoon.

"Sergeant Blackburn, I would expect you to be home asleep."

"Yes, sir. I just need to check—"

"You aren't going to skip work tonight, are you?"

"No. I'll be on the street by midnight."

"All right. But I don't like our men to walk around exhausted, so what do you need here?"

Blackburn lowered his voice. "Actually, what I need is a favor that only you can provide, Lieutenant."

Moses's heart skipped. He made a conscious effort to repress any show of excitement while he demurred, "I'm sure you give me too much credit."

"Not at all, sir." Blackburn dropped his voice to a near whisper. "I need access to personal property records. Specifically, anything at all that we have on the Nightingale family, of the Nightingale Dry Goods Emporium, and I need to do it now."

"The Nightingale family." Moses was interested. "That boy in the paper today?"

"Yes."

"Didn't the story say they were all killed?"

"It did."

"So the point is?"

"Sir, I just want to do something for this boy if I can, that's all. I want to know some things, such as, was he officially adopted? Did he take the family name legally? Things like that."

Moses was not the least inclined to help the boy who helped solve the Sullivan murder—a case that wasn't supposed to be solved at all. Pressure from the Widow Sullivan's high-and-mighty friends was raining down on him, and he knew it was just the sort of thing that could get him replaced.

But Moses also knew something Sergeant Blackburn did not, and that tipped the balance. "All right," he sighed as if the favor cost him money. "Go on back and get the Keeper to locate what you want. How long is this going to take?"

"Not long, I guess. Ten minutes?"

"Good. Then you'll go straight home and get some sleep, *yes*?"

"*Yes.*"

"Tone of voice, Sergeant—you're here to ask a favor."

"Yes, sir."

Moses had a new trick of pausing before rendering any decision whenever an underling was waiting for an answer. He used it now, allowing Blackburn to twist in the wind for a moment or two before waving him toward the relocated Record Keeping Department.

He had no fear of anything Blackburn might discover in a file Moses had already cleaned up for inspection. The only sensitive document was the one Moses had indirectly discovered while he was preparing to interview Mr. Tommie Kimbrough for his morgue work. It informed him that Tommie Kimbrough had a lien on file with the county against his house, and that the lien was held by the owner of the Nightingale Dry Goods Emporium. It seemed that Kimbrough had run up a huge accumulation of store credit over several years' time, but although Mr. Nightingale had won a court judgment against Kimbrough months earlier, he had only recently foreclosed on him. Perhaps up until then he hoped for payment.

That record, however, was no longer available to the public. The only copy was folded into the inside pocket of the ever-baggier uniform jacket belonging to Lt. Gregory Moses.

Moses stood and watched the sergeant disappear around the corner, then he turned and shambled back to his office, where he had been keeping Mr. Tommie Kimbrough himself cooling his heels for a good twenty minutes. Just to soften him up.

*Hallelujah!* thought Moses. He had a strong hunch that the foreclosure lien might be instrumental in his efforts to remain in place as Station Chief. It proved a serious vulnerability on the part of Tommie Kimbrough, who had strangely made a fat cash contribution to the SFPD at the same time that his house stood under foreclosure. The decades Moses spent in the Record Keeping Department had sensitized him to the negotiating potential that was often contained in one's financial oddities. He was ready to deal.

*Besides, this "gentleman" gives off a fishy aura*, Moses thought. *Just the sort of thing you might expect of a planted spy.*

————————

Blackburn headed straight back to his new apartment, less than a mile from the station. His eyes felt sandy and his whole body ached with the need for sleep, but he felt no regret at having taken the detour. The files clearly showed that Shane had been officially adopted by the Nightingale family, as required in order to move him into their home. He legitimately had the family name as his own, and though the Nightingale family will did not list Shane as an heir, Blackburn was sure the boy must have something coming to him. With a family business that big, it seemed certain there should be some sort of estate left over. He resolved not to say anything to Shane about any of it until he could find out whether there was something for the boy or not.

Blackburn had spent enough of his own boyhood being happily alone that he was not particularly troubled over Shane's isolation. He just hated the idea of the boy spending the foreseeable future doing nothing more than earning each day's meals. The fact that Shane was capable of such brutal clarity of thought certainly proved that he had some sort of extraordinary talent. The boy stood out in this city of displaced people, even though he appeared not to realize it.

If Blackburn kept the search to himself, then Shane would never miss what he never expected. On the other hand, if it turned out that there was anything there, then Blackburn would find some way to make sure this timid and fragile boy received what was due to him.

He was within a block of home. Relieved, he quickened his pace along the row of standing houses and made a beeline for his front door. There was just time for a few hours of rest before he was to spend his midnight shift dancing with the stumblebums down along the Barbary Coast.

---

Not far behind Blackburn, Vignette skipped along, darting from one concealment to another. In her master spy mode, she took pains to remain undetected even by the general public. To achieve that, she made sure to behave like a stupid little girl engrossed in playing some sort of game. It caused grown-ups to dismiss her and most kids to ignore her altogether. The others she could outrun.

That was the next best thing to being invisible. As long as she never got in anybody's way, she could sense that nobody noticed her. Later, they wouldn't remember she was there at all.

She slipped behind the thick pole of a gas streetlamp and peered out from behind it just in time to see Sergeant Blackburn pull a key from his pocket and stop in front of the sunken door to a garden apartment. She ducked out of sight while he let himself in. When she heard the door pulled shut, she stepped out and pretended to tie her shoe in order to sneak a good look at the big sergeant's apartment building.

So this was where he lived. Vignette decided that the best thing to do was to spook around the neighborhood for a while, get a feel for the area. And, she realized, to quickly locate any food that was looking to get stolen. She was starting to feel like she didn't weigh anything at all, as if a puff of breeze would blow her over.

First things first, then. She caught a whiff of something wonderful in the air. Not far away, somebody was doing some baking. Baked things were often set out to cool. Within moments, she was off on the trail of the luxurious aroma like a bloodhound on two legs.

"Sit down, sit down," Moses casually waved to Kimbrough. "No need for formalities with you, Mr. Kimbrough." Moses walked around his side of the desk and sat, making it a point to give Tommie a generous smile.

He noticed that Kimbrough's face glistened with tiny beads of sweat—the worried face of an obvious spy, Moses reckoned, a spy who was the tool of somebody up in the department brass. He would find out, but right now he was in no hurry. They were on his turf.

Kimbrough realized it was his turn to speak. "Of course I'm still upset over Private, uh—over the private's death. But I'll tell you anything I can."

"As long as it's the truth, you mean," Moses interrupted with a scowl.

"What?" Tommie almost gasped the word.

Moses broke out laughing. "I'm joking with you! Please! We are among friends here, aren't we?"

Kimbrough broke into a relieved smile. "Oh. Of course! We certainly are!"

Moses did a change-up on him and made a serious face. "It is most unfortunate, however."

"Oh, absolutely! That poor man! Did he, ah, have a wife and children?"

"I didn't mean him."

"...Ah." Tommie waited. When nothing happened, he added, "What did you mean?"

"The volunteer program at the morgue. There's just no way to continue it for the time being, even as badly as the help is needed there. It's just too dangerous." Moses leaned forward and made sure to remove any trace of joy from his voice.

"I am so grateful for your help. It's most impressive that a man of your means would voluntarily occupy his time amid the stench of rotting bodies. I'm sure the department can relocate you to a hospital or something where you can make the same sorts of drawings."

Tommie was unconcerned with the news, having already accomplished his goal. Now he simply needed to make sure his tracks were covered with regard to the dead private.

Moses paused and maintained his benign smile until Kimbrough realized it was his turn. "Well, Lieutenant, I'm sure that will be—"

"Because as I said, we are among friends."

"Um, yes."

"Good!" Moses pounded the desktop for emphasis. "We understand each other!" He stared at Kimbrough with a meaningless smile.

"So, ah, Lieutenant, should I give you my formal statement about Private, ah, Private..."

"The late private?"

"Yes."

"No."

"No?"

"Why would I trouble you? You wrote out a very nice statement for the duty sergeant. And after you were so kind as to spend time doing volunteer work in our city morgue, in spite of your own troubles."

"Troubles?"

"But nobody needs to know." Moses winked and gave a conspiratorial grin. He pulled the notice from his jacket and placed it on the desk. He opened it flat and turned it toward Kimbrough for easy reading, then watched his glance drop down onto the page. Kimbrough's eyes widened in surprise. All the color drained from his face.

"You see," Lieutenant Moses went on, "I pulled this from the files before anybody could see it. Since the quake, nobody has checked any private property details except where owners request it. And because your house was in an untouched zone, ordinarily nobody would have found this. In which case you wouldn't have needed my help at all."

He looked straight at Kimbrough again, who had now shrunken into his chair. Still, Moses was careful not to gloat while he pulled the linchpin.

"Sergeant Blackburn just happened to be rummaging through the Nightingale files today, and might have accidentally come across this dangerous document." He gave a reassuring smile. "*If* it had been there..."

And that was it, Moses assured himself. After today, no matter how high up the ladder this little lump of shit was connected, nobody could say Moses failed to show Mr. Tommie Kimbrough proper respect. Even while he gave him the bum's rush out the door.

"So you see, Mr. Kimbrough, we are among friends here. Certain troublemakers could misunderstand and become *very* concerned as to how you made a large cash donation here while you have a foreclosure notice on your house."

Kimbrough's mouth began to move like a drowning fish. Nothing came out.

"Rest assured," Moses soothed, "a friend like me sees no reason to point out this little fact to anybody."

"I told him I would pay him!" Tommie hissed. "I kept telling him!"

"I believe you! Greedy bastard tried to break your back, didn't he?"

"Exactly! That's exactly what he tried to do."

"And if he died in the earthquake along with who-knows-how-many other people, maybe that was just the Almighty Lord taking care of things for you."

"Yes!" Kimbrough practically shouted.

"Maybe the *real* settling of accounts is the way things finally shook out."

"It is! That's right! I knew it the moment the quake hit. It was so strong. It had to have been a *righteous* destruction!"

"Well, then!" Moses clapped his hands together and smiled yet again. "No cause for alarm, my friend." He snatched up the document and whipped it back inside his jacket. "I will keep it safe." Moses leaned in closer to Kimbrough and whispered, "Always."

"Perhaps," Kimbrough tentatively began, "I could...arrange to purchase that notice from you?"

"Purchase? Sir! You wound me. I would *never* try to rob a man who can't pay his mortgage."

"I *can* pay it. I could pay it anytime. It's just that—"

"No! You will never have to spend a penny to assure yourself that this document is safely hidden. As long as I am Station Chief, you have my word: there is nothing to fear." He patted his jacket pocket and added, "From this."

Moses's impression of Kimbrough at that moment was that the little man could not decide whether to sigh in relief or shit himself. The wheels inside Kimbrough's skull were turning so hard, the lieutenant could almost hear them creaking.

Kimbrough stood, offered Moses his confused thanks, and shuffled out. It was perfect. Moses didn't say anything Kimbrough could repeat without pulling himself down at the same time. He was willing to bet that whoever was using Kimbrough would never hear another bad report about Gregory Moses from that moment forward.

"Acting Station Chief." The term scalded him as if it was meant to imply that he was only *acting* like the station chief but wasn't fooling anybody.

Except Moses had just placed this Kimbrough fool under his thumb, a man who somehow possessed both cash and connections. And now Kimbrough clearly understood that his own well-being was a direct result of how well or how poorly things went for Lieutenant Gregory Moses.

*With friends like these*, Moses chuckled to himself, *you don't need real ones.*

⸻

Sunset over the Pacific was spectacular when viewed from the third story of Tommie's home. He caught a glimpse through the window while he opened the lid on his new glass-topped cage for the plague-infested rat, but he ignored the ocean scene. There was no time to regard the view. Nature's ability to paint a pretty picture was far less compelling to him than Her ability to place the power of life and death directly into his hands.

He felt so filled with anticipation that the strain made his fingers quiver, so he kept his moves slow and deliberate in opening the experimental box and getting ready for the transfer.

The box was about two feet long and two feet wide, six inches high, with a solid floor and a lift-up glass top. The inside was painted solid white. Tommie donned protective leather gloves, then opened the nearby lunch pail and retrieved the rat. It squirmed in his grip until, with the utmost care, he released it into the white box and quickly clamped down the glass top.

The box was otherwise empty, as it had to be, in order for Tommie to do a foolproof check for the presence of fleas. The tiny bugs made the phenomenon of scattershot infection too dangerous. But since the rat had ingested enough of the plague victim's flesh to guarantee its own infection, he needed no fleas on his rat. The white box would let him know. If the ice was enough to put the fleas into a dormant state, then the rat would be safe enough to handle as long as it was not allowed to bite.

Minutes passed. No fleas appeared anywhere on the white background inside the box. Not a speck. He gave it some more time, just as a precaution, but still nothing else showed up, confirming what he already suspected.

Tommie had a highly effective killing machine under his control.

He stepped back from the box and let the rat sniff around its sterile environment. "One more hour, I think. Although I'm certain you're clean," Tommie fairly cooed. "Then you can eat, and eat, and eat."

How nice it would be, Tommie thought, if the rat could break its fast on Lieutenant Moses. *But you can't have everything*, he reminded himself.

He decided to distract himself for the night, so he whirled on down to his locked changing room and spent a few hours carefully transforming himself into a lovely female. Then Tommie walked, hips rocking provocatively from side to side, all the way down to the Barbary Coast district. The pain of the garments and shoes served to make the experience all the more real. It helped to prepare him for the kill while he trolled the back alleys for robbers and rapists.

However, such killings were less satisfying to him now. True, they helped pass the time, but he knew from experience that they could never rise to the level of art. There was not enough to savor.

By eleven p.m., the fresh sourdough loaf Vignette managed to purloin earlier that evening sat heavy in her stomach. She wouldn't need to eat again before morning. As soon as she finished off the last of it, she crawled out from behind the bushes growing across from Blackburn's place, hopped to her feet, and brushed herself off. The street was quiet.

She moved off in a direction that took her by one of the sergeant's windows. When she passed by, she caught a glimpse of him through the opened curtains. He had on a clean uniform and was strapping on his weapon belt. She already knew he worked at night, so she felt no surprise to see him preparing to leave at this hour. To her, that just meant she had learned all she could about him, for now. After tonight, she would know where to find him if she had to.

With that, Vignette the master spy took off at a trot. Her mission for the day had been fairly easy, so far. However, the secret following, the spying, even stealing the food—none of that was the most difficult part. There was no way to avoid it any longer. It was time to face the real challenge: to find Shane and tell him about the secret—the gigantic secret—she ran away from St. Adrian's to reveal.

It was shortly after Shane was adopted out of St. Adrian's by the Nightingale family when Vignette, in disguise as Mary Kathleen, was poking around the headmaster's office. She spotted Shane's name on one of the files Friar John was careless about locking up. That was when she learned the truth about how and why Shane wound up there as a four-year-old, and why his existence was officially erased as soon as the Nightingales took him in.

But she had no intention of telling him that. No, her story was going to be far better for both of them.

It took her half an hour to cover the distance from Sergeant Blackburn's place to the Mission Dolores. There she hurried past the wrecked remains of the newer brick church and the solid front doors of the unharmed old Mission. She stopped at the cemetery gate. The strenuous walk had kept her tension at bay so far, but when she lifted the latch and opened the gate, the screech of its rusting hinges nearly knocked her backward.

She had now reached the moment to put all of her experience to the test. The goal today was to use her ability for something much more challenging than the little tricks she employed to make life better for herself around St. Adrian's. If only she could get Shane to believe what she intended to tell him, it would completely change her life for the better. His too, she dared to assume.

Inside the gate, she squinted through the midnight blackness to the back of the cemetery. There was a toolshed back there, with a glow of lantern light coming from inside. She quietly moved into the darkened graveyard and slipped through the shadows hovering between twisted tree branches and grave markers.

She drew close enough to the shed to hear a boy's voice. Moments later she recognized it as Shane's. He was speaking at a rapid clip, but she didn't hear any replies from whoever he was talking to. She tiptoed to the door of the shed and spotted Shane inside, pacing back and forth with a newspaper folded in one hand and a lantern in the other. Now she could see that he wasn't having a conversation, he was reading the paper out loud.

Dozens of tiny memories flooded through her, glimpses of Shane over the past several years, while they lived out their lives among a changing group of strangers. She would recognize Shane's quietly confident demeanor anywhere in the world. Now while she listened to him read with easy confidence, she could not help comparing his refined skill with words to her own struggles to read and write. Neither was her strong suit. She instantly admired him for it.

Somebody who could read like *that*, Vignette figured, could probably accomplish anything she needed to get done...

# 13

IMMEDIATELY FOLLOWING

"Shane?"

A girl's voice. Whispering. Shane dropped the paper and stumbled back until he hit the wall and nearly broke the lamp. He stared toward the door, but the lantern made everything outside dissolve in blackness. Then the voice came again, from close by.

"Sorry if I startled you. You all right?" The girl stepped forward and stopped just before the doorway. She was nearly his height. Skinny as a post.

He recognized her as one of the girls from St. Adrian's but couldn't think of her name. He also couldn't think of a good reason why any of the kids from that place would be here at the Mission, especially after midnight. She appeared to be by herself, but who could say whether anybody else lurked out there?

"Wh-who—who...ah-ah-are...y-yuh-you?" he asked.

She stared at him in surprise. "Are you all right?" She glanced down at the paper lying on the dirt floor. Shane reflexively stepped over to it and picked it up. But he didn't answer her.

"Since you asked, everybody calls me Vignette, and I'm a master spy."

She gave him a *ta-dah!* grin, as if that explained something.

Shane could manage no other reply but to stare at her.

"All right, that's not what they call me at St. Adrian's. You don't remember my name, do you? That's fine. Actually, it's good. They used to call me Mary Kathleen, so I would grow up to be a fat housewife. But now I'm Vignette—a vignette is a little story, you see?

"I ran away, Shane. Today. I'm gonna sneak back in tonight and steal my stuff, and then I'm gone from there for good."

"*So nobody else sent you?*" Shane tried to ask. "Suh-suh-suh-so nobuh-nobuh-nobody else seh-seh-sent you?" He felt his heartbeat beginning to slow down. Maybe it was all right. If others were out there, by now they surely would have already stormed inside.

He thought he saw a look of sadness flash across her face. "Shane, you didn't used to talk like that. I mean, you always got your words out just fine. And it's funny, but when you were reading just now, you didn't stutter at all. It sounded just like you. What happened?"

He gave her a look of frustration.

"Never mind, then. Too many words." She pointed at the paper. "So when you read out loud, you can talk without a problem. Is that right?"

Shane nodded, wondering why he was the one answering questions.

"Read me something."

Shane scowled at her.

"No really. I know you can. I heard you! Come on, just a line or two."

Shane had the definite feeling that he should insist that she get out before one of the priests spotted her and he got into trouble. But she was a familiar face from the first place he had lived since he could remember. She knew his name. He had never paid much attention to her, since she was a couple of years younger. But he remembered that whenever she passed by, there always seemed to be somebody yelling for her.

He picked up the article and began to read. "'Police have finally put an end to the practice of looting by chasing down a secret list of suspected perpetrators—'"

"That's it!" she shouted with glee. "That's how you sound! I recognize that voice!"

He had to smile at her reaction. So he nodded and mimicked her *ta-dah!*

grin. He struck a mock formal pose and repeated her new name. "Vign—" He stopped himself, took a deep breath, and started again. "Vignette," he said, mimicking a stage actor.

She laughed in delight and clapped her hands. He started to laugh with her but suddenly realized how dangerous it might be if they were overheard. He jumped up, startling her when he lurched past her and grabbed the door to the shed. He pulled the door closed, turned to her, and pointed outside.

"All right," she whispered. "We'll keep it quiet here."

He nodded and sat down on the dirt floor again.

His principal memory of Vignette as Mary Kathleen was that she seemed to flutter about the place like a butterfly that drank too much coffee. Once in a while, she would engage him in conversation or some little game. He would generally play along, but he never did anything to encourage her attention. Male and female fraternization was heavily discouraged by Friar John and his Helpers.

"Um, well," Vignette began, "I might as well just come out and tell you, right? I mean you must be wondering exactly why I'm here. I would be, if I were you. So here it is. I'm not—my name isn't really Mary Kathleen. I told you that, right? *They* named me that. I never told them to. They're not my parents. They can't name me. That's all. So I'm Vignette because I like the name and I picked it out myself."

She leaned toward him. "Vignette is a master spy. I mean it. She can do things. I can, I mean. And one of the things I used to do at St. Adrian's is get in trouble on purpose so I would be forced to clean Friar John's office as punishment. That's where you can really learn things, if you pay attention.

"See, he never tried to look at me in the shower, so I couldn't get him to give me money. Did they do that to you? Instead, sometimes I would read things he left lying out on his desk. I'm not such a good reader, but you know, I get the gist of it.

"They know a lot about some of us, Shane. About what happened to us, I mean. Things like why we were put there, or who our families were. Did you know that?"

Shane had never asked himself whether Friar John might know

anything else about him. Suddenly, he couldn't imagine why he never raised the question.

Vignette went on, "So I had what you might call a hobby, where I tried to find out where some of us came from. You know, what our stories were. And even though most of us are just found on doorways or something, sometimes the Helpers know things that they don't let on. Extremely interesting things."

Shane was starting to get impatient for her to get to the point. It must have shown on his face, because she sped up.

"Shane, you don't ever remember a time when I wasn't around St. Adrian's, do you? 'Cause I don't remember when you weren't there. I was small when they found me, maybe only two. And you were four, right?"

He nodded, wondering how she knew that.

"They didn't get us at the same time, but it was pretty close. A few days." Vignette steeled herself, then she leaped into her plan, unhesitating. *Just do it like you mean it,* she reminded herself. *The key is to talk too fast to let them think.*

"And so the file said that the notes that got left with us were done in the same handwriting. You hear me? They were done on the same sort of paper. And the friars think we came from the same people! But they never tell the kids things like that, because they don't want you to know if you have a brother or a sister. It's easier to adopt everyone out one at a time."

She looked at him with an expression of grim, cold truth. Then she made the *ta-dah!* smile again.

Shane's need to speak was so strong that he felt as if he would explode. He started once and got nothing out, then stopped, gritted his teeth in frustration, and tried again. No good.

Vignette watched in concern until he gave up and shook his head. At that point she chimed in, "Wait a minute!" She picked up Shane's notebook and handed it to him. "Here, take this. Write down what you want to say here." She giggled again with anticipation, then went on. "Okay, first write down, 'My name is Shane.'"

He had no desire for games at this hour, but he cooperated and wrote down, "My name is Shane," just to make her happy.

"Good!" she whispered. "Next, if somebody asks you where you live, you might say, 'I live in San Francisco,' right?"

He nodded.

"Good!" she cried out in excitement. "So write that down! You live in San Francisco!"

He cooperated, resigned to playing along. She was irritating, but at least his loneliness was gone. Just as he finished that sentence, she added the last one.

"Yes! Now just write this: 'I would never leave my sister all alone on the streets.'"

He looked up at her.

"Just write it down! I swear, I don't recall you being slow like this. 'I would never leave my sister all alone on the streets.'"

He couldn't keep from grinning while he shook his head, but he complied and wrote out the words.

"That's perfect!" she exclaimed, leaning around to look at his work. "Now, I'm going to ask you three questions, and all you have to do is read the answers right there off of your page, get it?"

Shane looked skeptical.

"No, really. Try it! Here we go: What is your name?" She tapped her fingertip on the paper. He looked down at it and read—

"Shane Nightingale." His voice was clear and strong, and the words came out with no effort at all. He stopped with a jolt and looked at her. When their eyes met, he laughed with astonishment before he could stop himself.

Vignette grinned from ear to ear and continued. "Okay, then, and where do you live?"

Shane looked at the next words on the page and read them out loud. "I live in San Francisco."

His voice had never been stronger. He laughed with delight. Vignette laughed along with him, then popped up to take an exaggerated bow.

"All right, *now*," she went on with a twinkle in her eyes. "Tell me what you have to say about your sister?" She pointed at the page.

While Shane read the words, he could feel the wry smile stretching his lips. "I would never leave my sister all alone on the streets."

Vignette grinned even bigger. "I didn't think you would." She stood up, took a deep breath, and brushed herself off. Shane was so dulled by amazement that she reached over and easily snatched the tablet out of his hand. She tossed it back onto the shelf and turned to him, glowing with mischievous delight.

"Now...your memory is good enough that you can still picture that page in your mind, can't you?"

Shane could still see the page with the three little statements written out, one by one. He nodded.

She giggled in anticipation and rubbed her hands together. "So I'm going to ask you three questions now. And all you're going to do is *read* what you can see there on the page in your memory. Don't try to *talk*, just *read*. So: Hi. My name is Vignette. What's your name?"

"...Shane Nightingale."

They both laughed to hear it work so well again.

"My, what a perfect voice you have, Mr. Nightingale. So tell me, where do you live?"

"I live in San Francisco!" he said triumphantly.

"And now, what do you have to say about your sister?"

Shane found it impossible to suppress the smile pulling at both sides of his face. "I would never leave my sister all alone on the streets."

In that moment, Shane decided that as strange as it was to meet his sister this way, it was no more odd than many other things in recent days. And yet what could such a thing even mean, to have a sister in a place like this? And what did it mean to be an older brother, knowing what he knew about himself?

At least he was convinced she didn't mean any harm. She was bossy, but so playful about it that it made him want to play along with her.

"I'm going to go back and get my stuff," she said while she teased the door open and peeked outside. She looked back at him and nodded, confirming that it was all clear out there. But before she could step out, Shane reached over to her and took her arm.

"Ah-ah-ah-are yuh-yuh-yuh-you—"

"Write it down!" she urged.

He scribbled his question and thrust the tablet at her.

"No, don't hand it to me—read it. Read it out loud!"

"Are you really my sister?" He read the words with ease.

She paused for a moment to look into his eyes, though she kept her thoughts away from him. *This is the test that always comes. You pass it by sticking to your story.* Light as a feather, she stepped up to him and kissed him on the cheek.

"They just didn't want us to know," she whispered. She turned and started out the door.

And then she was gone.

Shane sat quietly for a few moments, trying to digest what had just happened there inside his little toolshed. Someone from the orphanage finally came looking for him, but it was not as he had feared. Nobody wanted to drag him back or make trouble for him. The fact was, he had a real sister, a flesh-and-blood little sister, and she wanted to be with him. She wanted to be with him. What a thing.

*That's perfect*, he said to himself, in the voice that never stuttered. His life was broken into dozens of pieces. He lived in a toolshed in a cemetery. And now his younger sister manifested out of the midnight fog and just wanted to "leave her stuff" with him.

What would happen when she returned? The padres wouldn't let them live there together. Would she go off somewhere else to sleep every day and then drop by here for tea and cookies? How much could she be seen around the place before the padres began to ask questions? How much longer after that until they became concerned? And once the priests were concerned, what reason would they have to tolerate his presence any longer?

Was she there to doom them both?

But the main thing, no matter how he might try to twist and turn it, was the promise she had him make.

*I would never leave my sister all alone on the streets.*

Yes, the idea came from her. But the moment he felt his mouth make the words, he knew he was speaking the truth. He could never turn his back on her. Not now. The timing was perfect, because if she discovered they were brother and sister earlier, then the two of them might have been adopted into the Nightingale home together.

Which meant he would have had to listen to her die. Because of him.

His skull was home to tornadoes. Finding out he had a family member alive was the one bit of news he had never prepared himself to hear. The weight of it was crushing.

The inevitable question that naturally followed hit him with a thud: How would he protect her from the secret load he carried after his failure in the Nightingale house? He would have to make up a complete story to cover the family's deaths. Then for the rest of their lives he would have to remember to never slip, never drop the lie. He could not allow her to hear a word about the source of the knowledge he possessed regarding things a human creature will sometimes do—things it is best not to know too much about. What he could not guess was how much Vignette knew about such things herself.

Tommie Kimbrough lay on an expensive area rug purchased on credit from the Nightingale Dry Goods Emporium, fondly gazing at his experiment. After nearly twenty-four hours, not a single dark speck showed on the pristine white interior of the glass-topped box. And since the rat feasted on the body at the morgue, it had to be filled with plague now. Tommie rolled slightly to get a better look at the sophisticated medical book purchased by mail from Great Britain for twenty pounds, sterling. He found the listing for "Black Plague" and skipped down to the part that concerned him.

*...the most powerful form of the plague bacillus manifests as Septicemic Plague. In this form, it is generally transmitted to humans from the bite of infected rats. The effects develop lethality faster than any other plague form: death in a single day, from onset of symptoms. The body turns purple, then black in the death process, resulting from widely disseminated intravascular coagulation. This particularly virulent disease is 100 percent fatal.*

Reverberations went through him in powerful waves.

*One hundred percent fatal.*

*One hundred percent fatal.*

*One hundred percent fatal.*

"And they die in a day!" he spoke in the same tone of voice a new mother might use in telling of her child's first steps.

Dreams do come true. "Septicemic plague." He rolled the words around in his mouth. A term worthy of poetry.

Inside the stark white box, Tommie's furry black guest still appeared healthy and not in overt distress. The rodent paced a little this way and that, half-hearted, smart enough to know it was going nowhere. No doubt beginning to suffer pangs of rodent hunger, that instinctive need to bite, chew, and swallow.

And now that Tommie had confirmed the rat carried no dangerous fleas, the tiny animal was suddenly so much more than an unusual personal pet. It was Death on four little legs.

*And best of all,* Tommie mused, *this little creature works for me like the Grim Reaper works for God.*

# 14

---

## A NEW MURDER SCENE

RANDALL BLACKBURN STOOD at the entrance to the narrow service alley behind the Dash Theater on Pacific Street, one of the fortunate Barbary Coast brothels that came through the disaster without any serious problems. He had just been pulled to that spot by the "theater manager" and now stood staring down at the body of what appeared to be The Surgeon's latest victim. What was the total now? Fourteen? He was losing count.

There was no need for close examination to determine the big man was dead; the body lay in a large pool of blood.

He leaned in closer. And there, the familiar wound at the back of the neck. The body was massive. This victim was young, twenty to twenty-five. Most likely one of the dockside stevedores.

He noted with some relief that the victim's pants were still fastened and there was no sign of castration. *Maybe passers-by forced her to quit work early and disappear?*

No matter what else, he was certain that if this killing was indeed done by The Surgeon, she would place a note on the body, leaving her individual stamp on the crime. Intuition told him she was beginning to value the credit as much as the crime itself.

He paused, then set his jaw hard while he performed a nasty task. There was nothing else to do but go through the dead man's pockets. He steeled himself to jostle the corpse and find the note. The "reward" would be to read The Surgeon's next taunting diatribe.

At moments like this one, he felt a passing wave of embarrassment. His mother would have a heart attack if she could see how he spent his time. His father would be astounded that their quiet and tentative boy had grown up to fight with monstrous people on a daily basis, and that some of them compared badly to wild animals. Blackburn was glad his parents preferred to avoid the city and instead let him come up north to visit.

He exhaled more heavily than he intended, then stepped over to the sprawled form to look into the shadows and see...

The note.

This time rolled into a tiny tube and tucked between the man's lips, like an unlit cigarillo. Blackburn plucked up the tube and unrolled it.

*Search for me in every hour*
*But know you'll not find me*
*Until I greet you at a time and place*
*Of my own choosing.*

The tone of the poem implied the investigator's sense of tension in the chase and mocked him for it at the same time. Blackburn realized the writer was trying to push the timing of the investigation, amp up the immediacy. It seemed counterintuitive. For some reason or other, she was straining to get on with it all. The feel of it reminded him of a locomotive running balls-out while begging for the braking effect of an uphill stretch.

The verbal message, such as it was, would likely prove useless to the investigation, but the rising desperation it expressed was a hopeful conclusion for Blackburn. He rerolled the note and tucked it into his vest pocket for safekeeping until he turned it in. Then stood up. There was nothing else to do here but call for a coroner's wagon and begin all the routine procedures. He shook his head in disgust.

This newest murder underscored the same feeling that seemed to be holding most of the city in its grip; everything was out of control and might never get better. Since the day of the disaster, life on the rougher side of San Francisco's streets had gone completely downhill. Nearly every time Blackburn had to arrest someone, their story of despair poured out of them. The survivors' shock and pain were universal. For a surprising number of them it was pervasive enough to feel their faith shaken to the core. Some responded to the trauma of what the papers were now calling the "Great Earthquake and Fires" by giving up all pretense of morality and falling into extreme hedonism.

With the worst being this living mockery of a "surgeon."

He hated to think of Shane Nightingale wandering around these streets alone with no one to assure his safety. For an instant, he wondered what would happen if the boy ever ran into a monster like this one. He started to push the thought out of his head until an idea struck him; there was another possibility.

If the same unusual display of deductive talent shown by the boy in the Sullivan murder could be repeated with this case, then this Shane Nightingale fellow might be Blackburn's best opportunity to unlock the mystery of The Surgeon.

---

Vignette figured most of the people who were up and around outdoors after midnight were unlikely to be the type to rush to her aid if something bad happened, so she moved at a constant dog trot all the way back to St. Adrian's. She was less than half a block from the front entrance and already looking around for an open window when she heard the big wooden door at the main entrance open. Lantern light painted a pale carpet on the ground.

She shaded herself from the moon against a large tree trunk and melded her body to its form. An instant later, she recognized the man carrying the lantern. Her muscles tensed. Friar John. He stepped outdoors accompanied by some ragged-looking boy. A street urchin by the look of him.

Her heart jumped. They were going to walk directly past her. There was no time to run off without being spotted, and once she emerged from the shadows into the moonlight, Friar John was sure to recognize her. She pushed herself tighter against the tree and willed herself to fade into the bark, to dissolve into the night's background. She took a deep breath and held it while they passed.

"All right, we're on our way," she heard Friar John saying to the boy. "Now you can tell me why Mr. Kimbrough has this 'emergency' at this hour."

"No, sir, I can't."

"He always comes *here* to see me. He must have told you something about why he wasn't coming this time?"

"Nope," the boy assured him, perhaps eager for a tip. "Don't know nothing, and that's the truth. Mr. Kimbrough said something about a newspaper. Don't know what he meant by it."

Vignette could just make out the words. At first, the name "Kimbrough" didn't mean anything, but when the boy mentioned a newspaper, the connection clicked into place. She had struggled through reading the article on Shane herself after she heard a couple of the Helpers talking about it. They were too busy swapping reminiscences of Shane at St. Adrian's to notice when she swiped the newspaper and sounded out enough of the wording to get the general idea and then replaced the paper before it was missed.

This Mr. Kimbrough was a slight man with a wiry build. Over the years she had spotted him paying visits to Friar John on numerous occasions. They always made such a point of meeting in private—in secret, it looked like to her—which guaranteed that one day she made sure to push her mop close to Friar John's door and watch them through the keyhole. She learned only enough to know that Mr. Kimbrough was there about Shane, but that made her curious enough to peek into Shane's file the next time Friar John was out.

She sounded out a few of the words until she got the main idea. Mr. Tommie Kimbrough was Shane's older half brother. Shane was a bastard son of Kimbrough's father and some other woman. Listed right there as a bastard. She understood the term.

They just weren't letting Shane know anything about it.

He had never even heard his own last name. When he arrived as a small boy, the record said he was badly beaten and disoriented. Later on, once it looked like he would actually survive, he had to relearn the most basic skills.

This Mr. Kimbrough made sure Shane remained at St. Adrian's with no knowledge of his family and no contact with his "half brother." Something about that cruel fact twisted blades of heat and sourness within her.

*He doesn't even know he's got a brother!* At the time, she stored the fact for future use, but then Shane was suddenly adopted out, disappearing in a single day and whisked away before she could tell him anything at all.

So Mr. Kimbrough had sent that messenger boy to Friar John to tell him to come at this hour. It occurred to Vignette that if Friar John wasn't bringing any Helpers along with him, he must be going in secret. *Why would he do that?*

This had something to do with Shane.

For reasons she didn't bother to consider, that was all it took. She resolved to follow Friar John wherever he was going.

First she needed to get inside, grab her stuff, do it quickly enough to get back out, and then catch up before she lost him. She spotted a well-located ground-floor window in the office section. It appeared to be closed, but she knew they were seldom locked. It had never occurred to anyone in that miserable place to protect themselves from kids trying to get in.

Once she was out in the main hallway, which was darkened for the night, she started toward her end of the girl's dorm. But her leather shoes, so perfect for running along the streets, were too noisy now. She slipped them off and carried them while she tiptoed down the long row of sleeping girls to her bed.

She had left the cigar box with her special mementos right out on the nightstand by her bed. The contents were perfectly safe in the open like that and had been ever since the word spread around about the two black eyes she put on a girl who tried to steal a bracelet from her. Vignette's Helper had searched around for it and found it in the girl's things, so the girl also got in trouble with the headmaster.

After that, she could have left her stuff in the middle of the hall and nobody would have touched it.

Not that she got away clean or anything. In return, she had to bathe after dinner every night for a week, using the bath area during the empty hours when no one else wanted to. She told herself at least she didn't have to rush. Her Helper didn't like it when she rushed.

She silently picked up the small cigar box holding her special mementos and set it on the bed. She removed her other pair of long pants from the hook on the wall and slipped them on over her own, then took down her only coat and put it on over everything. She had one dress but left it hanging on its peg. Instead, she picked up her shoes and the box, slipped back down the row of beds, and hurried into the main hallway. Her plan was as simple as a frontal attack: go out the main door at a full sprint and disappear into the night.

And since she would never be back, there would be no punishment this time. No forced bathing this time.

She sneak-rushed to the heavy front door without getting spotted, bent to slip her shoes back on and slop-tied the laces, but when she stood up to reach for the door latch, a huge hand closed around the back of her neck.

She smelled his familiar body odor. It identified him so bluntly, she made no attempt to turn and look at his face. His grip was firm, but the survivor in her already noticed it was not as hard as when she was in real trouble.

"You're supposed to tell me when you want to go out. So I can help cover for you." As always, the voice was deep and frighteningly gentle.

"I know! I know. I always do. It's just, tonight I had this emergency, and—"

"Oh, emergency!" He laughed and said in a little girl voice: "She had an emergency, that's all!" Her Helper shook his head. "No, Mary Kathleen. You went and put me in a tough spot this time. I'd lose my job for failing to report this to the Friars. Think of how much risk that is. For me."

His breath always smelled of sour tobacco and stale coffee. Her stomach lurched when he breathed on her.

"Well, I was hoping you could do me this one favor, what with the emergency and all—but I guess I ought to get clean first. Take me a hot bath. You know, do it now when none of the other kids are in there. So I can take all the time I need to get clean. Then the favor. Cover for me."

He turned her around to face him and then smiled in appreciation of her negotiating skills. "Hm...maybe this one time," he cooed as he released her. "You get along to that bath now. Cleanliness is important."

"Okay. I'll go put my stuff away and take off my clothes. Then it's off to the bath!"

Her Helper grinned in anticipation, and even as he did so she saw his eyes glaze over and a slack expression cross his face. He turned and headed off toward his office next door to the bathroom, the one with the little hole in the wall behind a flap. He was so eager to get his private performance that he didn't mind going ahead and waiting for her to enter. She pretended to head for her bunk area until she saw him turn and step into his office. Then after a count of three, she spun around and ran back to the front door, yanked it open, and flung herself through.

At that moment, Mary Kathleen disappeared at the doorway of St. Adrian's Home for Delinquents and Orphans, never to be seen again.

Vignette hit the front walkway at a dead run.

---

She only had to keep running for a few minutes before she caught sight of Friar John's lantern bobbing along up the street ahead. Relieved, she fell in half a block behind and patiently followed until they reached the Russian Hill district. She figured they had come about two miles by the time they reached a fancy three-story house inside one of the areas untouched by the fires. She could see where the flames had split in two and passed around this particular hilltop.

She huddled in the cold shadows and watched while Friar John knocked at the door of one of the fanciest houses at the top. When it swung open, the inner light revealed Mr. Kimbrough. He gestured for Friar John and the boy to come in, then he threw a cautious glance around the neighborhood. As soon as the door closed again, the entire front of the house went dark. She had clearly seen the lights inside while the door was open, so Mr. Kimbrough must have had heavy curtains that completely concealed any light at all from the windows. Vignette wondered why anybody would do that. A cold shiver ran up her back.

But at least she had accomplished her tasks for the day. She had already found out where Sergeant Blackburn lived, and now she knew where Shane's secret brother lived, too.

With that, she tucked her cigar box a little tighter under her arm and headed off for the Mission Dolores to strengthen her position as Shane's long-lost sister. She hoped he would be awake when she arrived and that he might have an idea of where they could get something to eat without paying for it. She had already burned through the sourdough loaf, but there had been no chance to check Friar John's office for spare change. Vignette already knew full well that when your pockets are empty, life runs you around on a short leash.

Tommie waved the friar and the messenger boy into his study. The boy looked nervously around, clearly not happy about being there, but he needed to hang around for his payment. Tommie was confident the boy's hope for his coins would keep him silent for a few minutes. That was all the time he needed.

"Sit down, Friar," he invited, ignoring the boy.

Friar John perched on the edge of the sofa and impatiently looked back up at him. "Well?"

Tommie couldn't resist an expression of mock innocence. "What?"

"*What?* Never in my life have I been summoned in the middle of the night by any but the sick and dying. I have—"

"Horseshit." Tommie kept his face blank. "The only time you get up in the middle of the night is when you want to visit one of your kiddies."

Friar John gasped in shock and jumped to his feet. "What in God's name do you—"

"*Joking!* Friar, I'm joking!"

"I see no humor at all in—"

"Perfect! Because I see no humor in this." He slammed down the newspaper article about Shane onto the table. Friar John leaned over, read briefly, and grew pale.

"You friars don't see a lot of newspapers, do you?"

"I saw it, as a matter of fact. What could I do?"

"Nothing, *now!*" Tommie bellowed. "You were *never* supposed to adopt him out. Never! What the hell have I been paying you for all these years?"

"Your payments don't keep our doors open, Mr. Kimbrough! And you are actually quite casual about making them. Meanwhile our expenses are unimaginable! The Nightingales offered a very generous fee for Shane. I have to think of the other children."

"Not before you think about *me*, you don't! I had *dealings* with that family, you understand? I never knew anything about Shane being adopted out! And to *them*? To the Nightingales? Are you crazy?"

"You haven't been to see us for over a year."

"So what? The checks keep coming, don't they?"

"You are very irregular about—"

"Everybody gets paid eventually! Everybody! What, you're a friar with no patience?" He leaned in closer and dropped his voice. "I realize it now; Mr. Nightingale started pushing me to take things on credit right after you adopted Shane out to him. Lots of things. Expensive things. It was almost as if he knew my weakness. Almost as if someone told him how to ensnare me, create a big debt, win a suit, take my home. Take my home from me. You sold that boy to Nightingale and then told Nightingale how to use my weakness against me to *steal my home!*"

Friar John's face turned pale. "I would never do something like that."

"You would do that and more, Friar."

Tommie took a deep breath, made a pleasant face, and gestured toward the messenger boy. "You don't need to see what I'm about to do to him," he practically sang.

And with that, he snatched up a cast-iron statuette and struck the boy so hard that the top of his head caved in under the force of the blow. Bits of brain and blood flared across the wall behind the boy while his limp body fell to one side.

"God Almighty!" Friar John shouted, staggering backward in shock. But he failed to move far enough away to save himself. Tommie took two quick steps closer to him and then swung again. This time he used less force, so Friar John only fell unconscious, to be saved for later. The spider's fly.

Shane stood looking at the cigar box Vignette held out to him. "That's it? This is all you have?" he quietly asked, though the actual words took him longer.

"Well," she began, then shrugged. Before Shane could react, she unbuttoned her pants and removed them, revealing another pair underneath. She held out the spare pair along with the box.

Shane exhaled with a smile and took the pants and the box. He stepped to the wall and put the box up on the top shelf, then hung her pants from one of the tool pegs.

She smiled back. "See? You can keep my stuff here. There's no way anybody can tell it belongs to me," she said. "And those pants would probably fit you. You can wear them, if you want. Give them back, though."

Shane tried to reply, "That's all right. People donate clothes here. They let me pick from it sometimes. I can probably get you another shirt." But he stalled on the third word and bogged down.

"Wait!" Vignette clapped her hands in glee. "This is when you do it! This is when you write it down first, then read it back to me."

Shane grabbed his writing pad and pencil and quickly scrawled the words, then held up the pad with a self-conscious grin and read aloud:

"'That's all right. People donate clothes here. They let me pick from it sometimes. I can probably get you another shirt.'" Not one stumble. He grinned and shook his head.

Vignette nodded. "Then I can always keep one set of clothes clean. See? It's good for me to have a brother already." She thought for a second and quickly added, "And don't you worry, having a sister out here will be good for you, too."

He grinned and sat on the dirt floor, made a motion of writing in the air with his finger.

"How?" he asked. The word came out strong and clear.

"I saw that!" she cried. "I saw you do that! You wrote in the air so you could see it inside your mind, and then you read what you could see. Right?"

He replied with a conspiratorial smile.

"That could work all the time, you know. I mean, if you could learn to make that a habit." Her face lit up. "Hey, see that? We worked that one out together, didn't we? So there you have it. Your first big blessing from having a sister! Isn't that right?"

He seemed to concentrate on the air for a moment and finally answered, "Right. But you still can't—can't—stay here. They'll cah-catch us."

Her face fell. "I know. You don't have to tell me that."

He concentrated again. "Do you know our last name?"

"...Um, no. I thought we could just use yours."

He turned to her in surprise, thought for a moment, then realized he liked the feel of the idea. He nodded. "But wh-wh-where will you live?"

This time her voice was much smaller, nearly a whisper. "I know they would never let a boy and girl stay together here. Usually, anyway. But what about family? They wouldn't think anything was wrong with that, would they? Why would they? Even holy men come from families with girls, don't they?"

Shane laughed and nodded.

"We could just go straight to them and say we're long-lost family who just found each other after the Great Earthquake. I can work, you know! I can work like the dickens. All I ever did at that stupid place was work."

"Yeah, I know."

"Besides," she softly went on, "Catholics really like big families, don't they? We're just family, that's all."

She studied Shane's face while he looked back at her with a resigned smile. Finally, he got to his feet, brushed himself off, and picked up one of the two sleeping blankets that were folded on the shelf. He tossed the other to her.

"Tomorrow," he managed to say. "We can tell them. Tonight, if...if...if they come, I'll be..." He gestured outdoors.

Vignette guessed the meaning. "You'll sleep out there in case anyone finds us before they know you're my brother because I'm your sister and all?"

Shane nodded, then his face darkened with a strange sort of sadness. He rested one hand on her shoulder, but no words came out.

She whispered, "You would take care of me, though, right? They'll see that it's only right for you to do that, won't they?"

He concentrated for a moment, then looked Vignette straight in the face. "They will. Or we'll both leave." He was clear on every syllable.

Shane silently held her gaze. Finally he grinned and pretended to punch her in the arm, then went out to sleep in the open cemetery, leaving her the lantern and his other blanket.

Vignette stood near the doorway and looked out into the darkness. It was as if everything she ever learned had prepared her for this day. She wrapped herself up in the blanket like a giant woolen hug and lay down on the cool dirt floor. In her circumstances it was as good as a beautiful feather bed. She fell into the untroubled sleep of victory.

Out in the graveyard, Shane made his way back to the grave next to the Mission wall. A sister. He had a sister. He was a brother. The strangeness of his life continued to amaze him. Somehow, he was being given some sort of a second chance at having a family. Life seemed to be asking if he had learned anything at all from his failure and humiliation.

Gratitude and exaltation overwhelmed him. He was ready to dare anyone in the world to ever try to scare him so badly that he would fail to help his sister. Never. Not this time. Never again.

It was the first night since the Nightingale horrors that he allowed himself to fall asleep before it was light outside.

# 15

---

HIGH ATOP FABULOUS RUSSIAN HILL

FRIAR JOHN TRIED TO REMAIN UNCONSCIOUS, but pain pulled him back up to consciousness like a half-drowned body returning to the surface. He opened his eyes and realized he was lying stretched out on his back with his hands securely bound and pinned behind him. He was looking up toward the ceiling: expensive stamped copper sheets.

Where was he?

Then all of his senses became alert and the fullness of his pain hit him with such terrible force that Friar John shrieked in shock. He screamed from his bowels to the top of his skull, and only then did he become aware that his mouth was jammed full of cloth and that the gag was tied down. His screams were stifled there. Only a few small bleats made it through his nose.

He finally raised his head an inch. It was just enough to get a look around, but the pain waves were rolling through him with such ferocious power that he forgot what he was looking for. Panic swept him. Only the feel of the rope around his neck kept him still. He tilted his head just enough to look down at himself and saw that he was rolled up in several layers of heavy fabric, roped shut. It was tied off tightly at his neck, leaving his head sticking out and the rest of him covered. His feet were tied together inside the wrapping, which was pinched tight below the soles of his shoes and tied off. That rope stretched across the floor to a large eyebolt purpose-sunk into the wooden floor. A few bits of sawdust still lined the hole.

Now the pain rolled through him in waves timed to every heartbeat. With his mouth sealed, most of his energy had to go into breathing through his swollen nostrils. He already knew the rope holding his neck was tied off somewhere behind him, probably to another eyebolt like the one beneath his feet. But the pain took all else away, making him forget everything except trying to wriggle and squirm out from under it, kicking at it, flailing his whole body around inside the heavy fabric cocoon.

Then he remembered. Tommie Kimbrough! Friar John had rolled the dice and hoped to collect the Nightingales' outrageously high fee without letting Kimbrough know about Shane's adoption. Using Kimbrough's reckless financial habits against him was supposed to be Friar John's own private joke, one for him to enjoy for years to come, a revenge upon Tommie for all his harassing visits, his late payments, and his surly, abusive attitude.

There was no reason for the plan not to work perfectly—all those years, and Kimbrough had never once asked to see Shane. He always just took Friar John's word about where Shane was and what Shane was doing and how his health happened to be. Friar John's only solemn duty was to immediately summon Kimbrough if Shane ever gave any indication that he remembered anything of his life before St. Adrian's. But Shane never had, not a word. Friar John was certain he never would.

He could have told Kimbrough that Shane got sick and died. Maybe he should have. But who could predict a thing like that news article? What were the odds, in a city whose population was only estimated and where feral children of all ages roamed? Everything should have worked perfectly well.

Then his recent memory cleared. He recalled seeing Kimbrough attack the boy, striking him over the head. *The blow must have killed the boy on the spot!* The memory came back of Kimbrough turning on him. That explained the pain in his head, then. But what about this other pain in his leg? It was more severe, more immediate.

The pain flared again. Teeth—biting—biting—biting. He tried to pull away, but the teeth only gnawed harder.

Friar John screamed into his gag. He screamed over and over, in pain and sheer horror at the realization that something was trapped inside the wrapping with him.

It was eating him alive.

He felt the four little paws scramble over his midsection and knew then that this thing chewing on him was a full-sized rat. The harder he tried to squirm away from the teeth, the more frightened and aggressive the rodent became. Teeth that could eat through cabin walls gave the trapped animal the power to vent its frustration on Friar John's mortal coil.

Friar John was only aware of the terror and revulsion; there was nothing to let him know that the blinding speed of bacterial replication had already gotten under way in his bloodstream before he had even regained consciousness. His wounds were soaked with the black rat's saliva, laced with a potent strain of the Black Death.

He tried to throw his upper body into a seated position, but his struggles yanked the rope more tightly around his neck. He felt it grab hard and tight. It snapped him back down to the floor with such force that he cracked the back of his head. After that, the rope never eased its grip, not even once he stopped moving. It became a garrote. Now his swollen nostrils had to pull air through his collapsed windpipe, while the cloth wadding packed his tongue down tighter than the dirt around a casket.

He struggled to breathe, pulling in thin wisps of air and shuddering with broken sobs on every exhale. His eyes were still focused up at the copper ceiling when Tommie Kimbrough stepped into view, glaring down at him.

Tommie pulled a chair next to Friar John's prostrated form and sat comfortably, fitting a factory-rolled cigarette into an ivory cigarette holder. He settled back and lit it with a long opera match. After he puffed out a smoke ring, he paused to let the ring grow wide, then blew a thin stream of smoke straight through it without disturbing the smoke ring itself.

Only then did he turn back, but by then Friar John was losing himself into the pain again and forgetting why Kimbrough was even there. When the rat took a violently aggressive bite and Friar John felt a chunk of his flesh torn away, his useless screams buried themselves in his wadded gag while his entire body convulsed.

Tommie stood back and patiently waited for Friar John to quiet down. He bent over and preened in front of a mirror for a while, but it became obvious that the headmaster was going to be useless for conversation as long as the screaming continued. Tommie glanced at the grandfather clock. Almost six. Barely daylight, but Friar John had already been out cold and feeding the rat for over three hours.

That was plenty of time for this phase of the experiment.

So Tommie reached down and pulled the slipknot from around Kimbrough's neck and peeled back the thin fabric torn from one of his old drapes. He rolled the layers down past the friar's groin area to reveal his special friend, wrapped in a little harness made of rawhide strips and tied to Kimbrough's leg by a few feet of cording—with nowhere to go and nothing to do but eat.

Tommie was amused by the way Friar John watched him with blazing intensity while he snatched up the rat and dropped it into a nearby glass-topped box. He had shown Friar John where his pain came from, but it was all right to reveal that much. It didn't tell the real story.

There was nothing to be done about the real story, anyway. Instead he poured the rest of his bourbon into the wound and ignored the fresh screams while he stuffed it with a wad of rags and bound it up just tight enough to keep up a firm pressure. There would be no bleeding to death here.

With that thought, Tommie realized he was quite possibly missing an opportunity. Why worry about keeping Friar John's plight a secret from him now? Why not tell him? Let him burn up his last few hours on Earth in the maximum state of terror. Who in all the world deserved it more? Because of Friar John's betrayal, it was Shane who flawed Tommie's finest hour of justifiable revenge. Friar John had sold Tommie out for money. He was Judas, with his thirty pieces of silver.

Tommie focused on Friar John's terror-bugged eyes while he pulled the heavy fabric back into place and tied it snug at the neckline. When he was all done, he spoke to the friar but did not deign to look at him.

"The most important thing about this experience for each of us, Friar John, is that we *savor* it." He thought for a moment, then laughed. "On second thought, it's important that *I* savor it. You? You can choose for yourself."

He gestured over to the box. "You think the bites hurt? They're nothing, Friar John. The bites are nothing! It's what they *do* that matters. So let me spare you the suspense—you'll be dead by this time tomorrow."

Friar John made a little whimpering sound and tried to shrink from him.

"What's that?" Tommie asked. "Oh, no, you misunderstand. *I'm* not going to be the one who kills you!" He pulled his chair a bit closer. "I'm merely hosting your experience.

"Let's start with symptoms. Ordinarily, you would already be feeling a nagging little tingle of sickness worming its way into you. You know the feeling, yes? Something is gnawing at you, but you still think you can just tough it out, right? Your mouth should be getting dry by now, but you probably can't tell with all that cloth stuffing. And your eyeballs, you know that feverish feeling when your eyes feel like they're too big for the sockets? The way it hurts just to turn your gaze one way or another? Ooh! Tell me when you get that. Or better yet, don't tell me and I'll try to guess."

Friar John slumped in despair and tried to turn his head away from Tommie. Tommie picked up a rag and used it to protect his hand while he reached down and grabbed Friar John's face and turned it back to him. The uncontrollable noises from his victim sounded like a cross between sobbing and strangulation.

"No, you probably haven't noticed your eyes yet, because your head still throbs from the thumping I had to give you, just to get you all calmed down and ready to receive." He smiled in satisfaction.

"But that's all right. Receive you did, and what you received is now growing inside you." Tommie broke into the silly voice he used for cute toddlers. "You are a garden, Friar John. Did you know that?"

He dropped the voice and continued. "But here's the thing—you'll *really* know the Devil is coming for you when the pain starts in your gut. Sharp pain, far worse than rat bites, according to my research. A few hours after that, your blood pressure will drop so low that you'll start feeling dizzy. Too dizzy to stand. Even lying flat, you'll still keep getting dizzier and dizzier. Finally, the whole world will turn into a carousel whirling so fast you can't hang on. You'll have to let go.

"And right up until that last instant, the pain in your gut will be like a stoked fire. Problem is, after you're so dizzy that you just can't help but puke yourself right on out of your body, I am afraid you will be going straight to Hell. Frightfully sorry. You know what for, though, yes? Oh, don't look at me that way. Of course you do."

He leaned in close to whisper to Friar John with sensual intimacy. "So since we only have a day or so, I propose we share in this whole experience. And if you agree, actually whether you do or not, why then I promise you that every step of the way—" He barked an involuntary laugh. "It will be just as new to me as it is to you!"

He picked up his knife and began to sharpen it on a pocket-sized whetting stone, then slowly brought the blade and stone to a point just under Friar John's nose.

"Now," Tommie began, "you little trouser-cough of a man, let's see if we can find a reason for me not to slowly carve away your entire face, like pulling a fat tick off a dog."

Friar John launched into another fierce set of convulsions. Tommie watched without comment for a few moments before he continued. "You would prefer that I not, then. Here's how you can guarantee that: for the sin of double-crossing me and adopting Shane out—*despite* having accepted my money for years to safeguard him—you will tell me where I can find him today."

He brought the knife edge to within a millimeter of Friar John's right eyeball and tested the edge with his thumb. "This thing could peel the skin off a gnat."

He reached behind Friar John's head and pulled the release knot. The gag fell out of his mouth. For a few moments, the headmaster could only gasp and wheeze. Tommie gave him a glass of whiskey and allowed him to drain it. *Why not?* Tommie thought. The condemned man and his last drink. "You can tell me now, or I can reintroduce our rodent friend."

"Mr. Kimbrough!" the headmaster gasped. "In the name of God!"

"I did not ask you about God, Friar John. I asked you where to find Shane."

"Yes! I'll do whatever you say! Please! Let me out!"

"So I'm going to have to get the rat again, then?"

"No! No! God! I'll tell you! I mean I don't know, but he didn't tell me exactly where, he just said Shane is living at one of the Missions. Here in the city."

"Who said that?"

"A policeman. A sergeant. Name of Blackburn. He's with the City Hall Station. He's the one who knows, not me! I don't know! He never told me! I would tell you! I swear on the Blessed Virgin Moth—"

Tommie clubbed him over the head with the same heavy statuette. Not too hard this time. In the hush that followed, he stepped back and took a breath of relief. The silence was sweet. He replaced the gag cloths and quickly tied the wad back in place before Friar John could shake off the effects of the blow.

"I'm afraid you're too noisy to leave without a gag, and I have a vital errand. I'll be back in a few hours at the most. Now, this is very important, so listen carefully: I want you to pay close attention to your symptoms as they come over you so that we can talk all about it when I get back. No memory problems allowed, now, all right? I'll be pressing for clear answers, so stay awake and pay attention." He poked Friar John in the scalp a few times with the tip of the blade, just for emphasis.

"I'll take those grunts for acquiescence."

Tommie stood up and gave Friar John's bindings a once-over to ensure there would be no escape. Then with a cheerful wave, he left him in his thick fabric cocoon while he went upstairs to get dressed.

----

Late that morning, Shane and Vignette began working side by side near the front of the long carry-away line. Rumor had it that the padres were exhausted from all the physical labor of toting away the crumbled remains of the big modern church while avoiding damage to the older one next to it.

Years of prayer and meditation left them ill-equipped for heavy labor. More workers had to be brought in. Shane was under no pressure to work there because of his night schedule, but he knew nobody would turn him away if he felt like joining in.

Vignette donned the larger of her two pairs of pants, plus a thick and baggy shirt. With her short-cropped hair, she looked as much like a boy as Shane did. Nobody questioned her presence there, as long as she kept working. It was not a time and place where a person's identity mattered, so long as they could stay sober and work like a mule. The job paid nothing in wages, but there would be soup, bread, and coffee waiting for the hungry workers at lunchtime. That slim promise alone was enough to replace every one of the exhausted padres with a civilian worker who, months before, would not have considered toiling at such a difficult endeavor.

The food line was already being constructed, and now the workers could catch whiffs of the meal that was about to open up for them. They worked at top speed without realizing they were doing it. Shane and Vignette were caught up in the rhythm of the line as they passed bricks hand over hand toward the debris bins. Shane had spent the last several passes with his eyes fixed in space, imagining words written in block letters. When he could see them clearly enough, he read them out loud to Vignette while he handed her a brick. "Don't stop until everybody else does."

She handed the brick to the man behind her and turned back to Shane while he took another brick from the man in front of him. "What if we're the last ones there and they run out of food?"

He shook his head but gestured for her to wait. They passed four more bricks back down the line before he could respond. "They won't," he told her with a knowing smile. "I know people here."

Minutes later, one of the cooks blew a big lunch whistle and all the workers dropped their tools. The hungry people had just enough restraint left to avoid stampeding the table, so Shane and Vignette made it there among the first arrivals. Both were as hypnotized by the sight and smell of the meal as everyone else while they picked up tin dinner plates, bowls, and eating utensils, then began to move down the long table while the cooks doled out servings. The line compacted down into a tightening mass, and they felt themselves pushed along by the gathering force of everyone's hungry anticipation.

"Shane!" called out an adult male voice. "I'm proud of you for working today, but when will you sleep?"

Shane turned from the food table to see portly Father Carlos Ignatius standing behind him. It occurred to him that Father Ignatius had the look of a man who wanted to cut in line and get his lunch with minimal delay.

"Oh! Fah-Fah-Fah-Father. Hi." He made a gesture by holding his thumb and forefinger close together. "Juh-just a lit—just a little longer."

"Ah!" Father Ignatius smiled, looking around as if enjoying the view from that part of the line. "And who is your friend?" he politely inquired.

"Vignette," Shane stupidly began. Fortunately his stutter only let him blurt out, "Vin-Vin—"

"Vinny," Vignette interrupted with a masculine scowl. "We're brothers. Just found each other. After the quake and all. Everybody else bought the farm. All of them."

"Ah! *Brothers!*" cried the father as if a miracle had unfolded. He looked around with an expression that invited all to witness. "You were separated by the terrible earthquake, and yet you have discovered each other once again at the Mission Dolores!" He called out to everyone within earshot. "Isn't that wonderful?"

Everyone was impatient for a meal. More than one glared at the padre and grumbled about how some people were decent enough to stand in line.

"Two young *muchachos*," Father Ignatius rhapsodized. "*Hermanos*, who both thought they were alone in the world, but no! The Lord looked after them!"

The good father was rolling now. He was much too grateful for being in the company of this miraculous occurrence to worry about miniscule things like lines and places in them.

Vinny piped up in a boyish voice, loud enough to be heard by everyone in the area. "Thank you, Father. But since we saved your place in line for you, why don't you get in here and grab a plate?"

"Oh!" replied the happy friar without missing a beat. "That's right! I suppose I should. And thank you again, *chico*."

"It's our pleasure, Father. We'll be seeing you around, since we're both living out in the shed and guarding the cemetery. Looters. *Hah!* If we even *see* one, we'll set off a ruckus they'll hear for miles!"

Shane shot Vignette a panicked look, convinced she was about to say something that would draw the wrong attention to them. He was ready to move out into the streets with her if he had to, but he hated the idea of letting that happen.

"Oh. Really?" Father Ignatius replied. "Both? Then you've gotten permission—" He paused. "Yes. Fitting. Well, then. I'll see you at mass, no?" He smiled and lost interest in them while he loaded up his bowl and plate.

"Yes, Father. Both of us. We do everything together."

"*Bueno*, then," the hungry friar replied, eyeing his ample lunch. He smiled around at the nearby workers. "Thank you, everyone. Blessings upon you." He continued to smile while he walked off with his food and left the others to worry whether there would be enough or not.

Shane paid close attention to a number of the workers, who seemed to accept Shane and Vignette as actual brothers who lived out in the cemetery, apparently with permission. Something told him that as long as he and Vignette kept quiet and didn't cause any trouble, rumor could serve them as well as fact.

Now along with everything else, he had a sister to look after, and this time he knew with cold certainty that without hesitating, he would sacrifice himself to keep her safe.

# 16

## THE CITY HALL MORGUE

THE LATE MAY MORNING AIR was misty cold, ignoring summer. Tommie had eaten nothing at all for over two days, flushing himself out with gallons of water to achieve maximum inner purity. At this point he was feeling lighter than air, filled by an unusual sort of electrical charge. He walked all the way to the City Hall Station from his place up on Russian Hill, just to burn off some energy. In contrast to the frosty temperatures outdoors, his body radiated heat like a powerful gaslight. He nearly felt himself glowing.

By the time he entered the station house and found his way to Lieutenant Gregory Moses, Tommie was prepared to overwhelm that shrinking lieutenant and quietly coerce him to tell everything he knew about the surviving boy Shane—and about his connection to Sergeant Randall Blackburn, one of the lieutenant's own men.

Tommie didn't doubt any scraps of willpower remaining in the lieutenant's corpulent form would quickly dissolve in his presence. Afterward, Lieutenant Moses would feel proud to have been of service to one of his betters.

Moses left his blank stare on Tommie Kimbrough's face while his internal gears whirred. He had to wonder just how much a fool they thought him to be, these faceless higher-ups in the department brass who sent Kimbrough to test him yet again. Their low opinion of his intelligence grieved him more than whatever it was that they were doing to try to take away his position. Steal his job. Give it to their nephew or their bartender or anybody they might want to influence and control with a favor.

Thank God only men could be hired for SFPD, or competition would eat him alive. Moses knew if a woman could saunter into City Hall and start fornicating her way through the department brass, she would knock him so far out of the running, they wouldn't just dream up an excuse to fire him, they would probably confiscate his uniform and push him out the back door in his skivvies. Leaving him an unemployed mockery of a fat man standing there in his red long johns with the button-up ass flap, looking for a handout.

Not while the self-improved Gregory Moses was alive.

He was astonished that they would judge him to be such a fool. Did they have no *idea* of the kind of mental skills necessary to run the Record Keeping Department? Of course they didn't. None of them did.

And yet here he was being presented with this little popinjay of a man, who pressured him to give out information about Sergeant Blackburn and that Nightingale kid from the newspaper. Moses threw a glance up at the only other occupant waiting on the guest bench. Some attorney sniffing around for Sergeant Blackburn with a few questions. Moses thought about offering a professional courtesy to the attorney and allowing him to wait in the breakroom. He felt better about himself for having thought of it, since nobody else there would.

Then he remembered Kimbrough and forgot the attorney. "Well, the best I can tell you is to guess Sergeant Blackburn is home asleep at this hour, Mr. Kimbrough." He smiled a smile of kindness. "He works a midnight shift, you see."

"No, Lieutenant," Kimbrough the Rich Guy replied. "As I just said, I don't need to speak with him right now. At this moment. But, well, you know how much I support the work of our police."

"Oh yes."

"And after reading the article, I just couldn't stop wondering how the sergeant met the boy. Or whatever has happened to the boy since then."

"It's only been a few days."

"A lot can happen in a few days."

Moses briefly noticed that Kimbrough seemed to be trying to glare at him with a strange intensity.

"I'm afraid I wouldn't be able to tell you. If you want to come back at around eleven thirty tonight, maybe you can catch him before he goes back on duty. See if he's willing to talk to you."

Moses watched Tommie's face darken. He had struck a nerve. He fought the urge to taunt him and drive the needle further in.

"Lieutenant Moses," Kimbrough began, "I'm only taking this personal and direct route because I know how busy our city leaders are with the reconstruction efforts, and I hate to bother them for favors just because they are willing to do them for me. It seems unfair."

Moses could no longer keep his contempt bottled. "It must be a real tribulation for you to have that much money."

"It's a civic obligation, the way I see it."

"Like the obligation to pay your bills?"

"Exactly."

"Such as the mortgage bills on your house. That sort of thing, yes?"

There was a long, hot pause. Kimbrough's face darkened again. When he finally spoke, his voice was soft and in measured tones. "I wonder if the lieutenant has reconsidered my offer to buy that foreclosure notice?"

"Oh, please! Absolutely unnecessary! Save your money, sir!" He leaned close to him and whispered, "Your secret is safe with me..." He gave a smile that would curdle fresh milk.

Moses picked up the big duty roster and started going over names. A moment later he looked up again, as if he were surprised to see Tommie Kimbrough still in front of his desk. He gave him one more vague smile and then dropped his eyes back to the roster. A few moments later he glanced up again. Kimbrough was gone.

He worked for another ten or fifteen minutes before Randall Blackburn came strolling out of the rear office area. The sight gave Moses a pleasurable reminder that he had sent Tommie Kimbrough away dissatisfied.

"All right, Lieutenant," Blackburn said. "That's it on all the paperwork for this latest one. Fingers crossed, we'll get some funding for extra officers."

"We'll have to see, Sergeant, but we've been down that road. Meanwhile, this gentleman over here has been waiting for the last thirty minutes, just to see you."

The attorney stood and walked over to him and extended his hand. He was a tense-looking young man with a suit that was perhaps a size too small. "Gabriel Towels, Sergeant. Esquire."

"Mr. Towels, I'm way overdue to go home and sleep."

"Yes, sir. I'll just—" He looked around as if there must be spies. "Can we talk somewhere private?"

"Use the office," Moses told them with a wave. "Time to make a few rounds." He walked out and left the two men alone.

Blackburn sighed. "All right, Mr. Towels, if we could just—"

He held up a copy of the newspaper. "The article about Shane Nightingale—"

"That again?"

"What do you mean?"

"Never mind. What about it?"

"Sergeant, I represent the Great Republic Insurance Company, and part of my duty is to locate benefactors of our policies in the wake of the earthquake and resulting fires."

"Good. And you have a check for me?"

Towels ignored that. "Until the article, we had no idea that anyone in the Nightingale family survived. Nobody filed any claims, even though Mr. Nightingale owned three apartment buildings. Now, although his business was not covered, under the law they had to have fire insurance on the apartment buildings."

"Right, what does this mean?"

"We are not one of those companies who are trying to avoid their obligations to clients, Sergeant. We owe the Nightingale family twenty-seven thousand, five hundred seventy dollars and forty-two cents."

"Forty-two cents."

"We're thorough."

"You're looking for Shane Nightingale so you can give him money?"

"Yes. And he does not need to be a named heir to claim the money, as long as nobody else in the family survives to step ahead of him."

"Shane's rich, then? That money is his?"

"Well, not rich. Perhaps someday, if he invests well. But the point is, we can have a check in his hands within a few days, as soon as he signs the papers."

Blackburn felt an idiot grin spread from ear to ear. He was about to watch Shane Nightingale's life turn around on a dime and speed off in a whole new direction. For once, he was going to see a deserving kid get an honest break.

He clapped Attorney Towels on the shoulders, accepted his business card, and promised to bring Shane in to see him right away. Then he was out the door and on his way to the Mission Dolores, full of glee at the chance to be the bearer of this news.

While he hurried along, he once again failed to notice that he was being followed. And since the chaotic atmosphere of reconstruction was everywhere, offering a thousand points of distraction to disguise another's presence, Tommie Kimbrough discreetly tagged along unseen.

Blackburn and his secret tail reached the old Mission in less than fifteen minutes. He went in and excitedly checked around for Shane, who was nowhere to be found. But when he peeked into the rear toolshed, he saw that Shane's meager belongings were still in there. So it seemed Shane was missing out on his daytime sleep, too.

*Oh, well*, he told himself. *The money will still be there tomorrow.*

He decided to stop by again early the next morning, after his shift, then headed home to catch a few hours of sleep.

This time there was nobody waiting to follow him. Tommie had already started back toward Russian Hill, now that he knew exactly where to find the person who spoiled his perfect crime.

---

Shane worked to keep up with Vignette while they jostled and pressed their way through the crowded outdoor marketplace. Even though she was two years younger, she seemed to have some sort of motor inside. Her legs kept pumping away while his grew heavy.

Vignette also seemed to make it a point to keep him laughing just hard enough that he could rarely get in a full breath. She threw him questions that only required short answers, then gave him a second or two to respond. After that, if he still wasn't ready to answer, she began chanting random letters and numbers while he fought to keep up his concentration.

Every time she managed to make him stumble, they both laughed together. The thing keeping them on the same wave was that they both sensed how quickly Shane's ability was growing as a result of this little game. It tickled because it worked. Shane felt himself flooded with emotions of gratitude he had not felt since the day of his adoption.

Finally, she whipped into an alleyway and grabbed his sleeve when he passed. A second later she had pulled him into the shadows underneath a stairway.

"Look!" she beamed. She opened up her baggy shirt to pull out a loaf of bread and a large cooked turkey leg. Shane's jaw dropped.

"Where did you geh-geh-geh—"

"You were right behind me!" she interrupted. "Where do you think I got it?" She put her face right up in front of his and bugged her eyes out him.

Shane broke into a grin, overwhelmed by her combination of lively innocence, street smarts, and warmth. And now, to see her casually demonstrate her mastery of petty theft, the whole picture twisted his funny bone until he had to let go and laugh.

"You're feeling guilty, right?" She prodded him and giggled. "You think we should give it back, don't you?" She tore the loaf in half, then pulled a chunk of turkey off of the leg and handed it to him, along with his half of the bread.

He took it, bit off a mouthful of bread, and followed with a large bite of the turkey leg. Then he nodded and said, *"You're right. Let's give it b ack."* But all that came out was "You're rihh, leth givih—" followed by a cloud of bread crumbs and turkey bits.

They both screamed with laughter. Shane's sense of relief while the laughter poured out of him was so deep and so strong that all he could do was ride along with it. He decided laughing to death wouldn't be a bad way to go; he just hated the thought of missing out on more time with his sister.

---

Thick drapes blocked the early afternoon light out of Blackburn's little garden apartment. He had been forced to accept the first place he could find because of the severe housing shortage, but he was grateful to have somewhere to go after work that was private and quiet. The artificial twilight inside was restful, giving the place a quiet feel that was the antithesis of his working life. On other days at this time, he lay sound asleep after the prior night's shift. He slept on this day, also, but there was no peace in it. Images of his wife haunted him as they sometimes did. She appeared to him, the same as always, holding their swaddled newborn daughter in such a way that he could not see the baby's face.

He had let the grim surgeon talk him into not viewing the newborn's remains. What was there to see? they asked him. The infant died in childbirth, shortly after the mother succumbed to blood loss.

And so he never got to see their baby. As often as his wife's image came to him, the one thing that never varied was that she held their new baby so tightly, he could see nothing of the child. He knew the baby had been a girl; someone told him, but no matter how many times his wife and child visited his sleep, he never got a glimpse of his daughter's face.

Blackburn sat up with a gasp. He focused his eyes on the blanket and made himself take slow breaths until the room began to hold still and his head cleared. The heavy curtains rustled slightly at the open windows, and the breeze gradually cleared the cobwebs from his brain.

He checked his watch; it was barely afternoon, too early to get up for work. Dropping back onto the mattress, he closed his eyes with a deep sigh. He felt stirred up inside, with the sort of emotional hangover that sometimes hit him after having to break up a married couple in the middle of a vicious fight.

But the dream images were already fading. Sleep began to pull at him. He closed his eyes and took a couple of deep breaths, and then he was out again.

Not long after sundown, Tommie paced back and forth across the floor of his study, angrily stepping over Friar John's prostrate form with each pass. He had already tied his victim down once again by the feet and neck, but the friar was so far gone now that restraints were an overstatement. Tommie was astounded by the speed of this infection. Friar John's face had already turned several shades of red, purple, and black. His eyes were blank. He only moved when he convulsed with yet another sharp gut pain.

Tommie tried yelling into Friar John's ear again, hoping to force some awareness back into him. "I trusted you! And I *confided* in you that I have this difficulty with money. Parting with it is more painful for me than it is for you working morons. But all my bills get paid, eventually. It really is no one else's concern. And yet you used that against me. How did you persuade the Nightingales to adopt Shane, in particular? Did you offer incentives to encourage them not to take some other child?"

He turned and kicked Friar John in the ribs and got a satisfying grunt of shock and pain out of him. Friar John's eyes popped open and focused on Tommie, who was delighted to see that he was conscious again.

"Oh! Back with us, then? Lovely! They say many dying people often experience a final few moments of energy and clarity before they expire. How fortunate that this is the case with you. So I'll tell you what is happening.

"You are dying of the plague. You were supposed to be my experiment and I was going to record every aspect of your death, but the disease, as you may have noticed, has turned out to be far too strong for my needs. Much too quick." He pulled out his heavy-bladed knife and admired its edge.

"This knife, however, is a highly controllable instrument. Simple and effective. Some things, it seems, need no improving. I should have trusted it to deal with you. I could have spent days carving my initials over every square inch of your body, keeping you gloriously alive *and conscious* the entire time! Think of that! *Think* of it!"

Whether or not it was that image which did it, Friar John's eyes glazed over again. This time, he continued sinking. He seemed to shrink within his cocoon and melt into the floor.

"No!" Tommie cried. "Not yet, damn it!"

But as if Friar John were determined to spite Tommie Kimbrough, he completed the act of dying and paid no regard to Tommie's demands. The last air wheezed out of his lungs in that familiar death rattle which Tommie knew always signaled an end to his special recreations.

He stomped the floor. "It's too soon!" Yet even as he spoke the words, he began moving toward the side door leading to his garage and stable. He knew it would take half an hour to hook up the buggy.

*All this work*, Tommie lamented. The time and effort, the personal risk he had expended—all of it wasted. This strain of disease was so powerfully toxic, it killed within hours. And it rendered a victim unconscious long before that. The vile germ was hardly slower than using a gun.

The only priceless moment had been the look on Friar John's face when Tommie bludgeoned the boy to death in his presence. The sweetest moments never last. Tommie was discovering that when it came to motivating a victim, terror worked far better than pain.

It was certainly more entertaining for him.

So after all of this, it was not going to be enough to merely kill The Bastard. Tommie needed to terrorize him first, then destroy him. The boy's simple existence was a claim on Tommie's wealth. The destruction of his father's bastard son wouldn't just be a killing; it would be an exorcism.

# 17

## ON THE BARBARY COAST

BLACKBURN PICKED HIS WAY along the broken sidewalk. Every step carried him past crowded temporary dwellings and lean-to tents serving to replace the buildings of the Barbary Coast district. The neighborhood was decimated when the fires swept through. Citizens' committees were clamoring for changes to the district, and a sea change of public image for the entire district seemed inevitable.

Little had improved so far. Familiar faces swirled all around him in the darkness, popping in and out of the lantern light and the campfire shadows. True denizens of the bottom-dwelling existence had gravitated back to the old Barbary Coast area like homing pigeons. No matter what happened to the real estate itself, the location, location, location, was still near the ships. The ships brought cargo, and many times the cargo included alcohol. Sailors needed somewhere to blow off steam and get rid of their pesky money. And so alcohol continued to propel an ongoing dark party that randomly rotated through the neighborhood.

Blackburn was the lone force of order wandering the district, the cold point of contact where the law's carriage wheels met the cobblestones. But tonight he felt his energy sagging, even though there were several hours left on his shift. The corruption of nearly everyone and everything around him seemed to be a lesson that his efforts on behalf of justice were wasted there. The civic powers that controlled him and paid his wages could be dethroned with a single shaking of the earth, but the low criminals displayed a resistance to change that rivaled rats and roaches. While the original natives of the region learned to live off the land, the Barbary Coast denizens triumphed at the art of survival by learning to live off the garbage.

In a small tent less than ten yards away, he caught a clear view of some poker player turning over the table, grabbing up the pot, and fleeing into the darkness. It took another second or two before Blackburn noticed that his own feet were not moving in that direction. He was perfectly capable, but to him, the culprit was the same petty thief who had fled from him a thousand times before: easy to chase down, difficult to beat into submission, time-consuming to arrest, and pointless to rehabilitate. They were chipping away at Blackburn's life, one street fight at a time.

He watched for another moment while the thief fled with the howling players hot behind him, then he turned and walked away. "Bastards," he muttered.

He left them to work out their own difficulties. What was he doing? In the days before the quake, his self-delusion was much easier to maintain amid the red-lighted windows, loud piano music, and raucous laughter of the Barbary Coast. The doomed women in their gowns and layered makeup looked so much better under the tinted gaslights of the old dance hall atmosphere. Now, their desperation was plain in their ragged appearance and their aggressive, angry manner. Makeup was seldom seen. Quick contact in its basest form was all their clients could expect.

Blackburn bumped into them in the shadows under stairways, stepped over them rutting like pigs in back alleys, arrested them when they did it out in full view, but ignored them on any other occasion. Nothing stopped it. The word was out, anything goes in the Barbary Coast. Hanging over the city like a dark cloud, the idea wormed its way into the brains of anyone with nothing else to anchor down their life. *Come to the Barbary Coast! Sell your soul to willing buyers, or if you have the cash, buy someone else's...*

His energy dropped again. What was he doing? He felt so demoralized, it was hard to walk.

He stepped into a lean-to "bar" with two small tables, both occupied, and rapped his nightstick on the nearest one. The two men seated there promptly got up and hustled away. He sat down and motioned for the barkeep to bring him a beer, then he turned his back to the outside world and asked himself once again what the hell he was doing. After all his years on the force, he still walked the Barbary Coast beat.

*This is what they think of you.*

His disgust and resentment burned so deeply that the beer glass was empty before he knew it. His parents never brought him up to risk himself in this way. How would he explain it to them, when he could no longer explain it to himself? As a "guardian of society," who was he actually protecting?

His original goal of working his way up to the rank of detective seemed like a bad joke to him now. Chasing down thieves and arresting wife beaters was never going to bring him the sort of action that moves an officer up the ranks. His beat could kill him at the drop of a hat, but it wasn't going to get him any glory.

As for the city mucky-mucks who gave him his orders, reports were coming in to City Hall of officials whose mansions were not covered for earthquake damage, so they set fire to their own homes, which all had fire insurance as required. Entire insurance companies were now teetering on the brink of bankruptcy while these hogs helped to collapse the system, all so they could build themselves bigger mansions next time. They accepted the humble pay of public servants and somehow got filthy rich in office.

What was he doing? Life had slapped him to the ground so hard all those years ago, it was tough not to take it as a direct repudiation from God. In a single day, his wife and infant daughter disappeared, leaving him haunted by the sense that if he had chosen some other line of work, their deaths would not have happened. And yet after almost ten years of burying his grief and rage in dedication to his work, this is where it put him: seated in a nasty, smoke-stained tent that served as a temporary tavern of the crudest possible nature, drinking alcohol on duty, right out in the open among the very people he patrolled every night. And so what? he asked himself.

So what?

It was still dark out while Tommie drove his one-horse rig up to the northern tip of the San Francisco peninsula. He steered the big draft animal down the rough dirt road leading to the rocky shoreline. The Pacific Ocean flowed into the San Francisco Bay through the narrow Golden Gate, and Tommie parked near the tightest part of the strait. The opposite shore lay less than a mile away, swallowed in the darkness and the fog. A relentless current of six or seven miles an hour swept everything before it into the bay when tides were rising and then back out to the open sea when they drained away.

With a little push, any floating object would either join the rush toward the bayside shoreline or disappear out to sea and over the western horizon, all depending on the direction of the tides. At several points during the drive, Tommie found himself debating which had greater merit: letting a body disappear at sea to dissolve in anonymity, or causing a bold statement to wash up onto one of the bay's public beaches.

He appreciated the value of secrecy, living as he did behind veils of it, but he was repeatedly swamped by the giddy sensations rushing through him when he pictured the unsuspecting beach-goers who might encounter his handiwork and vomit on the spot. Tommie appreciated humor.

Humor won out. He decided to dispose of the body while the tide was coming in, guaranteeing that Friar John would have himself one final opportunity to present his naked carcass to the view of small children.

*Whatever's left of him by then*, Tommie cackled to himself. Given the nibbly fishes, this time he might even accomplish the castration by using Mother Nature instead of a heavy-bladed knife.

The darkened sea break was deserted at that hour, and he had no problem avoiding detection while he parked the buggy and stepped around to the back. He grabbed Friar John's wrapped carcass by the ropes and pulled the fabric cocoon onto the ground. The water's edge was only a few yards away at that point, but to get the body there he would have to traverse a row of jagged boulders and fist-sized rocks.

Tommie was wiry and fit, but he was a good six inches shorter than his passenger and lighter by thirty or forty pounds. He would have to drag the cocoon by its ropes, but that was just as well. To carry the thing any distance involved far too much close contact, given the virulence of the disease. So Tommie put his strength into it and dragged his burden across the rocks, yard by gasping yard, until he was nearly at the water's edge.

He squinted at the ground by the faint starlight and saw that the water was receding, but so far it was barely down from the high water mark. This tide would be headed back out to sea for hours yet before it returned back through the Golden Gate and into the bay. If he pushed the carcass in now, it would sail off, be lost to history, and a very funny joke would go untold.

Tommie wedged the cocoon tightly between two large rocks, where it would safely remain until the rising tide returned. Then the power of Nature herself would pry it loose and send it on its way. With just a bit of luck, the friar would be swept into the bay and beached somewhere visible. Tommie sliced open the cocoon so Friar John could bid the world farewell in all of his bloated and rotting repulsiveness, pink and purple and red and black. It would be his very last opportunity to personally show the world what old Mister Nightingale really looked like inside.

---

Blackburn quit his shift at four a.m. for the first time in his life, feeling well assured that nobody would ever find out. His mood improved as soon as he walked away from his beat and started for the Mission Dolores. It was a relief to be on his way to deliver good news to a deserving kid.

He didn't even feel anxious about how things might turn out until he had the Mission's cemetery gate in sight, but he stopped there when the questions hit him: How was he going to do this? Build the boy up to it and spring it gently? Give it to him straight and let him decide whether or not to be upset on his own? Blackburn felt the ignorance of his bachelorhood; how much protection did a young fellow that age need, anyway?

He opened the gate and gently closed it behind him. Now that he was there, he felt no urge to rush into things, so he quietly glided through the darkness toward the toolshed. When he drew closer, he saw lantern light shining within the shed. The door was open. In the shadows of the outer wall next to the door, he saw Shane sitting with another small person. The other one had the appearance of a skinny boy, but there was femininity to the posture and movements. The child employed a theatrical array of gestures when speaking, and the pair seemed to be engrossed in conversation.

They kept their voices down, whether out of respect for the dead or the fear of disturbing the resident priests. He realized there was no reason to stand in the darkness and eavesdrop on them.

"Shane?" Blackburn called out. Both kids immediately whipped around to face him. He got close enough to offer a reassuring smile and wave. "It's just me, Shane—Sergeant Blackburn. How are you doing?" He saw the other one, probably a girl, regard him with mild curiosity, but Shane had that same trapped-animal look again.

Both stood up, waiting for him to let them know what was going on. He decided to just plunge in and let the chips fall.

"I'm actually here with some news, Shane. Good news."

Blackburn could tell Shane was racking his brain for what sort of good news a police officer was likely to bring him. He realized that he wouldn't care to be surprised that way himself, so he decided to jump to it.

"All right. This is it, then. Hold on to your hat." He took a deep breath before continuing. "You know, the interesting thing is that we've got whole insurance companies that are going into bankruptcy now. You know what bankruptcy means? It means to fail, to go broke. Because so many people are coming up with every trick they can think of to make a claim for money they've got no right to receive. But you, Shane, you never went to City Hall to check, and you never went to some attorney to look into it, and you never talked to the insurance company people. They told me."

Blackburn gave him an admiring smile. "You're a bit young to deal with insurance people, but this gentleman here"—he handed Shane the business card for Attorney Gabriel Towels—"is a lawyer for the insurance company that covered Mr. Nightingale's other properties."

"Prop-properties?" Shane asked, still uncomprehending.

"A few small apartment buildings, a few other things. Anyway, these people have figured it all out down to the last penny, and this man told me that you have a lot of money waiting for you. We aren't talking about the kind of money that you go out and spend on a party or a bunch of clothing or things like that, either, Shane. This is enough to change your life all around. He said even though it won't make you rich forever, it'll take care of you if you're careful with it."

The priests in the monastery lacked Blackburn's experience at reading strangers. Now that he was closer to them, he felt certain the other child was female. In fact, he recognized her now as one of the kids from the orphanage. She leaned toward Shane and whispered, "See it and read it."

Shane stared into space for a second, then turned to Blackburn and announced, "There must be some mistake."

Blackburn noticed that Shane didn't falter but decided not to mention it.

"Well, don't say that so fast," the girl cautioned. She glanced over at Blackburn and gave a little sigh, then smiled at him. "I guess you recognize me. I saw you in the office at St. Adrian's because I used to get in trouble on purpose so they would make me clean in there and I could look for our files."

"Excuse me?" he asked. "I don't know what that means."

"I'm Shane's sister. They called me Mary Kathleen when I met you, but my real name is Vignette. And I finally found our file, the one for Shane and me that proves we're brother and sister. They were never going to tell us! Can you believe that? All so they could adopt us out easier. You know, without a lot of kicking and screaming."

"Ah. That's why you're here, then."

"...Obviously."

"Good. All right. Good, then. Now Shane, you need to go over and see that man as soon as you can. If you want to go later this afternoon after we've both had a chance to catch some sleep, I'll come by and go with you."

"Well, would that be soon enough?" Vignette asked. "Maybe we should get something to eat and go on over as soon as they open up."

Blackburn laughed. "You can, but I bet it's a solid idea to have an adult with you who's on your side, and I have to get some shut-eye."

Shane slowly shook his head. "Are you sure about this?" he quietly asked. His eyes tracked back and forth while silently he "read" his next line. "Are these people sure this is right?"

"City records prove you were formally adopted by the Nightingales."

"I mo-mostly worked for them."

"Doesn't matter. This money is legally your family estate."

"A family estate." Vignette repeated the words with solemn wonder.

Shane laughed and relaxed a little. "Sergeant, believe me, they would nev-nev-never leave me mon-money."

"Right. Interesting part, that. They don't have a will saying you can or can't have it, or that anybody else can, either. Maybe it burned up with the house. After the disaster, you *are* the Nightingale family, Shane. You're it. And so it just doesn't matter what anybody else wanted anymore."

He tried to make his own vision appear inside their minds. "You could go to school. A great private school!"

Shane's face suddenly lit up so it nearly glowed. His eyes darted back and forth for a moment, then he concentrated and asked, "I can share this with my sister, right?"

"I'm pretty sure you can, pal. You can both go to school. You can have decent lives." He clapped him on the shoulder and shook his hand. "Congratulations, son. Things are going to change!"

Shane stepped back to the toolshed and sat back against the wall, reeling. He rubbed his forehead with his palm, but this time he made no effort to speak.

Vignette smiled at Blackburn, then turned away and dreamily looked up into the sky. The impact of the news made her shudder, even though her arms were wrapped around herself. Her teeth chattered while she stepped over to Shane and sat beside him.

"Shane. It's like we just got permission to stay alive." She squinted into the thought and nodded. "It's a sign. It makes sense. I think it makes a lot of sense."

Shane stared at his watch hanging on the wall, then turned to Blackburn and cleared his throat. "Do you think we could meet here at four o'clock this afternoon? We'll be done working by then, so...I mean, would you come?"

Blackburn noticed that this time Shane got through two entire sentences without stuttering at all.

Tommie felt strangely out of place while he drove his rig up the road leading to St. Adrian's. He nearly always walked when he was in full dress and makeup, risking the beat cops for the joy of attracting predators. Here, however, high up in the buggy seat in full splendor as an ersatz female, he felt uncomfortably exposed. The hour was late. The rolling ocean fog was thick. There was scant traffic on the streets while he drove in isolation.

When the first destination approached, he pulled the draft horse to a stop across from the main offices of St. Adrian's Home for Delinquents and Orphans. The gas lines to light the streetlamps had not been reconnected yet in this neighborhood, so there was only faint moonlight to betray him. In moonlight, Tommie knew he appeared to the world as a mere silhouette.

The office windows were all dark. There was no one to look out and see the well-dressed lady getting down from her buggy. No one would have been alarmed if they did. An unusually astute observer might have noticed she carried an oil lantern, but that was to be expected for a woman alone in this darkened neighborhood. Nothing to arouse suspicion at all. She walked briskly toward the offices, moving with a feminine sway that developed into a little skip, at which point she used her forward momentum to swing the oil lamp in a wide arc and hurl it ahead of her with forceful power.

The lamp flew straight through the glass of one of the windows and shattered inside, spraying oil in all directions. There was a pause of barely two seconds before a low wave of flame appeared, rising from the office floor. It quickly became big enough to expand under its own power and would soon consume everything in the office, all files, every document telling anything about a little bastard who now went by the name of Shane Nightingale.

It was a morally clean crime; Tommie knew the housing area was in another building, so all of St. Adrian's delinquents and orphans would survive to join the bucket brigade before the fire crews arrived to watch the place burn.

Tommie sauntered back to the buggy and climbed in. When he glanced back toward the offices, the fire was already growing, though it would take several minutes for the flames to become apparent and visible through the fog. There was plenty of time to vacate the vicinity and appear at the

Mission Dolores and be mistaken for a grieving lady who is visiting a grave, or perhaps praying at the beautiful Mission altar. Tommie would be safe there. Because what kind of person disturbs a grieving woman in a graveyard?

Now, with Friar John out of the picture and the orphanage records destroyed, The Bastard's history was now eliminated. The boy calling himself "Shane Nightingale" had just been moved one step closer to not existing at all.

# 18

## MISSION DOLORES CEMETERY

VIGNETTE WAS RELIEVED to see the morning sun finally beginning to cook off the fog. Ever since Sergeant Blackburn left, she and Shane were so excited that they expended their extra energy with a long stream of boring physical chores. The work helped relax the nerves but barely relieved the stunned sense of disbelief gripping both of them. She saw Shane was affected as deeply as she was, even though he labored to keep his reaction to himself. She felt grateful that he had accepted her so completely. He had not only embraced her as his sister, his first thought on hearing about his good fortune was to bring her into it. They were family now.

She came to him with such blind hope in her heart, and Shane had actually showed himself to be the extraordinary young man she needed him to be. For the first time, it was safe to finally let go and love someone— a boy, especially—who would not go away. A boy who wouldn't hurt her, a boy who actually cared about what happened to her.

For the past hour, they had both been using the Mission's long-straw brooms to clean the walkways between the graves. Shane told her how he made it a point of doing something every day that the padres could easily see, to demonstrate his value to them. Vignette's pragmatic side grasped that. She had already worn a good inch off the broom's bristles.

Shane also cautioned her to avoid disturbing any mourners who might come through after sunrise. Sometimes people liked to stop in and leave flowers at the grave and pray. It was important to leave them undisturbed.

So far that day they had the place to themselves, except for a single lady standing off in the shadows in a far corner. Vignette couldn't tell which grave the woman was visiting, but whoever it was seemed to be deep in prayer. Shane was so used to visitors passing through that he ignored the woman.

There was no need for either of them to speak with her. Vignette was glad for that. Every adult they had to interact with had the power to give them trouble or grief of some kind, so if this particular adult wanted to be left alone, that was good. One less thing.

Vignette worked away, making sure Shane noticed she was not one to shrink from a little effort. She sneaked glances at him, still half expecting him to turn to her and begin his explanation of why he really couldn't accept her in his life. Instead, he just kept working.

The rush of love and gratitude for him felt like it must be the next best thing to romance. Surely a thousand times safer. The whole situation with this boy was a space she could occupy, a place where she could live.

A few morning birds sang in the overhead branches, but the only other sound in the cemetery was the whisking of the brooms over stone and mortar surfaces. The pair could speak back and forth at barely more than a whisper and still hear each other.

"I'm almost finished over here," she announced.

"Me, too. Just about. Cou-cou-cou—"

"Read it."

"...Couple of minutes." He smiled and shook his head.

"All right, then. After that, why can't we both go sleep in the shed? They know we're family and all."

She saw Shane stop sweeping for a moment, then he shrugged and said, "Well, right. Since they know us now, I think..." He paused, then continued. "They wouldn't fire us. I mean, we've shown them we're honest and we work hard."

Vignette burst out laughing and clapped her hands together.

"What's so—"

"You're talking about how to keep your cleanup job! You just got rich!" She laughed out loud and whirled with the broom, but Shane grabbed her shoulder and brought her to a halt.

"Vignette. Wait. We heard a story about money. Right? Do you have any money? Do I? If we celebrate we could jinx it."

She wanted to argue. It hurt to be rebuked by her new brother. But she also heard the truth in his words: it's foolish to celebrate something before you know if it's true.

*But what if it is true?* her inner voice repeated. *What if it is? What if this time there is no monster? What if shadows are only shadows, and everything works out all right?* She wanted to believe that with every cell in her body. Then Shane spoke up.

"But...wouldn't it be something if that money really was there for us?"

They both beamed at that one, telepathic with shared joy. Shane collected their brooms and went to drop them back inside the Mission's custodial closet, tactfully leaving Vignette free to go ahead and undress before climbing into her sleeping blanket. She stepped into the dark shed, ready to remove her pants and shirt and hang them up before her brother returned. Her brother. Her brother Shane. It struck her that everything was working out so much better than she had dared to hope.

A thin forearm snapped around her from behind and caught her by the neck with animal strength. Before Vignette could make a sound, she felt herself yanked upward and lifted until her toes barely brushed the floor.

In an instant she realized she must have done something to infuriate Shane. He had attacked her for some reason. It made no sense, but it fit her experience.

In the next instant, a few of her old skills kicked in—the arm was already reaching around her over her right shoulder, so she instinctively turned her head to the left to take the pressure off of her windpipe. When she did, she got a peripheral look at her the assailant.

It was not Shane. Not Shane. *Not Shane!*

It was the woman from the cemetery...

Vignette was so used to having grown-ups mad at her that she wasn't particularly shocked by the fact that one of them was attacking her; she just couldn't imagine what caused this adult's anger.

Acting on instinct, Vignette already had both hands clasped around the arm under her chin, but she still struggled for air under the vise grip. At last she felt the woman's breath on her face when her attacker put her lips next to her ear and spoke in a husky whisper.

"I like turning the boys into girls. But I've always done it after they're dead. Small courtesy of the trade. However, I'm afraid your case calls for me to float you out to sea, up at the Golden Gate. You'll still be alive *after* I do it!"

Vignette's strangled voice could only manage a broken rasp. "I'm already a girl, you shit head!"

She heard a grunt of surprise. The pressure eased on her throat.

The crazy woman grasped both of Vignette's shoulders in an iron clutch and turned her face to the light. When the woman spoke this time, there was no more whisper. And at full voice, she sounded more like a man.

"Who the hell are you?" the attacker demanded.

"Vignette."

"*What?*"

"My name! Vignette! They call me...My name's Vignette!"

"I see. 'Vignette.' My goodness. Royalty. If you're a girl, why is your hair chopped so short?"

"They always cut it off for punishment."

Shane's voice boomed from the doorway. "What are you doing!"

To Vignette, the sense of authority in those four words made her new brother sound more like a grown man than a twelve-year-old. Dangerous like a man.

Shane stood outlined in the doorway. He glared at the crazy woman with an intensity Vignette had never seen before, even among the friars. He looked like he could turn into a wolf. She never wanted anybody to look at her like that.

"I said, what do you want?" Shane snarled. His entire body was shivering in fear, but his fists were clenched and his face was red.

"Ah, Shane," the woman replied, as if they were at a tea. She threw a glance at Vignette. "I thought she was you." She turned to Vignette with an apologetic little grin. "Sorry. It was the short hair. Tsk! You must have really been a bad girl!"

Shane hurried over to Vignette and planted himself in front of his sister, blocking the woman. He drilled his gaze into Vignette's eyes and barked a single order. "Run!"

Everything about the way he said it forced Vignette's muscles into motion. The adrenaline of her survival drive blasted through her, and she was out the door and speeding through the graveyard toward the front gate before she even realized she had decided to obey him.

The springs of her legs fully unwound and sent her flying past the tombstones while the growing whoosh of runner's wind filled her ears. She maintained that speed all the way to the border of the Mission grounds, across the road, down the block, and around the corner. She sprinted several more blocks before she grew tired enough to slow to an easy dog trot.

She thought about looking for a cop but wondered what she was supposed to tell a policeman that would get him to help Shane and not the crazy woman. Vignette thought of most adults as unpredictable and dangerous, and the police could be just as crazy as any other adult. Except they also had the power to put you in jail. Shoot her? Probably not. She could still slip into the Helpless Little Girl character pretty well. It had protected her so many times already.

What, then? She tripped on a loose brick and fell to her hands, but pushed off the ground and sprang back to her feet, hardly missing a step. Still with no clear answer, she considered going back to the Mission, but Shane's order left no room for it. She needed to trust her older brother if they were going to work as a team. No matter how much he needed her.

True, during that moment there in the toolshed doorway, he projected the very picture of rage. The fangs of a wolf. Nevertheless, his display of ferocity gave her comfort. Surely, she told herself, the creature she saw there could deal with that nasty woman.

It struck Vignette that there was one adult both she and Shane could trust. And if she had been paying more attention to her own legs, she would realize that ever since she left the Mission, her feet had been heading in the direction of Sergeant Randall Blackburn's place.

# 19

CHINATOWN

IT TOOK SHANE A WHILE to wake up. After a long struggle with his senses, he realized his eyes were actually seeing something, but barely so. All they could deliver to his brain was a general darkness showing faint illumination. A moment later he realized he was lying face up and staring at a broken and jumbled version of what should have been a ceiling. It occurred to him that he must be underneath one of the city's many collapsed buildings.

His attention was seized by a long and hard bolt of pain running the length of his back. He finally recognized he was bound to a wide construction beam by several windings of thick rope, with the rope tight enough to cause the beam to dig into him. His feet were just touching the floor, on tiptoe, with his ankles bound to the beam by another turn of rope.

The pain in his head was intense and unrelenting, impossible to ignore. Something had struck him hard, with such force that it could have just as easily killed him. It hurt to breathe, it hurt to think. He knew it was good news to still be alive, but he couldn't feel that part of it.

At the edge of his vision, a thin rectangle of faint light spilled across the floor. His line of sight caught just enough to see a workman's oil lamp perched on the floor, gated to emit a narrow beam. Its dim yellow-orange glow cast a patchwork of jagged shadows. He strained his eyes until they focused on a few broken signs with Chinese characters on them. That gave a strong hint of the location, and since he already knew Chinatown was swept by the fires, he also knew this artificial dungeon only existed because the building was mostly stone and masonry. He was underneath an artificial mountain.

The throbbing in his head was as intense as he had known it to be from a well-thrown fist. Every heartbeat sent another sharp stab. He winced at the worst ones while he wrestled with his thoughts. He was alert enough to realize something terrible was happening, but every time he pushed his memory, he only got deeper pains.

After a few more minutes, he became aware of another presence in the room with him, the sound of a slight scuff along the broken floor. He heard somebody nearby take a deep breath. Body warmth loomed close. A moving shadow hovered just beneath his chin, right up near his throat. Hot breath ricocheted off of his skin.

"Shane," came the whisper.

The sound of his name stabbed him like a shard of broken glass. The voice was that of an adult, but that was all he could guess about it.

"Shane, do you know me?"

With that second phrase, a singular burst of fear shot through him. It was the voice. That voice! There were only a few words, so it was impossible to be certain, but still...

The face of a strange-looking woman rose up into his view. Her makeup was badly smeared, and when she brought her eyes close to his, her breath was hot and sour.

"Do you know me?" the woman asked again, speaking in full voice this time while she revealed herself. To Shane's astonishment, the voice had changed. Shifted, as if the words were spoken by a male.

The woman reached both arms upward over her head and grasped handfuls of her own hair, as if to pull it out. But instead, it came off as a wig, which she raised up to arm's length, instantly becoming a short-haired young man in smeared makeup.

This time he looked Shane directly in the eyes. "I said, do you know me?"

With those six words, it sank in for Shane. His body knew before his brain did, and his bladder emptied down his pant leg and over his shoes.

"I've nev-nev...I've never...never seen—"

"Stop! Because it seems extraordinary for you to claim not to know me, since you tried to club me over the head with a hand shovel this morning, forcing me to defend myself. If you don't know me, you have no reason to try to kill me, do you?

"No, Shane, there'll be no easy death for you. Because I know what you are now. I clearly see your purpose. You are here to torment me in this life. I tried to be rid of you, but then some treasonous bastard arranges for you to be in one of the few places where you could reappear in my life. Like a stubborn weed."

He paced while he spoke, feeling his own rhythm. "A relentless weed. So! Big things coming for you! Things that work best while you're still alive, too! I would say 'good for you, you'll still be alive,' but as far as the 'good for you' part, that would be spreading falsehoods." Tommie giggled at his cleverness.

Shane tried to recapture the rage he possessed earlier, when he first discovered this maniac there in the toolshed, menacing his sister Vignette. But the magic powers of his rage and the strength it could impart were gone, evaporated.

The claw of dread in his stomach began to suck the life from the rest of him. He felt the old sense of his powerlessness rapidly returning, bringing the same invisible monster that held him so petrified and useless during all of the Devil's hours in the Nightingale house.

"Do you remember my name?" asked the man in a dress.

"I don't kn-kn-know your name."

"Oh, I believe you do. You used to, Shane. You used to say it."

"I don't—"

"The name is Tommie. T-O-M-M-I-E. You can say it."

"Tommie," Shane repeated.

And that's when the magic happened. Saying the name aloud did it.

He spoke without hesitation, because he was only mimicking what he had just heard. So the word came out loud and clear. And a little rush of strength and confidence followed from the sound of his own clear speech. The sense of helplessness over his frustration paled next to his need to strike out at this killer in some way. He concentrated on the next words he wanted to say, determined to send them out strong and clear. He wrote them out in his mind's eye and then read them back, just the way his sister taught him.

"In the Nightingale house, you never once told them your name. Why? Were you ashamed? Was that it?"

Through the haze of pain that blurred his thinking, Shane saw Tommie snap around to stare at him in shock. Now there was no doubting it, for either of them. Each one was face-to-face with the only other living person who knew what actually happened there.

"Ashamed?" Tommie spoke the word as though he had never heard it before. "I was the living embodiment of Judgment Day! Is your brain defective? I dished out nothing this family hadn't earned! Don't try to tell me about them being some sort of innocent group, either. They were willing to take *my house* for themselves."

He showed Shane a cynical grin. "And shame on you for telling the newspapers the Nightingales all died in the earthquake..."

"I never told the papers anything," Shane replied in a low, steady voice. It had occurred to him to imitate someone who wasn't afraid. "Somebody else told them those things."

Tommie leaned toward him and stuck his face within inches of his own. "Then where did they *get* the story from, eh? Somebody got it from you at some *point*, didn't they? Do we have to speak to each other as if you're stupid?"

But Shane had already seen it—Tommie was late with his reply. He had faltered. Shane felt another rush of confidence, enough to allow himself to become aware of how much rage was boiling away inside him. The rage channeled his fear into a bolt of lightning. It started a fire so quickly, he felt new strength explode through him. He tested himself by daring to let Tommie know he remembered the insanity the killer revealed inside the Nightingale house.

"You did every evil thing to those women," Shane said. "Except for—

except for—" He fumbled for the right term, but all the words he had heard to describe it were nasty street words, and he would not use them here. "The thing that men and women do together. That's the only crime you didn't do. But it wasn't because of your conscience, right?"

Shane had the last word out before he realized that he had spoken all those words without a hint of a stammer. Tommie seemed to notice, too; he flashed a nervous glance at Shane. And in that one moment, Tommie Kimbrough looked nothing at all like a cocky killer.

The moment did not last.

---

Blackburn was a light sleeper under most circumstances and could not help but hear the knocking at his front door. But since he was only a couple of hours into slumber and had a full shift coming up that night, he lay still, hoping the noise would stop.

It did not.

A light, rapid set of knocks came. Then a slight pause. Then another burst. And with no more warning than that, it became as relentless as a woodpecker who just finished a pot of coffee.

Who could it be? The idea of a visitor never crossed his mind. Most likely a neighbor, he groused. Some little neighborhood difficulty they wanted him to sort out, having heard that a policeman lived there.

"Oh, what the hell." He sat up, climbed out of bed, and picked up his robe, donning it on his way to the door. As soon as he had it tied, he reached forward and pulled the door open.

It was the girl from the cemetery shed. Panting hard, still dressed like a boy.

"Hi." She smoothed out the front of her shirt.

"Shane's sister...um..."

"Vignette."

"Vignette. Are you all right? Because I was sleeping, and—"

"Shane is in trouble."

She shot him a look so earnest, he snapped out of the remaining fog of sleep. "All right, then. Vignette. Try to keep it simple and just tell me what's going on."

"This woman came to the cemetery. We never saw her before. For a long time, she just stood by a grave, praying. We thought she was praying. But when Shane took the brooms back inside, I was in the toolshed because we wanted to go to sleep, but she sneaked up behind me and grabbed me from behind. Around the neck like this." She pressed her forearm to her throat.

Blackburn was taking in every word, and it struck him that Vignette was describing all this in a strange voice. Her calmness had an eerie feel.

"She wasn't that much bigger than me, but she was strong. Her arm around my neck was thin, but she could grip like a man."

"A man?" Blackburn felt his pulse step up a few beats. "What makes you say that? Just because she had strong arms?"

"No, not just that. She was strong all over. She leaned back and lifted me up off of the ground so that even my toes couldn't touch it, and I was— my throat was squeezed in her arm and so I had to turn my head just to be able to breathe, and she held me up in the air like nothing."

"Do you have any idea why she would—"

"She thought I was *Shane*! See? Because she just sneaked up behind me and all my hair got chopped off last month and I have the clothes on so that, you know, she actually thought I was him. And she said she was going to turn me into a girl and then throw me out in the ocean up at the Golden Gate. She said that she liked to turn boys into girls."

"What do you think she meant by that?"

"She said she used to do it after they were dead, but now she was going to do it while I was still alive, except that when I told her I was a girl, that's when she realized I wasn't Shane. Which is when Shane showed up and scared her off. Just at that moment! You should have seen it! Then he yelled for me to run and get out of there. So I did. But he didn't say anything else, you know, like where I was supposed to go or what he wanted me to do or anything. So I came here."

She laughed a little bit. "Actually, it's more like my feet came here and just took me along."

Blackburn kept his voice low and smooth. "All right, then. This woman thought you were Shane. And you heard her say she wants to turn Shane into a girl. Did you see a knife? Anything with a heavy blade?"

"No, but still. You see why I came here."

"I do. All right, wait right there," Blackburn replied. The dread was already working its way through him. He darted back in and threw on civilian clothing, strapped on his service revolver, and tucked a pair of cuffs into his back pocket. Then he hurried back outside.

"Let's go." He walked away, moving out into the street.

He sensed her following along behind him, so he waved down a passing two-seater buggy and showed his badge. "This is an emergency. Can you drive us to the Mission Dolores?"

The policeman's badge was enough for the driver to reluctantly agree. Blackburn lifted Vignette into the carriage and jumped in after her. In less than five minutes, they were at the Mission and the two-seater was clattering away into the distance. Blackburn insisted that Vignette wait outside the main gate, then hurried through it, across the graveyard and all the way back to the toolshed. No one was around, and he strained his ears for any sounds. The silence was near perfect, tinged only by the scraping of crickets and light rushes of breeze through the upper branches. Was she still here? Nearby? Close?

There was every reason to believe this woman could be The Surgeon. The small frame, the reference to castration. But here? So far away from the waterfront where she had always struck before?

And now a piece of fresh hell. Striking out at children.

Blackburn felt his own anxiety slow everything down; the time it took him to cross the width of the cemetery felt longer than the ride to the Mission. All along the footpath, he listened for any sound that might give something away. He kept his hearing tuned until he had nearly reached the closed door of the shed. Still there were no sounds of struggle from inside. No voices.

He reached forward with his left hand, resting the right hand on his gun, then grasped the handle and yanked the door open.

Nothing. He peered in, his eyes adjusted a bit—still nothing. The shed and its contents appeared undisturbed. The sleeping blankets were still stacked on the wall shelf. The tools were in good order.

He was thankful to see there was no blood anywhere and no sign of physical struggle. But that left him with nothing. After scanning in all directions, he stepped back onto the walkway and headed toward the front gate. He needed to find out what else Vignette remembered. And for now, he planned to keep her with him as much as possible. Despite circumstances, she was still safer with him than on her own, knocking about in the city.

It was time to head for the station house. This mad killer could no longer be dismissed. Whatever drove The Surgeon to her grisly work had now turned its hunger onto innocent citizens, wandering inland far from the waterfront dives. Blackburn had seen far too much of this monster's handiwork to be able to tolerate the idea of Shane captive in her company.

He had to convince Lieutenant Moses that the station must immediately issue enough resources to hunt this killer down and get The Surgeon off of San Francisco's streets *before the day was out.*

He knew the odds of Shane surviving longer than a day were scant. The demands of hostage holding were too great. With a hostage, you not only needed a reliable hiding place, which stopped the conversation in most cases, but even with a safe haven, you and your hostage or hostages needed basic sustenance. Your presence with hostile captives must not be heard or otherwise detected, and your needs for support would be unending. You have to keep them alive or they are worth nothing more than the troubles a dead body brings.

⸻

Lieutenant Moses had lost so much weight, he was overwhelmed with delight when at last he was able to close the buttons on a pair of brand-new uniform pants and a tailored shirt. Unhappily, now that he was a few hours into his long shift, there was no denying he had been far too optimistic in donning the new pants. Even when he stood as straight as possible, the crotch dug into him hard enough to make him mildly nauseous. When he tried bending over to pick up anything, the damned trousers gave him a silent kick to the scrotum. He felt like he was trapped in a pipe from the waist down.

Moses felt all the more foolish for it, knowing that he brought all of it on himself. Events of the night before saturated his judgment. He had simply felt so relieved and confident while he was getting dressed for work that morning when he pulled out the new outfit—which he had not planned to wear for another two or three weeks—sheer euphoria clouded his judgment.

But still, still, his first sexual experience in many years had been an overwhelming personal event, just short of spiritual ecstasy. And upon waking now that morning with a wonderful glow upon him? It felt natural to commemorate the occasion with the new outfit.

The night before, he had taken a quiet, predawn stroll through the prisoners' cells on both the male and female sides, personally seeing to it everything was shipshape. He started with the men. Inmates on the male side were either all asleep or smart enough to fake sleeping until he passed through.

Then he headed for the women's side. It consisted of a single cell. There was just the one woman in custody.

Her section was sealed off, as was the men's, so that no night guard was needed for entry. He stepped inside, and out of professional consideration for the prisoner, carefully pulled the door closed without making a sound. He locked it for proper security.

Lt. Moses paused at the door for a moment. His breathing was fast and shallow, and he felt mildly dizzy. The anticipatory sensations swimming through him felt better than anything he had ever experienced. He drank up the wonderful swirls of pleasure.

Before he knew it—and certainly before he had taken a moment to think it over and perhaps ask himself if he had a plan—he was standing at the cell of prisoner Elsie Sullivan, currently held without bail until her murder trial commenced. He already knew she spent most of her stay huddling with her bevy of attorneys and uptown sympathizers. Moses felt nothing against the woman personally, but her presence in his jail did make things politically difficult for him. All the investigators knew she was guilty, but she had certain civic bigwigs in her personal circle who strongly objected to the charges.

In the darkness, Moses could only hope he was not staring down at the sleeping form of his own destruction: a proud woman who might be inclined to punish him for her stay in his jail after she is cleared. Inevitably cleared. Nevertheless, he was captivated by the sheer sexual pleasure of being so close to her. This was a woman of the top tier of San Francisco society. He could never expect to occupy the same room with her, let alone have her in his power like this. Alone, helpless before him. Trapped behind thick iron bars.

He caught a faint whiff of Mrs. Sullivan's aroma, and the two sensations combined to buckle his knees. In moments, Moses was kneeling right next to the bars, and then the bars were all that separated him from her sleeping form. Her face was only a few inches from his.

Moses knew how dangerous it was to risk having one of his own men walk in, discovering the lieutenant on his knees next to her. But the simple scent of her skin held him in chains. He closed his eyes to the danger of discovery and concentrated on separating out the smells of her hair, her skin, her breath. He leaned his ample cheek into the cool iron bars, pushing his flesh to get as close as possible to hers.

Over recent days, he had stolen glances at her on more than one occasion, in fact whenever he could find business that would pass him close to her cell. His state of yearning made him ridiculous in his own eyes. He felt, in that heated moment, that he would willingly give up the position of Station Chief for the chance to rub his face over every square inch of her body. Nothing else in this life could have been more compelling to him.

He flinched when Elsie Sullivan turned in her sleep, rotating until she was flat on her back. His eyes had somewhat adjusted to the darkness, so he could tell hers remained closed. He relaxed a bit, taking just a moment to study her breasts beneath the fabric of her gown. When he glanced at her face again, her eyes were open. Staring straight up at him.

He froze. A moment passed. Then another.

When finally she spoke, her voice was soft, conspiratorial.

"Well, you're going to have a hard time explaining why you're on your knees, there, aren't you, Lieutenant?"

He leaped to his feet with all of the speed his newer and slimmer form could display. "No! No, I—I was checking! Just looking around for that damned thing. Where is it?"

"Psst!" she hissed to him with a coy little smile.

It was magical, Moses thought, the way this sweat-stained bundle of body odor and toilet funk metamorphosed into a playful kitten right before his eyes.

"Don't worry," she whispered. "It's all right with me. I'm glad for the company." She smiled and sat up, leaning against the bars until she was close enough to touch. Moses realized that if he still had his cheek pressed to the bars, he would be feeling her skin against his own. The thought overcame him, and he nearly shamed himself in his pants. He was only restrained by maximum will.

For the next whirlwind hour, the conversation was glorious and all so easy. Gregory Moses had never known he could be so witty, so entertaining. And when things got a bit quiet, he impressed both of them with his deeper, philosophical side. Elsie Sullivan was utterly captivated, and she even lowered herself before him and confessed that if she had ever been lucky enough to find such a man as Gregory Moses in her own life, no doubt things would have gone much differently for her. Surely far better.

Moses could see her point. It broke his heart to think of how a ravishing creature like this—who, it turned out, was not at all like the stuffy and removed person he would have guessed her to be—had been unfairly driven into this dungeon.

And Sweet Lord, when she reached through the bars to work her magic with her hands, he fell into a trance unlike anything he had ever known. She guided him through every movement with the delightful nastiness of a secret best friend. It only took a few moments for a lifetime of sexual repression to explode out of him. Lieutenant Moses cried out without meaning to. He was so lost in ecstasy, he could not have stopped the process if the entire Committee of Fifty walked into the cell block holding fat candles. He would be left stuck, writhing on the floor. Powerless to prevent his boner from publicly destroying him.

But such a horror was not to be. The night passed without harm.

Afterward everything that followed seemed natural to him. After all, why on earth would he let this delightful woman rot away inside that dingy jail cell? Did Moses obtain his current position in order to gain power he didn't bother to use? Not that he could recall.

Within hours, he found a sympathetic judge who wrote up a bail order, in an amount just high enough to sound harsh if word got out. Within two hours of that, the attorney for the lovely Widow Sullivan had posted bond and escorted his client back to her large and tastefully beautified home. Moses was not yet aware of the only mar on his plan, which was the corrupted nature of the police department and its tendency to leak useful information to substantial donors.

For his part, Gregory Moses was a man transformed. He experienced levels of confidence in his manhood such as he had never known. He felt it when he woke up the morning after her release and throughout the early part of the day.

He had yet to solve the new pants problem when the two new detectives Gibbon and Mummery came stomping into the station with such an annoying display of laughter and brash confidence that he made a mental note to punish them later.

The two detectives were also accompanied by two uniformed officers, men Moses recognized. He was just about to point out that this was *precisely* the sort of casual attitude he did not tolerate under his watch, when Detective Gibbon loudly announced that Lieutenant Moses was under arrest. Moses was charged with committing an assault of a sexual manner upon the Widow Elsie Sullivan while she was in police custody.

Moses may as well have been struck down by a thunderbolt. He put out an arm to brace himself against the closest wall.

Detective Mummery stood giggling into his uniform glove while Detective Gibbon called for the two officers to handcuff Lieutenant Moses—right there inside of his own station.

Moses was so stunned, he could only gasp for air. Speech had not returned yet. His head swam. In his state of trauma, he barely noticed Sergeant Randall Blackburn step to the front of the crowd. The sergeant also had some kid with him, a boy, it looked like. Maybe a girl.

"Lieutenant Moses—?" Blackburn began, but Detective Mummery stepped forward with a sneer and raised his hand.

"The lieutenant is under arrest, Sergeant Blackburn. I'll have to ask you to step back."

Moses watched Blackburn comply, but the sergeant looked confused and stared at him. As soon as Moses saw the genuine surprise on Blackburn's face, he knew the man had no part in this.

But of course, he realized; it made sense that Blackburn was no part of any plot. The man was only a sergeant. No, this variation on hell came from somebody much higher up in the structure, somebody who could order the arrest of a Station Chief.

In the next instant, the answer leaped up before him. Tommie Kimbrough.

The sonofabitch must have betrayed him! He used his fancy contacts to get some sort of false confession from the Widow Sullivan. The little fellow had thumbed his nose at Moses and even dared to ignore the fact that Moses knew all about the foreclosure notice.

Kimbrough was daring Moses to move against him.

A rush of anger filled him until there was no room left for fear. Every muscle in his body twitched for the chance to spring, although bound up as he was, the only weapon left to him was verbal. So while the officers escorted him across the station floor and toward the stairs leading down to the jail, he craned his head around until he could see Sergeant Blackburn, who stood aghast.

"Sergeant!" Moses hollered. "I found a foreclosure notice on Tommie Kimbrough. It fell out of the file on the Nightingale family!" The officers kept pulling Moses along. He was nearly at the door.

"Nightingale foreclosed on Kimbrough's house! A few days later *they were all dead!*"

For Moses, the stairway door slammed at that point and cut off the sight of Sergeant Blackburn's astonished face, staring. He had to assume Blackburn heard enough. If the fellow was worth half of what people estimated, he was going to drop everything and make sure to find out anything he could about Tommie Kimbrough.

Moses felt some measure of satisfaction, knowing Kimbrough would never walk away from his betrayal with a smile on his face. But he also realized with dawning dismay that he had just committed his final act as the Acting Station Chief. The wild ride that began with the collapse of City Hall on the morning of the Great Earthquake was over now, just as his fears had always projected. All that sacrificed sleep, never a day off. For nothing. New thin clothes. For nothing.

The ability to look at himself in a mirror without feeling his heart sink: gone now.

---

Blackburn stood amid the chaos on the station house floor and saw that everyone was captivated with the hot gossip about Lieutenant Moses. He glanced down at Vignette, and as soon as their eyes met, they both shared the obvious question. How was he going to handle this? For Blackburn, the general question resolved into the specific challenges of how, amid a broken command structure, he was supposed to get clearance to round up a group of beat cops and detectives and spread them out in an organized manhunt for a monster of a killer and his twelve-year-old kidnap victim?

Vignette tapped him on the arm and motioned for him to bend close to her. When he did, she put her mouth next to his ear and whispered, "I know where Mr. Kimbrough lives. I followed Friar John there when Mr. Kimbrough sent for him. It was late at night."

Blackburn considered that. The headmaster of St. Adrian's had travelled in the middle of the night to the home of Tommie Kimbrough?

He took Vignette's hand, turned around, and walked out of the station house.

---

The early afternoon streets were busy up on fabulous Russian Hill. Ice wagons, coal wagons, fish wagons, meat wagons, commerce makers with domestic merchandise shared street space with pleasure seekers of every stripe, all passing their horse-drawn carriages within inches of one another or giving resentful room to the rare automobile banging and smoking its way up the hills. Blackburn's street sense told him that at this hour on a busy day, a policeman and a little girl could walk up to a lovely three-story Victorian residence and be accepted as making a simple house call. Charity work, perhaps.

The front door was set far enough off of the street that no one besides Vignette saw him take a casual look all around before he rammed his shoulder hard enough for the lock to immediately give way. The door swung open. They were inside a moment later. He pushed the door closed and set it back on the latch to conceal any damage from the other side.

Inside, the curtains had all been pulled shut and the house was dark. They stood at the door for a moment to let their eyes adjust. There was a claustrophobic feeling to the air, out of place in a house this large.

There was a lot to see. Three times as much furniture as the place needed. Several times as many lamps, statues, and wall ornaments. On top of the furnishings themselves was what appeared to be an accumulation of heaps of paper trash. Years' worth of newspapers stacked in bundles and tied with rope. The bundles were piled to shoulder height all along the walls. The whole place smelled of musty paper.

His eyesight finally resolved enough to distinguish thin trails cleared through the piles of junk. Each cleared trail had a specific purpose and led to a chair, a sofa, a shelf. "Wait here," he told Vignette. Then he moved off down the trash trail leading to the stairway.

"All right."

She followed him anyway a few feet behind. He ignored the fact that she ignored him, and they moved up the stairs to the third floor, climbing between rows of books and bundles of newspapers that lined both sides. He planned to begin searching from the top down, but the surprise sight on the top floor simplified his task. With the exception of a few storage closets stuffed with linens, most of it was bare, with plain wood floors. The walls were lined with mirrors. One of those new vacuum sweeping machines was parked in a corner.

There was a horizontal ballet bar mounted on freestanding supports in the middle of the room. The person using it would get a full self-view from every angle, a private visual world consisting only of their image.

Blackburn turned and went back down to the second floor with Vignette shadowing him. The view there was much more like the down-stairs area: excessive levels of furnishings with knickknacks stuffed into every bit of open space. Trails carved through the mass included access to a bathroom, a sitting room with barely enough space for one person to sit, and a bedroom so stuffed with unnecessary items that even half of the bed was piled high, leaving the other half for sleeping.

His interest peaked when he tried the knob on the final unopened door on that floor and found it locked. This doorknob, unlike the other glass doorknobs throughout the house, was made of delicately carved ivory. The doorplate appeared to be gold.

He took a step back and kicked the door open, noticing that Vignette barely flinched.

"Hold it now, what's all this?" The words popped out of him all on their own. He stood in the doorway of what appeared to be the boudoir of a whorehouse madam: red velvet was draped everywhere, even the wallpaper was embossed with red-and-gold fleur-de-lis patterns.

This room was neither barren nor packed. A single chaise longue occupied one end of the room with a lamp and reading table. On the other end was an elaborate dressing table fit for a Broadway actress, piled with an array of makeup items and half a dozen colorful female wigs. Next to the mirror stood a rack of elaborate dresses and walking outfits, appropriate shoes lined up below.

*Turn boys into girls...* And these were, no doubt, the same outfits that would be described by witnesses who saw a "small-boned woman" near the crime scenes around the Barbary Coast. He turned to see Vignette staring up at him.

"All right, now," he whispered. "You have to see everything? Look around inside of here and meet The Surgeon."

"I've heard about her," Vignette bluffed with toughness she did not feel. "You think I don't know things? She's some crazy killer lady."

"Right. Except it turns out, here, she's a man after all. A man who dresses like a woman. That's what all this is. Right here is where Mr. Tommie Kimbrough has been turning himself into The Surgeon. And whatever he was talking about doing up at the Golden Gate, it looks like he might be already headed out that way."

Vignette nodded and quietly replied, "And he's got Shane..."

# 20

HIGH ATOP FABULOUS RUSSIAN HILL

AFTER SHANE GAVE HIMSELF up for dead, he was amazed to feel himself gripped by utter fearlessness born of rage. A transformation began inside of him. Because of it, his fervent wish to reclaim the bold stance he was able to make for Vignette not only came true, it arrived as a sum multiplied.

All of the anger he had barely sensed within himself in the past now overflowed and demanded release. His lifelong concern about how anyone else might perceive him fell away and dissolved. Every part of him that formed while he was playing the role of "good orphan" to encourage his adoption, or that of a docile house servant hoping to avoid his return to the orphanage, all of it was gone now.

The shame that caused Shane's stutter also left him. Now the voice that boomed out of him was nothing he recognized as his own. "You bastard! Damn you into Hell!"

Tommie backhanded him across the mouth with such force that Shane was knocked into momentary silence. It left his head ringing.

"Who are *you* calling a bastard?" Tommie hissed. "You don't know what you're talking about!" He paused to practice his breathing while he paced back and forth. Finally he made himself calm and continued.

"I'm the *real son*, you miserable larva! I'm the real heir! You're just my father's little 'oops,' some son of a whore that Daddy was careless enough to impregnate!"

"There, you see?" Shane shot back. "You are out of your mind! I don't have anything in common with you! You think that I'm your bro—"

Tommie struck him again. Harder this time. The room swam, and Shane's vision blurred.

"You will *not* use that word! I do *not* think you are my brother! Christ, that's the whole *point!* You are a piece of garbage our father and his slut left behind. She should have kept you in her shitty little world! It's all you ever deserved, anyway! What have you ever done to earn anything, any privilege? Who the hell are you?"

Shane just stared at him. He had been forced into silence, but the rage still fueled him, demanding release.

Tommie sneered. "Oh, not feeling so talkative now? You were quite the tough little guy there for a few seconds, weren't you? You never would have known anything about this, and I never would have known anything about you, if my parents—*my* parents—hadn't found me naked with a couple of the neighborhood boys. Is that justice? Is that the way for me to find out I have a bastard son of a bitch for a half brother, and that I am completely disinherited in his favor, just because of who I am?"

"You are getting crazier by the minute, mister."

"My, aren't we confident? What happened to your stu-stu-stutter, bastard boy?"

"It decided to leave so I could tell you you're going to rot in Hell."

"The bastard boy is a fortune-teller! He knows my future!"

"That's right."

"You don't look that powerful, under the circumstances. Hadn't you noticed?"

"You're the one who didn't notice. You didn't notice me in the Nightingale house. And I heard everything. For a day and a half, I heard it all."

Tommie's triumphant look faltered for just an instant, but he quickly restored it. Shane went ahead anyway.

"So what about our half sister, Vignette? Did she have the same mother as I did?"

Tommie looked at him, puzzled, then just shook his head. "You'll be glad to know that the father who intended all your life to leave his bastard in poverty is dead. And so is the bitch who was willing to throw me away. Her own son, just because I was different. Different from them. They killed each other."

"You killed them."

There was a long pause. Shane could not see what Tommie was doing. Finally, from a corner behind him, he heard, "You don't know that."

"Oh, I know it. Because I know you. I listened to your pathetic babbling for all that time. And after a while, I could tell that half of the time, you didn't know whether you were talking out loud or not. Sometimes one of them would answer you when you said something, and it would surprise you. Because you didn't know you spoke out loud."

Tommie focused a stare on him as if he were a lab specimen. "Interesting, you're still not stuttering." He gave Shane a pouty smile and a little wink. "Shane, Shane. Were you faking it all along? A fake stutter? Why? To get girls, perhaps?" He whispered conspiratorially, "I know you're at that age..."

Shane ignored the question. What difference would the answer make? He possessed the power to turn a burning ray of light onto Tommie Kimbrough. And he knew the exact combination of words to make it happen.

Shane took a deep breath and once again squeezed every muscle in his body to keep his voice from faltering. He looked straight into Tommie's eyes and held his gaze.

"Sorry. I have to empty you out."

This time Tommie could not conceal his shock. Shane saw the blood rush to Tommie's face. And off in the back of Shane's mind, a part of him wondered how a man who has slaughtered innocent people as a source of joy could still have the ability to blush at all.

Tommie gave an incredulous little giggle, then asked, "You're going to do what?"

"You know what it means. I heard you say it. I heard you tell all about it.

It's just something you were thinking out loud. Without even knowing you were talking! But I heard it. Even after they were all dead and I knew for sure you had nobody to talk to, you kept right on arguing with your demons. I listened. I was inside of your head."

Tommie leaped forward and flashed his heavy-bladed knife directly under Shane's nose. "Shut up! You shut the hell up!"

"You started that way with each one. 'I have to empty you out.' Three times, I heard you say that. And with Mrs. Nightingale, the first one, you even made her guess what it meant to say 'I have to empty you out.' She wasn't that frightened at first, was she?"

"I didn't want her frightened at first. I wanted to experience her intact personality. I wanted to hear her speak while she was still thinking she could bluster her way out of everything. She thought she still had a life to defend."

"And you used your knife. Little cuts. Hour after hour, until you dissolved her into a babbling, grown-up baby."

"That's the part I love. Watching all of their haughty pride dissolve, their opinions, their judgments, their rejections. Everything that makes one a unique creation eventually collapses into the same infantile shrieks and babbling. And that, my friend, is triumph."

"Triumph over who?"

"*Whom!*... And what do you mean?"

"Well, that's what confuses me. Because while you were killing Mrs. Nightingale, you kept talking to her like she was your father. Telling her how you're just as much a man as she is. Only you weren't talking to her; you meant your father. And you hate your father for rejecting his only son. Only you weren't killing him, because you already did that.

"And Amy, the older daughter. Did you know you were talking out loud when you started pretending she was your mother, bawling her out for not keeping her husband at home so that he couldn't sire a bastard son? Did you think that you were alone and safe while all that came spilling out of you? You did, didn't you?"

Tommie turned to face Shane. His eyes seemed to sink back into his head.

"Now I know exactly how I'll do it. I'll leave you tied to that beam and haul you out to the Golden Gate *before* I go to work on you. If I start here, I may not be able to stop myself and you'll bleed out before we get you into the water.

"And then, just before you and your beam go into the water, I'm going to treat you to exactly one hundred little slices from your head to your toes. Your blood in the water will draw sharks from incredible distances. And there are plenty of them lurking around the mouth of the bay. I trust they will eat you slowly, because of the beam, you know. Surely it will slow down their rate of consumption so you can *savor* the experience of being eaten alive at sea. Eh?"

Shane leveled his gaze. "You killed your mother and father for money."

"I killed them for throwing my life away!"

"But you killed yourself too, all those years ago," Shane added. "Ever since then, you've just been walking around with a dead thing where your soul should be."

"How poetic," Tommie sniffed. He snatched up a writing pen, dipped it in an ink bottle, and announced, "I have this custom, just this little thing I do. Sort of a trademark, lately." He picked up a small notebook, opened it, and dictated to himself while he wrote:

"Even if The Last Nightingale could be revived, how would it tolerate the cure? Knowing Life merely awaits to devour it again..."

He read it over silently two or three times, then happily exclaimed, "It will work perfectly for your suicide note, little bastard brother!" He dropped the notebook into a large section of oilskin. He folded it snugly and tied it with thick twine.

"There. Waterproof. Good enough so the note will still be readable when they find it on your body. In case there's anything left of you to wash up on shore. Probably not too much, though. Sharks and whatnot."

Tommie tucked the oilskin envelope into his coat pocket, then reached down into some box Shane could not see. When he stood, he produced a thick muslin potato sack. He stepped up to Shane and raised the sack overhead, then Tommie let his mask of civilization fall away. His dead-eyed face melted into the expression of a man who could never be at peace with the outside world.

A moment later, the bag swooped down over Shane's head and everything went pitch black. He felt Tommie's hands pulling the bag down over his shoulders, and a rope was tied around his shoulders and chest, keeping the sack in place. Next he felt the harsh blow from the thick board that bashed him across the side of his head, but only for an instant before unconsciousness overtook him.

---

Twilight was rapidly dropping into darkness while the horse-drawn taxi clipped along at a brisk trot on its way back to the Mission Dolores. Vignette struggled to grasp the rapid turn of events. As usual, when she let herself get caught up in the business of grown-ups, she found herself stuck between shouting men, without being able to figure out what the problem was. Sergeant Blackburn had raced her away from Tommie Kimbrough's house and back to the station to get more men to go capture him. But everybody was all excited about the fat man in charge who was arrested that day. Nobody would help because there was no boss around to give orders.

Now Sergeant Blackburn had her in this cab, forcing her to return to the Mission to wait all alone in that stupid toolshed without Shane—because of course nobody could let a *girl* go along to catch a murderer. Worst of all, Sergeant Blackburn seemed to shake off her best attempts to manipulate him with her claims of being too scared to go back home.

He just smiled at her. "You have to wait where it's safe, Vignette."

"Shane's out there. If he can be there, I can be there!"

The sergeant laughed out loud at that, and he didn't bother to argue with her. She was glad to see him laugh, since his face seemed so tired and worried. Maybe it was safe to ask him.

"Why wouldn't the other cops help us?"

"It's called command confusion."

"They didn't seem all that confused."

He laughed again, a little. "Yeah. They all seemed crystal clear about not wanting to be of any help."

This was good, Vignette thought. She had him talking, and he seemed to be feeling friendlier at the moment. Maybe if she could keep this up...

"If I was with you, I could still wait in the taxi, and then if either of you got hurt, I could start helping to bandage you up while we run for a doctor! You can't argue with that!"

"Got me there. I can't argue."

"So can I come?"

"No."

They rounded the corner and pulled up next to the Mission. She flashed him her very best look of betrayal and hurt, but he just put his hand on her shoulder and smiled.

"I want you to wait here so I know you're safe, because if I have to worry about you, I might not be able to do my best to help Shane."

"If we're together, we can look in two different directions at the same time!"

"Vignette, this perpetrator is madness itself." He lifted her down and put her at the curb. "I have to go."

She refused to let herself cry, but the worry and fear were too much for her. She turned and fled back into the cemetery, to at least be around the place where her brother lived.

Once she was gone, the cabbie turned in his seat and asked, "What now, sir?"

"Well, that's the thing, actually," Blackburn replied. "I need this carriage to drive up to the Golden Gate. I'm on the trail of a man I believe has killed a couple dozen people so far. I expect to find him up there tonight, because he has one more victim to kill there."

"What, you mean *that's* what that little girl was talking about? A real killer? And you're after him?"

"I'm all there is, right now."

"Sir, you realize what you...there's no light at all up there! Can't see your ass, if you don't mind me sayin' so. Fog covers moonlight, starlight, all of it!"

"I believe you. That's why I'm prepared to offer you double your rate, all the way out there and back tonight."

"Very generous, sir. But I can't possibly risk my horse in that—"

"I'll triple your rate."

"Triple, now? Triple? Sir, you'll easily go down twenty dollars that way."

Blackburn pulled a twenty-dollar bill from his pocket, leaving himself with nothing but a few coins. "I have to go right now. You can either take the money to drive me up there, or you can take the money for renting your rig to me, and I'll have to drive it myself. But I'm telling you," Blackburn said, "I could sure use one more man along with me tonight."

"To go after a maniac."


Minutes later, Blackburn sat alone in the rented/commandeered hack, steering his way up to the Navy Presidio, a huge expanse of preserved land that fronted onto the strait of the Golden Gate. The search would require as much luck as skill, since there was plenty of deserted and rocky shoreline where the Pacific Ocean poured into the San Francisco Bay.

Just as the cabbie warned, the lack of light at this hour became a real obstacle at the northern tip of the peninsula. There were no structures anywhere. Early clouds sucked up any moonlight before it hit the earth. The air smelled of incoming rain.

He slowed the horse to a brisk walk and proceeded toward the shoreline. The sound of the wind was in his ears, topped by the clip-clop of the horse's gait. But that was it. He strained to hear any trace of voices or noise that might tip off another person's presence. Nothing came back to him. He slowed the horse to a gentle walk, letting it stumble along the rutted road at a slow walk, the only safe speed out there.

Even then, there was no sound in the air to guide him. Just the rushing wind and the big animal's steps. After a few more moments, he caught the first faint sounds of surf on the distant rocks. He leaned into each crash of a wave, straining to hear any voice in the pause between them. There was nothing, still nothing, just wind and waves and horse hooves, all in darkness so thick it held his vision down to a few yards.

Fear twisted his stomach and tightened his jaw. His muscled body felt the lack of sleep. The night and its obstacles seemed so huge, he wished that in such times he had some kind of abiding religious faith to sustain him. But it still seemed to him that when his wife and daughter were taken, God ripped his family away in one icy blow, telling him his ambition as a family man was denied. His heart had frozen to the spot on that day. Now he couldn't pray anymore for the same reason he couldn't "just start another family again," as people used to advise him. Back when they still bothered.

The casual disrespect he received in Vignette's presence from the officers around the station had left him with a bitter feeling in his chest, but he also knew that without an actual station chief to direct traffic, discipline was gone. Leaving him with nothing else to do but venture out to the Presidio alone and see if there wasn't some way a single police sergeant could ruin The Surgeon's plans for the night.

His frustration mounted at the slow pace while he drove the horse forward. It felt as if the elements conspired to slow him down. Soon the sounds of the sea became the dominant noise, combined with the rushing of the sea winds, the clatter of the buggy wheels on the rutted road, and the steady clop of the horse's walk. Now there was too much ambient noise for him to hear any signs of other people. He wondered how this was going to do any good.

In the seaward distance on his right-hand side, he could just make out the flashes from the rotating beam of the gas-powered marine searchlight. That fixed his current location near the narrowest part of the Golden Gate passage.

The chill in the air seeped through his light jacket, and a shiver rippled through him. At this point the mist hovering over the ocean water was dense enough to steal even that last hint of light. He pulled the carriage to a halt and tied back the reins. It was quieter then. Blackburn felt encouraged that he might hear something if he executed the rest of the search on foot.

---

Shane was in and out of consciousness throughout the rugged ride to the north shore in Tommie's horse-drawn wagon. He remained bound to the beam by several turns of thick rope. Time after time, he rolled back up to the surface of awareness and realized he could work his way out of the ropes, if only he could gather his strength and focus his energy. But that same strength flowed right back out of him each time, running on its own schedule and leaving him to sink back into nothingness.

When enough time passed that he could come back to the surface and stay, the thing that roused him was a sharp drop in temperature and the sensation of cold wind blowing across his body. Nearby wave blasts sounded like cannons, sending spray flying through the air. He shivered uncontrollably. There was almost nothing to see in the darkness and fog.

But in the background there was a slow and rhythmic pulse of light that had to be coming from one of the searchlights along the shoreline leading into the bay. Shane was instantly wide awake, gasping with fear when he realized the monster was about to make good on his threat to kill him at the Golden Gate.

Now he felt the beam dragged backward a few feet before the head of the beam was tilted up and rested upon a rock to hold him up at an angle. A few seconds later, the next searchlight strobe flashed across the feral grin on Tommie Kimbrough's hovering face. All traces of his dress and makeup were gone.

"I developed a whole new expertise in handling rats with the plague," Tommie said, "just for you. I was going to wait until you died that terrible death, then haul your carcass out here and push it into the surf."

Shane knew that his only chance of survival in this desolate place was to distract Tommie long enough to allow him to wriggle free of the bindings and make a run for it. With luck, he might disappear in the thick darkness.

"You think I don't remember anything before being at St. Adrian's," Shane began, "but you're wrong."

"Horseshit." Tommie pulled out his heavy-bladed knife and began testing the edge.

"'I have to empty you out.' I know why you say that."

"I'm going to start your hundred slices with small cuts, just enough to let you taste the blade for a while. After the first fifty or so, we'll go ahead and float you on out into the water. Before I push you off, well, I'll do the deep ones then." He smiled and added, "The ones that will bring the sharks."

"It's what our father said to you. After he caught you with the boys. He tried to whip you until everything sinful got knocked out of you. You think I don't remember?"

Tommie stared at him. When the searchlight flashed again, his face looked as cold as a fish. "Maybe the current will carry you on out to sea," he replied. "Maybe it will sweep you into the bay. But most likely the sharks will devour you within a few hours. Or a few minutes, even."

"They tried to make you out to be garbage! They tried to take away your future and throw away your life, even though you weren't hurting anybody. He tried to beat you until there was nothing left inside of you. So now you do it to the others because you're still trying to make our father and your mother stop!"

"*Shut up!*" Tommie screamed it at the top of his lungs, raising his knife high overhead, tensing to thrust it deep. Just before he began the downward stab, Shane pulled his arms from behind, tore the rope from around his neck with his right hand, and simultaneously blocked the stabbing motion with his left. He sat up just as Tommie stabbed downward again, this time driving the knife deep into the beam.

As Tommie struggled to pull the knife free, Shane kicked for his life against the ropes at his ankles until his feet finally pulled away. He tucked into a defensive ball just as Tommie thrust at him again, and an inch of the blade caught in his thigh. The pain made him scream into Tommie's face, but his survival instinct flooded him with strength.

He jumped away from the beam with the wound burning in his leg and howled with rage. He knew nobody else could hear him out there, but Tommie was the only audience he needed for his utter revulsion at the creature his so-called brother had become. He knew the scream was likely the last sound he would make in his life, and he was leaving no doubt about where he stood. The little boy who had shuddered helpless in the kitchen cupboard now faced the killer bare-handed. He poured every ounce of his life force into defiance.

It kept him from realizing what happened for a second or two after a single gunshot was fired from somewhere nearby. Tommie grunted with surprise when the bullet whizzed by inches from his head. He swore while he spun on his heels and sprinted in the opposite direction, vanishing in the inky blackness. When the search beam swung by again, there was no trace of The Surgeon.

Shane staggered under his own weight and fell to his knees in the rocky sand. He was so drained and exhausted that he barely flinched when a

sharp scuffing sound came from the beach next to him and Randall Blackburn appeared at his side. For an instant he wondered if he was dreaming
again, but he felt Blackburn's strong hands clutch him.

"Are you all right?" Blackburn asked.

"He stabbed my leg, Sergeant. I can't chase him."

"*Chase him?* Listen to me. You don't go anywhere. I mean it, Shane. Stay
right here. I've got a buggy up on the road, but you'll never find it alone,
especially not bleeding like that."

"All right, I know."

"I mean it!"

"I *know!*"

Shane felt Blackburn give him a reassuring squeeze on the shoulders,
then heard the big sergeant stand up and run off in the direction Tommie
had taken, along the waterline toward the big signal light. His footsteps
were surprisingly fast. They only receded in the distance for a moment
before they dissolved into the sounds of the ocean.

Shane huddled on the ground and wrapped his arms around his knees
to conserve his warmth. There was no way to tell what was happening with
Sergeant Blackburn, or when he might return. And the thought of Tommie
somehow getting the best of the big policeman was too awful to contem-
plate. He could only huddle and wait. In between the periodic sweeps of
the distant searchlight beam, it was as dark as the bottom of a well.

## DYING BADLY AT THE GOLDEN GATE

RANDALL BLACKBURN SPRINTED across the rocky sand into the opaque night. The flashes from the sweeping navigational beam gave him brief glimpses of his surroundings, barely enough to keep his direction oriented. He fell several times, abrading the skin on his palms and knees, sending him scrambling to recover his pistol. He lost valuable seconds with every stop, and the resistance of the darkness and the terrain made him growl in frustration. He could only hope Kimbrough was having the same difficulty, maybe more, with luck. Surely the madman would not continue to have the Devil's own luck the way he had done for so long around the Barbary Coast.

The thin strip of sandy beach ran out near the narrowest part of the strait and gave way to rocky shoreline. Blackburn stopped, using the sweeping searchlight beam to look for alternate routes. But all the land leading away from the Golden Gate was so flat, he knew Tommie would be visible in the beam at that moment if he fled in that direction. Blackburn decided his quarry must have continued over the rocky portion of the shoreline formed by a long stretch of seawall boulders the size of elephants.

Jagged fragments filled the spaces between, making for treacherous ground.

He jumped to the top of the first one, immediately caught his foot on a patch of slime, and went down face forward between the big rocks. He struck the fragmented stones with a series of impacts. A fiery burst shot through him when he felt the ribs on his right side crack and separate, jabbing his flesh from within. He screamed with pain, but his voice barely carried over the sounds of the surf. When he was able to pull himself to his feet, he felt as if he had a spear lodged in his side.

On any other occasion, in pursuit of any other fugitive, this would be the point where the chase was abandoned for another day. Even though he still had five shots left in his pistol, he was no longer sure his arm would hold steady enough to take aim.

But this quarry was The Surgeon. Nothing could blur the terrible joy the man took in his crimes—Blackburn had encountered his demonic leavings time and time again. The Surgeon had been attempting to kill Shane Nightingale at the moment Blackburn managed to creep up on them after their shouting match lured his attention. He knew if he had arrived a few seconds later, it would have been for nothing.

He pulled himself to the top of the boulder in front of him, waited for a flash from the searchlight, then leaped to the next one, crying out at the pain of the impact. At least this time his footing held. He managed to make it from rock to rock without falling again, timing his movement to the light beam. Each time it flashed by, he checked out his next potential landing spot on top of the next rock. After his first six or seven leaps, he caught a glint of reflection about twenty yards ahead. The searchlight beam reflected off the wet leather of Tommie Kimbrough's long coat, giving a sure fix on his position.

He felt his heartbeat jump into high speed and pump him with so much adrenaline that he barely noticed his broken ribs, throwing himself into a reckless pursuit and double-timing it to make two leaps per light flash. That closed the distance by at least half, but by then the rocks ran out again and there was another stretch of a narrow, sandy beach. He was close enough to hear Tommie's footsteps speed up on the flat ground and realized this would end it; his injuries did not permit him to catch the athletic killer.

He staggered to a halt, gasping, and managed to raise his gun by holding up his right arm with his left hand. He pointed the barrel in Tommie Kimbrough's general direction and waited for the next searchlight flash. When it came, he saw that The Surgeon was surprisingly close. He adjusted his aim in the flash of the light beam, then fired into the inky darkness where Kimbrough's form had just been. There was no way to tell if the shot found its mark. But now that he was back on a flat strip of beach, Blackburn was able to keep walking forward in the dark until the next pass of the beam. It finally arrived and swept the strip of rocky sand.

The beach was empty.

He spun in all directions, but there was nothing to see. He was forced to wait for each new sweep of the beam and look in one narrow direction during its brief moment of illumination.

And then at last, there it was, out on the water: the reflection of light off of the wet leather of Tommie's long coat. He was not far offshore, perhaps twenty-five yards, attempting to quietly drift off into the bay on the rising tide. He had escaped notice so far by not breaking the surface with his arms or legs.

Blackburn realized that with the current rising, Tommie could simply float his way right into the great bay for as long as he could stand the cold and then swim for any random landing point along the shoreline. Anyone who could outrun him across a beach lined with slippery boulders could manage to do that much.

There was no chance of swimming out to catch him with broken ribs. The Surgeon was making his escape, right out there in front of him. Blackburn's frustration was worse than the pain.

In desperation, he dropped to the ground and knelt on his right leg while keeping his left foot flat so that he could use his left knee to stabilize his shooting hand. Then he aimed in the general direction of Kimbrough's escape path and waited for the next flash. When the beam swept by, he got a solid fix on the coat's reflection and emptied five fast shots. He saw the second shot hit home just before the light went by and felt certain the third one also hit the mark. The last two were well-aimed guesses.

The next pass of the beam showed nothing but black water. He waited and watched for another pass, then another, and another. At last he caught the crucial glimpse, only a few yards from where Blackburn aimed his shots; the low, floating body rolled slowly in the current. He watched it for three more sweeps, growing more convinced with each one that he was looking at a floating carcass.

A flash of white foam exploded next to the body, and the long leather coat spun violently in the water. In attempting his ocean escape, he ended his life. Something out there had just taken the first bite.

The infamous "Surgeon" was now his own final victim.

When Blackburn heard a footstep behind him, he whirled with all the speed his fading strength allowed, wondering if Kimbrough had an accomplice. He was ready to go down using the empty pistol as a fighting club, but when he tried to raise his right arm, the pain was so sharp and intense that he lost his balance.

Shane grabbed him in time to keep him from falling to the ground. "Did you get him?"

"What? Shane? Yeah. I got him. But I told you to stay back there."

"I heard the shots. But are you sure?"

"Positive! I said stay there, as plain as—"

"No! Are you sure you got him?"

"Look out there, wait for the next flash."

A moment later, the beam swept across the water. The water was calm, and the rising tide was bare.

"You see him out there anywhere?"

"No."

"Well, I saw him out there. Big as life, with something already gnawing on his carcass and ruining his nice leather coat."

Shane strained his eyes to penetrate the darkness, hoping for any glimpse of Tommie Kimbrough's body, any confirmation that the killer was gone. He kept it up for a minute before he finally nodded and exhaled. "All right, then."

Blackburn sat down on the rocky shoreline with him. "He'll likely wash up somewhere close by. Whatever's left of him."

"What a shame." What Shane would have loved to do, given the chance, was to use his bare hands to tamp down the earth on top of Tommie Kimbrough's grave until it was as hard as stone. He turned to Blackburn.

"My leg is still bleeding, and you don't look so good."

Blackburn smiled when he noticed that Shane wasn't stuttering at all anymore, but under the circumstances he saw no reason to bring it up. He felt himself growing woozy enough to swallow his pride and let the kid help him to his feet. Then he placed his good left arm around Shane's shoulder and guided both of them on a slow trek back to his rented/commandeered taxi.

Vignette paced back and forth in the moonlit spaces between the cemetery trees, walking fast, digging her heels in with every step and spinning so hard on the turns that her knee joints hurt. Still nothing slowed her down. She needed the sense of focus she got from the violent pacing. The powerlessness of the moment was sheer torment.

In general, she tried not to hate being a girl, to loathe being small, to detest being young. But those were all the same qualities that prevented her from being of any use in helping Shane.

She could not lose him. She could not. She could never let the world give her a dream come true of a big brother—even if she had to goose the world pretty hard on several occasions to make it happen—and then have him taken away again, just like that.

At some point in whatever it was she was doing, she caught a flicker of shadow from the front area of the cemetery, up there by the main gate. The flicker happened again, showing that it wasn't a shadow, it was a silhouetted form. Approaching her.

Somebody was walking into the graveyard. One person, alone. Not a woman, but someone in pants and a shirt, someone with short hair like Shane's. Someone was walking like her brother walked, hurrying toward her, covering the last few steps to her with a beaming smile. When Shane put his arms around her without a single word, hugging her just right, not too strong, she had more joy and exaltation shooting through her than she could stand without breaking into pieces.

She returned the hug, gripping him hard, as hard as she could, trying to prevent herself from waking up and finding that Shane had turned into her pillow and it was all a dream.

At last, he stepped back, put one arm around her shoulder, and began to walk her toward the shed. She noticed that he was standing up very straight. He seemed taller.

"Would have got here sooner, but I had to drop off the taxi at the City Hall Station and get bandaged up over this cut on my leg. Sergeant Blackburn looked like he got kicked by a horse. His ribs are wrapped up tight. He's sleeping at the station. The taxi man drove me here."

"What? What? What the hell happened?"

"I'll tell you in the morning."

"In the *morning?!* Who cut you, Shane? Was it that crazy guy? How did you fight him off?"

"Vignette. I promise. Let me sleep, and I'll tell you tomorrow. We have to go see that lawyer, you know. We should sleep."

"Wait. Just wait. Do you mean to say it's all right to just go in there and go to sleep? It's safe to do that?"

He looked her straight in the eye. "That's what I'm saying. Sergeant Blackburn shot him, and he sank into the ocean. Sharks got him."

He opened the shed and stepped inside. "He's coming by tomorrow, even though he got pretty banged up." Shane went inside and lit the oil lantern. "He's going to stick up for us." He grabbed up both sleeping blankets, passed her one, and tossed the other over his shoulder.

She unfolded it and wrapped it around herself before lying down. "How are you doing that?"

"What?"

"*Talking*, Shane. Are you reading it first? Is that how you're doing it?"

"Well..."

"...*Well?*"

A wide grin spread across his face. "I'm getting faster, aren't I?"


Late the next afternoon, Randall Blackburn stood ramrod stiff under his rib bindings. From his place on one side of Attorney Towels's massive desk, he watched Shane sign the final insurance form. Blackburn signed next, as Shane's guardian and witness, making the transaction legal. And with that, he watched Shane Nightingale take possession of a bank account totaling close to twenty-eight thousand dollars of the Nightingale family estate.

It struck Blackburn that Shane looked like he would be sick at any moment. He wondered if it was just nerves. Whatever was going on, the boy certainly didn't look happy or relieved to be taking possession of this money.

Vignette had quietly taken a chair and let everybody go about their business, and it was clear that her reaction was the opposite to Shane's; she was fighting to control her excitement. The energy of it radiated out from her. Seeing her behave that way made it all the more strange not to see something similar from Shane.

A few minutes later, Blackburn escorted Shane and Vignette out of the building. When he spotted a small café that had reopened a few doors down the street, he guided the kids to it and pulled them inside. He waited until they were seated alone at a small table in the back, then pulled a folded newspaper from his coat pocket and set it on the table. At first, he left the paper there unopened.

"So," he began, "I guess nobody can blame you for being overwhelmed."

"I'm not. Maybe I am. I'm just...I don't know."

"Well, *I* know!" Vignette chimed in with a happy laugh. "I'm surprised you didn't faint yet! We are getting some food here, though, is that right?"

"In a minute," Blackburn assured her. "Why don't you look at the menu and pick out what you want?" He picked a menu up off of the table and handed it to her. She took it but held onto it as if the menu could bite.

Blackburn turned to Shane and lowered his voice. "Shane," he began, "you now have every reason in the world to begin a new life with your sister, and to do it as if you both plan to grow up and make a good accounting of yourselves."

He opened the paper and pointed to the afternoon's headline, and there it all was: how the half-eaten body of Tommie Kimbrough of Russian Hill had only been in the water for a few hours before the tricky currents swirled it up onto a public beach a few miles away. In spite of the deteriorated condition of the corpse, part of the body was protected by the leather coat, which was recovered, and the owner was identified by the wallet in the inside pocket. There was also a note wrapped in oilskin. It was assumed to be the guilty farewell of a killer who could no longer abide his sense of remorse. The identity of The Surgeon was now known.

"That note was supposed to be from me," Shane said. "He was going to put it in my pocket before he pushed me out into the water, so people would think it was my suicide note if there was anything left of me."

"I like the way it turned out better. Cuts down on paperwork." Blackburn stared at him. "This ends it for you. You see?"

"See what?"

"Now you know it for sure. He's gone, and you don't have to go around looking over your shoulder. You're free. So you don't have to spend any money running from him. You just need to use your money to build a future for both of you."

Shane looked from Blackburn to Vignette with a rueful smile. "You want to know a secret? He said we were half brothers. Me and him. He said we had the same father. He said that he was the one who gave me away to St. Adrian's after he got away with killing his parents—our parents—my father—the same—"

"Read it back," Vignette interjected.

He ignored her and added, "Which means that my father was Vignette's father, too."

Blackburn thought he saw Vignette go pale at that, but there was already too much else for him to think about.

Shane put a consoling hand on Vignette's shoulder. "I asked him to tell me what your real name was back then, but he just looked at me."

"I like Vignette. I don't care what they called me back when I was *born*. It's not my name *now*. At St. Adrian's they called me Mary Kathleen, but that's not my name anymore, either. Nope. We can forget all about that one."

At that moment, a realization hit Blackburn so hard that he whistled through his teeth and clapped his hands together. The other two gawked at him.

"Shane," he began, "that's it!" He laughed. "This is amazing! Listen to me—here's the best way in the world to get back at that maniac. If we can get our hands on the birth records, you and your sister will stand to inherit the entire Kimbrough estate. Even his house up there on Russian Hill!"

Once again, Shane's reaction seemed to come out of the blue. "No!" He jumped up from the table, eyes wide. "I don't want anything of his!"

"That's right!" Vignette quickly agreed. "Not from anybody like that."

Blackburn started to object, but Shane cut him off. "No! To hell with him."

"Yeah!" she agreed again.

"Those people weren't my family," he went on. "I don't want anything of theirs."

"Neither do I." Vignette nodded. "We would just have to be *reminded* all the time. We don't even want to look at the birth records!"

"What?" Shane turned to her.

"Why be reminded?"

"Oh. Good point, I guess."

Blackburn felt things slipping out of control. "Shane," he began, "I know you have a lot of reason to be just as angry as hell about all of this, but I have to stop you for a second there. We're probably talking about a great deal of money. That amount you already have now is enough to get you both started in life, and it can get you both the right schooling, but it won't support you for life."

"What's wrong with that? I never wanted to grow up and just sit around, anyway."

"What's the right schooling?" Vignette interrupted.

"Oh, you know," Blackburn smiled, "one where the teachers are so good that you actually learn to read and write without any problem."

Vignette blushed and closed the menu.

"Shane, how did you get so good with the written word?"

Shane shook his head. "If you stay quiet and read, they leave you alone."

"Staying quiet hurts too much," Vignette muttered.

"Well, I don't know if you were aware of the fire at St. Adrian's. It only got the offices, none of the kids were hurt. But tomorrow, the department's going to announce that Friar John was in there and the flames consumed him."

He sat back and gave the kids a moment to react. Neither one said a word. They both sat silently looking forward as if waiting for somebody to speak.

He nodded and spoke under his breath, "All right. No love lost."

He shifted in his seat and cleared his throat. "But as for the two of you, this is the thing—you can't come into this much money without people noticing. And there are plenty of adults who will steal from a kid without hesitating. That's why I signed off on the forms as your guardian. It wasn't just so you could get your money, but that unless you're protected, it will all disappear."

"Maybe we could live with you!" Vignette enthused.

Blackburn and Shane both turned to stare at her. There was an awkward pause.

Blackburn cleared his throat. "Actually, that's just what I planned to talk to you about. Both of you. I've saved most of my salary for a long time, and, well—I can get a place big enough for us. You don't have to stay, you're not my prisoners or anything, but somebody's got to look out for things while you two finish growing up. I guess I'm volunteering to do that, here."

"That sounds great!" Vignette immediately responded. Shane just stared with his mouth slightly open.

Blackburn went on. "We'll get you both into a good school."

"Shane could go to school first, if one of us needs to stay home."

Blackburn smiled at her and quietly asked, "What's your favorite thing on the menu? We can wait while you sound it out."

Vignette just scowled at him and pushed it aside. Shane snorted at that and said, "Get used to it. If I'm going, you're going."

"And you'll both have to learn how to cook. We'll all three take turns."

"What if we can't learn how?" Vignette asked.

"Then I expect that I won't be able to learn how, either, and that the three of us will be eating a lot of sandwiches." Shane and Vignette both laughed and groaned.

"All right, now," Blackburn grinned. "Let's order something to eat. Shane, read Vignette the choices. Then I have to get a taxi and lay up at home for a few days. It'll be a while before I can walk a beat. If I had to do it now, I'd be in trouble."

"Let us come to your place with you," Vignette pleaded.

Shane brightened up at that, adding, "We could take care of you!"

"We don't even need to go back there to that cemetery," Vignette said.

"Well, I have to get my watch."

"I'll go! You're too tired."

"I can do it, Vignette."

"Maybe, but so can I. And right now I bet I can run faster than you and get back quicker, too!"

Vignette and Shane played at arguing the point before deciding to go together, while Blackburn smiled and shook his head. The sound of their request had caught him completely off guard, but it felt like the first pass of rain over a desert. Even though he had known the issue was going to come up, he felt an equal mix of excitement and fear at hearing it. He had also been completely unprepared to feel his heart break open at the beautiful sound of two young voices telling him his company was something they actually wanted.

"I guess you're better off at my place than in a toolshed." He turned to Shane. "We'll have time to talk, too. I've got some other crimes on the books that you just might see into, like you did with the Sullivans. Like the way you managed Kimbrough. The way you can see certain things, it seems natural for you to do this work." He grinned and clapped him on the shoulder. "You can be my 'apprentice' and help me clear some cases."

Shane's face darkened. "Maybe. You know, sometime."

Blackburn let it go. "All right, then. But we're going to have to fill out a lot more forms to do this. So Vignette, what last name will you be using?"

"Well, I tell you one thing for sure, you can forget Kimbrough. I don't care what that guy said."

"Same for me," Shane agreed.

Vignette turned to Shane. "So you're keeping Nightingale, then?"

"I think so. I mean, sure." He thought for a moment, then added, "I need to. I need to carry the name."

Vignette nodded and turned to Blackburn. "We'll be using Nightingale."

Shane glanced at her, then smiled and nodded.

---

Later, on the taxi ride back to the little garden apartment which Randall Blackburn would soon exchange for a house with three bedrooms, he thought back to his late wife and the daughter he never got to know. It amazed him to think of how powerfully the heart of a young man can break over the loss of the love of his life. For almost ten years, he had locked his grief inside and hidden in his work, trying to make the need for a family leave him, trying to insulate himself against ever feeling such agony again. He had only succeeded in feeling nothing but a lot of isolation and loneliness. In spite of that, it seemed as natural as breathing for him to reverse direction and take these two young ones under his wing. He knew there would be nothing easy about it, and he could hardly wait to get started.

THE HIDDEN MAN
Book #2 in the Nightingale Detective series

**A determined detective must stop a murderous fanatic at the 1915 San Francisco World's Fair in this riveting second installment of the Nightingales Detective Series.**

Nine years after San Francisco's Great Earthquake and Fires, the city is on the brink of a new era.

But danger lurks behind the glittering façade, as a murderous fanatic stalks one of the fair's main attractions: the brilliant mesmerist J.D. Duncan. When J.D. receives a threatening note from his stalker, homicide detective Randall Blackburn and his adopted son must combine their intuitive profiling skills to solve a murder that hasn't happened yet.

Out of the public eye, Duncan is battling an even greater enemy: his own advancing early onset dementia, threatening to destroy the powerful memory and sharp mind that made him famous. As the detectives work to unmask his elusive stalker, J.D. will work twice as hard to hide his condition and keep doing the work that defines him—no matter what it takes.

*The Hidden Man* takes the reader on an unforgettable journey in this page-turner about a brilliant mesmerist, a vengeful killer, and the great fair that tied their fates together.

# ACKNOWLEDGMENTS

Landon and his brother, Cohen; Matthew and his brother, Daniel, two beautiful young boys and two rising young men. They are in this world to create respected places in their futures, all because of how they were nurtured at home.

With my thanks to editor Kate Schomaker for her application of skill to this manuscript, I also celebrate Severn River Publishing for giving a home to this book series. SRP is the brainchild of CEO Andrew Watts, to whom we are all grateful for this platform.

Excellent work by Amber Hudock, in Publishing, and Holly Sharp, in Marketing. I see them in an office building with tall glass windows and a spectacular skyline view, well deserved as evidenced by their efficiency in escorting this manuscript through the publication process. I imagine office walls groaning with first editions of their authors' books, while Cate Streissguth in Publishing and Keris Sirek in Finance perform their tasks, sipping oolong tea to meditative background audio. Maybe something by Kitaro, the early years. I am fortunate that Mo Metlen stepped up to guide me through the newsletter process, helping me reach you, the Reader.

My privilege of working with this team came out of the faith in this book series shown by literary agent Lindsay Guzzardo, representing for Martin Literary Management. Thank you, Lindsay. Every writer is grateful for faith shown in their work, and I am no different in that regard. Proving once again we are none of us an island; we are each peninsulas. Billions of little peninsulas, dangling away.

# ABOUT THE AUTHOR

Anthony Flacco is the New York Times and international bestselling author of *Impossible Odds: The Kidnapping of Jessica Buchanan and her Dramatic Rescue by SEAL Team Six,* which won the USA Book News Award for Best Autobiography of 2013. His *Tiny Dancer* was selected by Reader's Digest as their 2005 Editor's Choice for the magazine's commemorative 1000<sup>th</sup> Issue, and he received the 2009 USA Books News True Crime Award for *The Road Out of Hell: Sanford Clark and the True Story of the Wineville Murder.* Flacco's *The Last Nightingale,* book one of the Nightingale Detective series, was originally released to acclaimed reviews including a NYT rave, and was nominated by the International Thriller Writers (ITW) as one of the top five original paperback thrillers for 2007. Anthony resides in the beautiful Pacific Northwest.

anthonyflacco@severnriverbooks.com

Sign up for Anthony Flacco's reader list at
severnriverbooks.com/authors/anthony-flacco

# SELECTED REFERENCES

Douglas, John and Mark Olshaker (2019). *The Killer Across the Table: Unlocking the Secrets of Serial Killers and Predators with the FBI's Original Mindhunter*. New York: Dey St. at William Morrow/HarperCollins.

Stout, Martha, PhD (2005). *The Sociopath Next Door*. New York: Broadway Books.

Douglas, John and Mark Olshaker (1999). *The Anatomy of Motive*. New York: Scribner.

Egger, Steven A. (1998). *The Killers Among Us: Examination of Serial Murder and Its Investigation*. New Jersey: Prentice Hall.

Navarro, Joe and Marvin Karlins (2008). *What Every Body Is Saying: An Ex-FBI Agent's Guide to Speed-Reading People*. New York: HarperCollins

Harrison, Shirley (1993). *The Diary of Jack the Ripper: The Chilling Confessions of James Maybrick*. London: Smith Gryphon.

Holmes, Ronald M., and Stephen T. Holmes (1996). *Profiling Violent Crimes* (2nd edition). Thousand Oaks: Sage Publications.

Turvey, Brent E. (1997). *Criminal Profiling: An Introduction to Behavioral Science Analysis.* Elsevier, Academic Press.